MURDER'S A SWINE

MURDER'S
A SWINE

NAP LOMBARD

With an Introduction
by Martin Edwards

Poisoned Pen
PRESS

Introduction © 2022 by Martin Edwards
Murder's a Swine © 1943 by The Estate of Pamela
Hansford Johnson and Gordon Neil Stewart
Cover and internal design © 2022 by Sourcebooks
Cover image © Mary Evans Picture Library

Published by Poisoned Pen Press, an imprint of Sourcebooks,
in association with the British Library
P.O. Box 4410, Naperville, Illinois 60567-4410
(630) 961-3900
sourcebooks.com

Murder's a Swine was originally published in 1943 by Hutchinson
and Co. Ltd, New York, Melbourne and London.

Library of Congress Cataloging-in-Publication Data

Names: Lombard, Nap, author.
Title: Murder's a swine / Nap Lombard ; with an introduction by Martin
   Edwards.
Description: Naperville, Illinois : Poisoned Pen Press, [2022]
Identifiers: LCCN 2021014768 (print) | LCCN 2021014769
(ebook) | (trade paperback) | (epub)
Subjects: LCGFT: Detective and mystery fiction.
Classification: LCC PR6023.O433 M87 2022 (print) | LCC PR6023.O433
   (ebook) | DDC 823/.914--dc23
LC record available at https://lccn.loc.gov/2021014768
LC ebook record available at https://lccn.loc.gov/2021014769

Printed and bound in the United States of America.
SB 10 9 8 7 6 5 4 3 2 1

INTRODUCTION

MURDER'S A SWINE, KNOWN IN THE UNITED STATES AS *The Grinning Pig*, is an entertaining wartime mystery, first published in 1943. It was the second (and final) detective novel to appear under the name Nap Lombard, following *Tidy Death*. The rather mysterious pen-name masked the identities of a husband-and-wife writing duo, Gordon Neil Stewart and Pamela Hansford Johnson.

The couple had married in 1936, and when war broke out, they became ARP (i.e., Air Raid Precaution) wardens. They were stationed, as Deirdre David explains in *Pamela Hansford Johnson: a Writing Life*, "in the basement of 94 Cheyne Walk, Chelsea, near the highly plausible German bombing target of Battersea Power Station." In the opening lines of this novel, we are introduced to Clem Poplett, also a warden, in a story set in "the early days of the war, when air-raid wardens were thought funny." The atmosphere of the times is splendidly evoked, and I was amused by the jokey term "sitzkrieg," an alternative name for the more familiar concept of "the phoney war." As so often, an unpretentious and light-hearted detective story makes fascinating reading as a document of social history more than three-quarters of a century after the original publication.

In the company of a resident, Agnes Kinghof, Clem discovers a body nestling behind the sandbags in an air-raid shelter at Stewarts Court. Two of those floor plans so popular in vintage detective stories are supplied, one showing the flats in block 3 in the building.

The other shows flat 10, occupied by Mrs. Sibley, who is able to identify the corpse and set in train a murder investigation in which Agnes and her husband, Andrew, aid and abet (and sometimes get ahead of) Inspector Eggshell.

Pamela's time as a warden came to an end once she became pregnant. Already a published novelist, she amused herself by collaborating with her husband, a journalist, on a detective story. *Tidy Death* was published in 1940, and featured Agnes and Andrew, along with Andrew's cousin, Lord Whitestone, "who was someone of considerable importance at Scotland Yard," and who is nicknamed Lord Pig. The appearance of this novel, the follow-up, was delayed by wartime paper shortages.

Just as Stewarts Court takes its name from the co-authors' surname (and resembles, Deirdre David suggests, Beaufort Mansions, where the couple were living at the time), so the presentation of Agnes and Andrew contains elements of self-portraiture. It is possible, as David says, that the popularity of the *Thin Man* movies, starring William Powell and Myrna Loy, also provided some inspiration. The novel was sufficiently well-received in Britain and the U.S. ("Very British" said *Kirkus Reviews*, which *may* have been a compliment) to have encouraged Nap Lombard to produce another book. But none was ever forthcoming.

Gordon Neil Stewart (1912–99) came from a wealthy Australian family. The Stewarts moved to Paris during his teens and he subsequently settled in London. There he moved in literary circles, and met Pamela. He was also concerned with radical politics, and became a member of the Communist Party. During the war, he joined the British Army, serving in India and Burma. The couple had two children, and their daughter Lindsay became the second wife of the Liberal politician Lord Avebury.

Long periods of separation took a toll on the Stewarts' marriage, and they were divorced in 1949. He remarried the next year, and returned to Australia in 1955, publishing a couple of novels as well as nonfiction books. Following the divorce, however, his former wife had a much higher literary profile; in recent years she has been the subject of no fewer than three biographies.

Pamela Hansford Johnson (1912–81) was born in London, growing up in Clapham. She left school at sixteen, worked as a secretary, and began to publish poems. Becoming aware of Dylan Thomas (like her, he had recently won a prize in a poetry competition sponsored by the *Sunday Referee*), she wrote him a letter. When they finally met in February 1934, the correspondence ripened into romance. As Deirdre David puts it: "Dylan essentially changed her writing life from the composition of dreamy verses...to writing novels grounded in social and psychological realism." The title of her first published novel, *This Bed Thy Centre* (1935) is a quotation from Donne and was suggested by Dylan. Marriage was on the cards, but she was deterred by his drinking as well as by apprehension about his roving eye. She marked the end of their relationship by writing a poem called "By Mutual Consent."

Curiously, her relationship with C. P. (Charles Percy) Snow also began by way of correspondence. After their marriage in 1950, they proceeded to become a literary power couple. Snow's first novel, *Death under Sail* (1932) had been a detective story in the classic vein, but he was a man of many parts: a chemist who became a mainstream novelist as well as a civil servant and public figure, known for a famous lecture on "The Two Cultures" (i.e., literature and science, and the gulf between them) and even taking a role in Harold Wilson's Labour government after his elevation to the peerage in 1964. Both husband and wife shared an interest in crime, and Snow's final book, *A Coat of Varnish* (1979), was a rather sombre crime novel. Pamela not only attended the trial of the Moors Murderers but later wrote a book about them. But she and her second husband never wrote a whodunit together. Perhaps at that stage of their careers they would have regarded it as too frivolous a pastime.

Writing in *The Spectator* in 2018, when five of Pamela's mainstream novels were reissued, Philip Hensher described the Snows as "a formidable presence to writers of the time, dispensing approval or censure through book reviews, lectures and public patronage" and Pamela as "an immensely influential and powerful figure in the world of literature, plugged into the British Council's networks and much relied on in official circles." Hensher is evidently unimpressed by much of her fiction, but he concedes: "Johnson was an effective reporter from a particular streak of suburban London, and explored, almost without knowing, the mores and conventions of a forgotten way of living." This observation neatly captures one aspect of the appeal of *Murder's a Swine*.

The two Nap Lombard novels have long been out of print. I'm not clear how the two youthful authors divided the labour of producing the stories, although my guess is that Pamela did most of the writing, while her husband may have been responsible for the plot. I first became aware of the books many years ago, thanks to a passing reference in Julian Symons' magisterial *Bloody Murder*, but never managed to lay my hands on a copy of either of them until recently; if one could unearth a signed first edition of a Nap Lombard novel in a dust jacket, it would command a large sum on the collectors' market. When at last I read this book, I discovered that Symons' recollection that Nap Lombard's hero was "Lord Winterstone" was mistaken, but I'm glad that his words prompted me to track down *Murder's a Swine*.

This is a cheerful mystery. There is a political sub-plot, but it is treated lightly (although the authors' disdain for fascism is clear), while the Kinghofs employ a characteristically jokey trick to unmask the culprit. Even if Pamela didn't regard the Nap Lombard stories as highly as her more serious work, it's arguable that the detective novel was a form well-suited to her talents. More than that, I'm sure *Murder's a Swine* helped its original readers to forget, for an hour or two at least, the miseries of wartime. Writing this introduction at a time when the coronavirus pandemic continues to rage, it is easy to appreciate the virtues of light entertainment at a time of crisis. To be able to lose oneself in an enjoyable, unserious book is an underestimated pleasure.

Martin Edwards
www.martinedwardsbooks.com

"Father's in the pigsty,
You can tell him by his hat."

—Ancient Ditty

to
harold and consola

—Porcos ante Margaritas

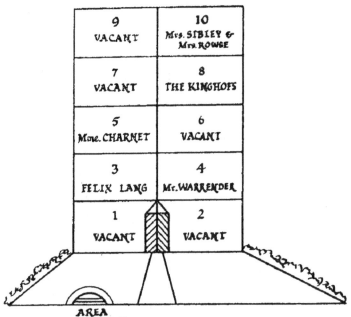

9 VACANT	10 Mrs. SIBLEY & Mrs. ROWSE
7 VACANT	8 THE KINGHOFS
5 Mme. CHARNET	6 VACANT
3 FELIX LANG	4 Mr. WARRENDER
1 VACANT	2 VACANT

AREA
ENTRANCE TO
WELL
(used as Air Raid Shelter; The
one in Block 2, where the corpse
was found, is similar.)

BLOCK 3, STEWARTS COURT

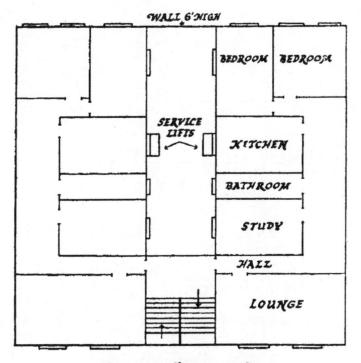

BLOCK 3, STEWARTS COURT
Mrs. Sibley's Flat: No. 10

Chapter One

IF CLEM POPLETT, YOUNGEST WARDEN AT THE POST IN Featherstone Mews, had done as he was told and continued his patrol instead of dodging in out of the rain to one of the area shelters in Stewarts Court, he would not have discovered his first corpse.

It happened like this. These were the early days of the war, when air-raid wardens were thought funny, the days when their duties consisted of patrolling the streets for hours on end, shouting Put Out That Light. This night in question, a January night, was bitterly cold, after a long spell of muggy weather, and the streets glistened beneath a coating of that delicate, almost invisible rain that soaks you through to your vest within three minutes. It was half-past eight, and Clem was not expected back to the comfort of the Post, to the fire and the dartboard, the cups of orange-coloured, stewed tea, the cards and the wireless, until nine. He was young, he had the face of an adored pet rabbit, he had red hair, he stood five feet four in his socks, and he was dreadfully cold and wet. And so it occurred to him to spend the last half-hour enjoying a cigarette in the second of one of those dismal shelters, between the blocks of flats, which had been made in the slender hope of protecting the public during air raids. Being no more than disguised tradesmen's entries, approached by a steep flight of stone stairs and emerging into a well where was the lift that served the five floors, the shelters were bleak, wet, comfortless and narrow as coffins. No fat man or woman would have had a hope of passing the sandbags that half obscured their doorways.

Clem sneaked down, not lighting his torch lest some Senior Warden should see him. He fumbled his way past the bags, guided himself along the soaking walls, and sat down on the long bench, which was scarcely wide enough to accommodate more than half of his small buttocks. They'll have to replace all them bags, he thought, they're growing grass already and they stink to hell.

He lit a cigarette, and as the match flared up saw that he was not alone. Facing him was Mrs. Agnes Clunkershill Kinghof, née Sidebotham, who lived in one of the flats overhead. Clem jumped, then said: "Good evening ma'am didn't see you nasty night." The match went out in time to conceal his blush. Mrs. Kinghof was plain of face, it is true; it was a birdlike face, with little beak, tiny pink mouth and two large, liquid eyes; but her torso was a poem and her legs the admiration of persons for miles around.[1] "Frozen music," the Senior Warden had called them. He was considered extremely original, and his remark had been orally cyclostyled, as it were, into several hundred copies.

"Very nasty night," said Mrs. Kinghof.

Her voice was entrancing. That, and her legs, had the

_____
1 See *Tidy Death*.

effect on very young men of making them feel both shy and dashing at once.

"You're Mr. Poplett, aren't you?"

"That's right," said Clem huskily.

"I know you well by sight. It always makes me feel safe to know that you're looking after us."

"Oh, I don't know about that," said Clem. Switching on his torch, he offered his cigarettes. Mrs. Kinghof thanked him and took one. Clem restored the darkness. "'Fraid I can't light us up, ma'am. The battery's nearly gone as it is, and I can't waste it. Got ticked off proper last week for wasting batteries."

They smoked in amicable silence.

"I expect," said Mrs. Kinghof after a while, "that you're wondering what on earth I'm doing in this sepulchre, when I might be in my own nice, warm, cosy flat four floors up in Block 3."

"Well, I had wondered," said Clem, "not that it's none of my business."

"The fact is, I've lost my key and I can't get in. The porter's got the only pass-key and his wife says he's gone to the pictures and won't be in till nine, so I'm just passing the time here till he gets back."

Clem sympathized and told her his own reasons for seeking the shelter's malodorous hospitality.

"Well, then, we ought to be grateful for each other's company." The pretty voice plunged through the darkness, sociable, eager. "Tell me, Mr. Poplett, how do you think the war's going? I'm not asking for military secrets, of course. My husband's coming home on leave tomorrow—he's been training militia men in Norfolk—and I'm hoping *he'll* tell me how it's going. No one seems to know."

"Seems to be going slow," said Clem, in the guarded voice of one who is in the know, but is not telling the secrets of the War Office to strangers.

"Dreadfully slow. My aunt, General Sidebotham, used to say—"

"Your aunt's a General?" Clem exclaimed, bewildered.

"Salvation Army—used to say that wars were wars when she was a young girl, and hadn't been the same since; but then, she was at Agincourt."

"Was she, now," Clem mused, and choked on his own smoke.

Mrs. Kinghof, seeing that at least she was entertaining her new friend successfully, plunged on. She was a kindly woman, and believed in bringing excitement into people's lives. "I believe she commanded a hundred bowmen. She was a tough old lady, and not really religious till later life. My husband admired her intensely, and she admired him."

Clem also liked Andrew Kinghof, that long, grey strip of a man who had sent a bottle of whisky, two hundred cigarettes, and a dozen American film magazines round to the Post at Christmas. Feeling that Mrs. Kinghof's conversation was a little beyond him and hoping to bring it on to more familiar grounds, he said:

"The Captain keeping well? I expect he thinks this is a rum show to the last war."

"Oh, he likes this one much better! He likes his wars to be quiet. Well, as I was saying, General Sidebotham was not really religious until she had turned ninety and by then it was high time. In middle life, she captured Prince Rupert at Marston Moor, and tore off his greaves. She was Cromwell's white hope. She called herself Perdition-to-All-Fornicators Sidebotham."

"If she's only ninety now," said Clem thoughtfully, "she must have been very young in Cromwell's day."

Mrs. Kinghof giggled. "All right, I'll talk sense. I'm sorry. But you know, Mr. Poplett, life's so dark and monotonous these days that one has an urge to infuse a little romance… if you know what I mean?"

He said he knew what she meant.

"Good," said Mrs. Kinghof. "Now I must tell you about my aunt's exploit in the American Civil War, when she chased Stonewall Jackson across the Potomac on ice-floes, with only one bloodhound and a borrowed borzoi… Mr. Poplett! This place smells horrible. What is it?"

"I think them sandbags is gone rotten."

"Oh, yes. But there's another smell too…as if a cat's got into the bags and died there."

Clem switched on his torch and put it on the seat, lighting up the shelter in dismal sort. He rose and went to the bags, which were germinating nicely. Several had already burst, and the others were straining at their stitches like sizeable bosoms at tight blouses. He began to pick away idly at the earthy structure, smelling and snuffling as he did so.

"Look out," said Mrs. Kinghof, "one of them's coming loose."

Clem stepped back just in time to catch a loosened bag that had toppled out from its companions, and as it fell into his arms he found himself nose to nose with a long dead face, phosphorescent, greenish-brown in the torch light, hideously blotched and even more hideously smelling.

His yelp of fright brought Mrs. Kinghof to her feet.

"What is it?"

His shaking finger answered her.

Mrs. Kinghof looked and swallowed. "All right, Mr.

Poplett, all right. We must think. Here, take a drink." She drew from her bag a quartern bottle of brandy and made him gulp at it. Then she took a long swig herself, and both, by common consent, bolted upstairs into the cold, wet cleanness of the streets.

Clem was liver-coloured with shock, Mrs. Kinghof only a faint shade ruddier.

She said bravely: "Don't worry about me, Mr. Poplett"—though he had shown no signs of worrying about her—"I'm used to corpses. My husband and I were involved in a little affair…just as nasty as this. That was murder. I should imagine this was murder, too, because it would be very difficult to build yourself into a heap of sandbags and then die… Mr. Poplett, you stay on guard here. I'm going to get a policeman. When he comes, you can tell him you just went into the shelter to see if anyone had been interfering with the lights—they do interfere, don't they?—I noticed someone had removed the bulb down there. All right. I won't be long."

Though it occurred to Clem that she might herself have put the dead gentleman in the sandbags and that he should detain her on suspicion, it did not occur with sufficient force to promote action of any kind. Miserably he watched while Mrs. Kinghof darted on lovely legs through the wet, her mackintosh gleaming like starry water, and he had one awful, paralysing moment of imagining that the corpse was crawling up the stairs behind him to pass its cold and earthy hands about his throat.

———

Mrs. Kinghof, who had been a mean centre-forward in the school hockey game, ran soundly and with good wind. She might have run for miles had not a car stopped at the street corner and a long gentleman, alighting, gathered her panting form to his heart.

"Andrew!"

"Darling! You look more beautiful than ever. I expect it's the black-out. Lots of people don't think you're beautiful, but I do. Where's the fire?"

"There's been a murder. I want a policeman. I love you, Andy. It's so nice to see you. What are you doing home?"

"Nothing doing, so I pushed off this afternoon instead of tomorrow morning. Who's murdered?"

"I don't know his name. He's in the sandbags. Clem Poplett found him. How long are you home for?"

"For heaven's sake, tell me a clear story! Oh, I'm due for a transfer, so I'll be home till they fix it up. Maybe only two days, maybe a week, maybe a fortnight." Mr. Kinghof shook his wife violently and kissed her.

"I want a policeman," said Agnes.

"Come on, tell me about it."

Panting, she told him. Mr. Kinghof, Captain in the Royal Artillery, aged forty-three—too nice-looking, said the disappointed women, for such a wife—dragged her into the car and with commendable presence of mind drove her round the corner to the police station. They returned with the Inspector and a young constable to find Mr. Poplett holding his post with the nervous determination of Casabianca. With him was a War Reserve policeman, in private life Colonel Eckersley Plumpfield, of 17 Carlyle Street.

The party descended into the shelter to view the body.

"Anyone know him?" the Inspector demanded.

No one did.

"Dig him out," the Inspector ordered, and the unhappy

constable, aided by the even less happy Mr. Poplett, went to work. It was easy work, for the whole structure of bags was on the point of collapse. Indeed, the Kinghofs and Colonel Plumpfield managed to back up the steps only a second before it fell on them.

The body was well nourished. It was that of a tall, plump man in the early sixties. His countenance, or such of it as could be seen through the initial blur of decomposition, was far from prepossessing, and a fish-shaped mole just below his right eye did little to improve matters. He was dressed simply in a warden's uniform: a navy-blue boiler suit with embroidered pocket. He wore nothing beneath it; on his sockless feet were very new Wellington boots of regulation A.R.P. pattern.

"Was this man a warden?" the Inspector asked Clem.

"Not that I know of, sir. Not unless he's a new man from some other part of the district. I know the personnel"— Clem put the accent on the second syllable—"pretty well, because it was me that had the giving-out of uniforms and they was all signed for by the perspective wearer."

"Interesting to find out if there's a warden going around without a uniform," said Mr. Kinghof.

The Inspector looked at him with displeasure. "I expect we'll be finding out everything like that, sir."

"There wouldn't have to be a warden without a suit," said Clem. "There's a whole stock in the basement at the Town Hall. People go in and come out all day, and almost anyone could have pinched one without being seen."

"I see. Thanks. I know you, don't I?"

"Clement Poplett, sir, Post C. That's the one in Featherstone Mews."

"Ah. Um. Well, Poplett, I think you might as well be

getting back there. I may want you again tomorrow, and you'll be called at the inquest."

"I'll keep my mouth shut," said Clem, staunchly, "not a word of this out of me."

"You can do as you please," the unappreciative Inspector told him, and Clem went gratefully back to his duty, mentally improvising his tale as he went.

"And I shan't need Mrs. Kinghof any more today. Have you got the address, Frankson?"

"8, 3 Block, Stewarts Court," said the constable.

Just then the doctor came, a bright little man called Patrickson, who loved a good crime and saw few of them.

"I'd as soon stick around for a while," said Agnes, pleasantly.

"Not down here, madam. Good night."

Mr. and Mrs. Kinghof retired to the top of the steps.

"We can't get in," said Agnes, "unless the porter's home from the pictures. I've lost my key."

Mr. Kinghof swore. "And I've left mine in Norfolk. Curse you, girl! For that, you can just cut along and see if Blake's home yet. I'll wait for you here."

She was some time gone, for Blake had dropped into the "Green Doe" on his way home and did not arrive back on his own doorstep till nine-thirty. In the meantime the doctor made his examination and Mr. Kinghof, eavesdropping, heard him say, "Not less than fourteen days or more than twenty, but that's only an opinion. The damp has helped him."

Mr. Kinghof, his curiosity satisfied, retired into the car, where he awaited his wife's return. She came up at last, tired, cross, and damp, dangling the key on her little finger.

"He wants it back first thing tomorrow. I'll go in and

make up the fire while you park the car. Have you had any supper? There's nothing in the house."

"Luckily for you," he shouted, as he drove off, "I had a snack at Chelmsford on my way through."

If there was no food, at least there was whisky. Within fifteen minutes, their tempers restored, they were sitting in the lounge before a bright fire, decanter, siphon, cigarettes, and potato crisps on the table before them.

"This is a nice place," said Andrew appreciatively, drawing his wife into the circle of his arm. "I like old-fashioned flats. What's the use of modern ones? Never room to swing even a mouse in, and flues jutting out all over the place. What are we paying for this?"

"Three pounds a week," Agnes replied, with satisfaction. Both persons of substance in their own rights, they could have afforded three times the amount.

"Wonderful. Know what it costs at Bingham Court? From five upwards, for nice, miserable little flats with the lavatory in the bathroom and the hall running through the bedrooms and the sink in the lounge. And we're only twenty minutes from town. You're a marvellous house-hunter, my dear."

They had moved five times in two years of married life. They were restless people.

"Everything's marvellous," Agnes murmured, a little affected by the whisky. "I hope you get a nice long leave so we can solve the murder."

"I'm afraid that isn't our murder," he answered with regret. "We don't even know the corpse."

"Oh, we will," she replied confidently.

———

The second shock of that night was heralded by a midnight visit from Mrs. Rowse, who was Phyllada Rounders, author of *The Saddest Girl in the Sixth,* and other popular stories for growing girls. Mrs. Rowse lived with her friend, Mrs. Adelaide Foster Sibley, and it was on the latter's account that she ran down, in pigtails and flannel dressing-gown, to summon the assistance of the Kinghofs.

It happened like this. Andrew and Agnes had been in bed for about an hour. Andrew was now asleep and Agnes, in a delightful golden drowse, was thinking how pleasant it was to have a husband. She was thinking so deeply about this that the sound of the service lift creaking up the wall and, after a few moments, creaking down again, did not strike her as a strange one. Nor was she particularly interested by a dim, catlike howl from the flat above followed by a tattoo of heels on the floor. Noisy devils, she thought mildly. Darling Andrew, how lovely it is to have him home. Damn the Army, I wish I were a vivandière, so I could watch him being a Captain. I wonder if he'll get into trouble for taking no action about the gunner who threw butter at the bombardier? Even if Andrew didn't like the bombardier, and said he wished it had been half a brick, he can't behave like that... I hope he stays home long enough to catch the murderer.

Then the door-bell rang, rang insistently through the stuffy darkness.

Agnes switched on the bedside lamp and sought for her gown and slippers. Andrew grunted and slept on. She ran down the passage, lit up the hall and opened the door. Mrs. Rowse, yellow flannel girdled about her shaking fat, her yellow-white plait whipping on her shoulders, precipitated herself into Agnes's arms.

"Oh, Mrs. Kinghof, Mrs. Kinghof! Can you come up?

It's terrible. Poor Adelaide's having hysterics and I can't deal with her. She saw a pig at the window."

Agnes raised a hand for silence. She must, she thought, allow this information to sink in.

"A pig, you said?"

"Yes, shining horribly… It was bluish, she told me… just the head. You see, I hadn't gone to bed. I was working in the study, finishing Chapter VII. I was just on the part where Fernia Prideaux is suspected of stealing Thelma Thombleson's lacrosse shoes and she can't clear herself so the girls send her to Coventry, and I suppose I was absorbed in my work, because Addie must have been screaming for at least a minute before I heard her…"

"Wait here," said Agnes sternly. "I'm going to fetch my husband."

In a moment or so she returned with him, sleepy-eyed, grumbling, cursing all pigs; but on seeing Mrs. Rowse's pitiable condition he spoke kindly to her and bade her tell her story.

"She says she was lying in bed, with the black-out curtains open—she always opens them before she goes to sleep as she must have fresh air—when she heard a tap on the window. She looked up, and there it was grinning at her—a pig's head, all shining and blue, with the snout pressed against the pane. Then it disappeared, and there was a long creaking noise, and then she just had hysterics."

"Nightmare?" Andrew enquired dubiously. "What did she have for dinner?"

"Look here," said Agnes, "the creaking was the service lift. I heard it, only it didn't strike me as funny that it should be working at midnight. The pig came up on that."

Andrew said, "You go up and try to calm Mrs. Sibley. I'm

going down the well to investigate. Mrs. Sibley's bedroom is in the same position as ours, isn't it, with the kitchen next door? Well, if someone went up on the lift and pushed the pig's head against the window, a second person must have been cranking the lift from below. Go on, darling, rush to Mrs. Sibley's aid, and yell out like fun if you see any more pigs. I'll hear you."

Chapter Two

WHEN SHE HAD GONE, TAKING WITH HER THE WEEPING Mrs. Rowse, Andrew got into trousers, sweater, and overcoat and went downstairs, out of the front door, through the third block area shelter into the well. His first discovery was that one person only had been concerned in the terrifying jest played upon Mrs. Sibley. On the lift stood an old paint-bucket, and wedged through the side of this, at an angle of forty-five degrees, was a long cane.

When the lift was hauled up to the level of Mrs. Sibley's kitchen sill, the top of the stick would have reached the middle of her bedroom window. Therefore the pig's head, if pig's head it was, had been fixed on the stick, and the joker himself had cranked the lift. A risky joke, surely? But there were few people in Block 3 who would have been likely to hear the midnight creaking save Mrs. Sibley, who had been meant to hear it, and Mrs. Kinghof, who had, in fact, actually heard it. Suppose the latter had looked out of her window. But she was notoriously a heavy sleeper. Her heavy sleeping was one of her favourite topics. Who else? Five of the flats had been evacuated at the start of war.[1] To the third block of Stewarts Court there were the flats. Numbers 1, 2, 6, 7, and 9 were vacant. The Kinghofs lived in Number 8, with Mesdames Sibley and Rowse immediately above in Number 10. Mr. Warrender, who was seldom seen by the tenants as he worked late nights at a Government office, lived in Number 4. Opposite him, to the left of the staircase, was Felix Lang, the medical student, who lived in Number 3. Above Mr. Lang was the Frenchwoman, Madame Charnet, who was a comparative newcomer. Well, Madame Charnet was deaf. Mr. Warrender slept at home only at week-ends. Mr. Lang—

Andrew heard a pleasant voice in his ear. "That you, Mr. Kinghof?"

By torchlight, he saw the young man, far from sober, far from dry, and far from dismal.

"Lang?"

"That's me. I say, I've locked myself out. Just come home, put my key in the door, opened it, took key out, dropped it in the hall, then found I'd dropped my wallet on the outside mat, stepped out to get it and the door swung to. Been to a party."

"So I see," said Andrew suspiciously.

"I was going to try and climb up the pipe. My window's open. Bit of a job, though, climbing, I mean. Been to a party. I suppose you couldn't crank me up on the lift?"

Andrew said sharply, "Was it you playing a fool joke with a pig's head?"

"Pig? What are you talking about, pig? Just got home, I tell you. Been to a party. Oh, 'This little piggy went to party, And this little piggy stopped a tome—'"

1 See plan in front of book.

"Shut up! Do you want to wake the dead?" Andrew's words echoed disagreeably in his own mind. "Lang, where was this party?"

"Party? How'sh'd I know? Been to lots. Don't know which one was the last."

"You may have to remember."

"Don' wanna remember. Wanna go home."

Mr. Lang sounded tearful. Andrew said suddenly: "Right! I'll shove you up on my shoulders and you can grab the pipe where it bends round."

"Wanna go up on the lift," said Mr. Lang fretfully. "Poor Felix wansh go on lift."

"Well, you can't! Get along now!" Andrew used his parade-ground voice. "I haven't got all night."

Bundling up the round young man, he assisted him on his way. Throwing, against all regulation, the light of his torch upwards, he saw Mr. Lang shin pretty featly up the pipe and disappear through his window.

If his story's true, thought Andrew, he was out… And Madame Charnet's deaf, and Warrender's at work, and Agnes is a sound sleeper…so whoever did this knew a great deal about the flats. "An inside job," he murmured importantly. Then he had an idea.

Leaving the well, he went up to a policeman who was guarding the entrance of Number 2 shelter, where a dead man had been unearthed earlier that evening.

"I say, officer!"

The constable did not respond very readily to this flattering form of address. He was feeling his position acutely. "Yes, sir?"

"Did you see anyone go into Number 3 shelter about twenty minutes ago?"

"No, sir."

"Sure?"

"Yes. What's up?"

"Nothing much. Perhaps you just weren't looking that way."

"Nobody's been near there. Nor near any of the shelters. Nobody."

"You didn't hear a service lift going up and down?" Andrew asked this rather hopelessly, hardly expecting that the noise could have been heard so far away.

"No, sir. Look here, what's the matter?"

"Oh, nothing. I'm Captain Kinghof, Number 8, Block 3. I just thought I heard someone mucking about the lift in our well. Must have been mistaken."

"Must've," said the constable. "No one's even been along the street."

"Sorry to have bothered you. Good night. Oh, I say, you guarding the scene of the crime?"

"Look here, who told you—"

"Oh, that's all right. You ask the Inspector. My wife was with young Poplett when he was found. Good night."

The constable glared, but did not answer.

Andrew went home, where he found his wife before the lounge fire finishing the whisky. After reproving her for her greed, he told her of his deductions, and of the odd behaviour of Mr. Lang.

"So you see, if no one went into the well from the street, someone got in there from inside the block. It's easy enough. Flat 2's vacant, and it was open tonight, because someone's been altering the lock—Blake, I suppose. I had a look at it as I came in. Anyone in this building could have gone into Number 2 and out of the window. And whoever played the pig-trick knew the habits of the residents pretty well."

"But, Andy—"

"I hate being called Andy."

"But, Andy, who could have done it? Only Madame Charnet or Mr. Warrender, if Felix Lang was really out, as he says."

"Only Charnet—but that's ridiculous—or Lang. Warrender's at work."

"That's where you're wrong. On my way down from drenching Mrs. Sibley with sal volatile I saw a light under his door, so I knocked, and asked him if he'd heard the lift. He said no, he'd had his gramophone on. He'd come back from work with a cold and was making a holiday of it. He's got a cold all right. Sneezed all over me, disgusting man."

"Did anyone hear his gramophone?"

"Don't be silly. The flats above and below his are empty."

"Then it must have been Lang! I mean, you can't imagine poor doddering Charnet climbing out of windows."

"But suppose Lang has an alibi?"

"If he had, the thing would become plain impossible; only I don't suppose we'll be able to investigate him. You can't badger the police about a silly thing like this."

"It's rather beastly, isn't it? Thank God we keep our blinds drawn. I'd be sick with fright if a pig looked in at me. Andy, I'm going round the local butchers tomorrow to see if they've sold a pig's head to anyone."

He took the glass fondly from her and ruffled her pretty blonde hair. "This isn't the way to spend my first night's leave. Come on, you."

They returned to bed. As Agnes clambered back into the mussed sheets her husband said, "What lovely legs you've got! I do love you. What fun we do have, don't we?"

"Fun!" Agnes agreed sleepily, turning upon him an

angel's smile that gave her a charm which might have startled the disappointed women, had they been fortunate
enough to see it.

———

Mr. Kinghof, who was accustomed to wearing battle-dress
around the place, put on his dress uniform the next morning
to accompany his wife on a round of the butchers' shops.
He fancied it would be as well to look as impressive as possible. They drew a blank. At shop after shop they met with
uncomprehending stares, and at several of the multiple
stores with that frozen variation of the horse-laugh that was,
in later stages of the war, to become so familiar to customers who were not Our Registered. They returned disconso-
lately, wandering along from saloon bar to saloon, and filled
in the rest of the time before lunch by looking at the book-
stall in James Crescent, at the cinema posters, and into the
window of the theatrical costumiers who had been exhibit-
ing a cavalier's suit for so long that the moths had founded a
colony in the feathers around the black hat. When they got
back to Number 8, they met Mrs. Sibley on the stairs.

If she were fatter than Mrs. Rowse, she was far more delicate. Her face was yellowish under her dyed black hair, and
her cheeks trembled with every step she took. Obviously,
she was badly shaken. It would be a comfort to her if Mrs.
Kinghof would climb the remaining flight to take a glass of
sherry with her.

They assented, writing off as a bad debt the headache
that would follow Mrs. Sibley's Sunnymaloo sherry imposed
on Dunhill's whisky, and went in her wake up into her clut-
tered flat, where stuffed birds and fish, Chinese fern-pots,

whatnots, gold pier glasses, and walnut chiffoniers jostled one another like creatures in a bad dream. Mrs. Rowse was not to be seen.

"She's working," Mrs. Sibley whispered reverently. "She's got to the part where Fernia Prideaux hoists the Union Jack on the refugee girls' bicycle shed. We mustn't disturb her."

They spoke in hushed voices.

"Tell me, Mr. Kinghof, have you come to any conclusion about the…animal?" Mrs. Sibley swallowed, and became a shade whiter.

"We have thought the matter over," said Andrew portentously, "and come to the conclusion that you must have had a very distressing nightmare. No—don't say anything. If it should recur, then I think you should see your medical man; but for the moment I should wipe the whole affair out of your mind."

Mrs. Sibley's face crumpled with such an expression of affront that Agnes hastily interposed a subject that she felt might divert her hostess.

"Yes, do try, because horrible as your experience has been, something much more horrible happened last night! They found a man, a dead man—"

"…very dead," said Andrew.

"…walled up in the sandbags, in No. 2 Block shelter! In fact, I and an air-raid warden found him."

Mrs. Sibley's eyes bulged and a trickle of sherry ran down her chin. "A murder?"

"Well, we're not sure yet. But I should think so, wouldn't you?"

"Who was he?"

"No one knows. The police are trying to find out."

"I must get Mrs. Rowse. She always says to me, 'Addie,

never fail to bring to my notice anything that may be copy, anything that may prove valuable to my work.'" Mrs. Sibley rose, took from the mantelpiece a toy shillelagh tied with emerald ribbon and beat a tattoo on the wall.

"I shouldn't have thought murders were in her line," Agnes murmured. "There weren't any in the school stories I used to read."

"Mrs. Rowse never knows what she may wish to write. 'One day,' she says, 'I hope to write an English epic.' Ah, there you are, dear!"

The author wandered in, pen in hand, ink on the lace vest tucked down the vee of her purple marocain morning gown, and her lips were moving over fair words. "'Fernia tossed her mane of auburn hair. "You may think I'm a common thief," she said, "but I'll show you, I'm British!" Thelma Thombleson sneered vindictively...' Yes, dear, what is it?"

"There's been a murder in No. 2 shelter!" Mrs. Sibley cried.

"'—sneered vindictively, fingering her prefect's medal.' A murder? Goodness, what next?"

"I should think that would be enough," said Andrew, "for the time being. We don't know it's murder, Mrs. Rowse." He sketched the story for her benefit.

"Now tell me," she said, squatting on a fat pouffe at his feet and patting his knee in intimate fashion, "because all this is grist to my mill. What did he look like? Omit nothing. You are observant, I know it. Omit no tiny detail. What may seem insignificant to you may not seem so to me."

"Well," said Andrew briskly, with the air of one who is pleased to oblige, "he was tall, fat, sixtyish and had no clothes on—"

"Oh!" Mrs. Rowse commented faintly.

"Except for an A.R.P. overall and Wellington boots. He had just begun to decompose and he was smothered in wet earth and sand."

"He had a long, thin nose," Agnes continued, "slightly hooked, and a very small mouth. His eyebrows were tufty and thick and under his left eye he had a reddish birthmark rather like a fish—"

There came an unnerving thump. Mrs. Sibley had fainted.

For the second time in twenty-four hours she was restored with sal volatile. When she opened her eyes she said, "That's my brother, Reg. Reg Coppenstall. I haven't seen him for thirty years."

——

This was shock number three; but before lunch Andrew and Agnes were to receive shock number four. They left Mrs. Sibley in the care of her friend, telling her that they would immediately convey her statement to the police. They had just left the flat when Andrew, who had held the door open to permit his wife's egress, gave an exclamation of disgust and turned to inspect the Sibley portal.

It was an ordinary sort of door, coated with rather dingy white paint, the handle and letter-box polished by a careless daily help (Mrs. Sibley kept no maid) who had left smears of Bluebell in the mouldings. Today, however, it presented an extraordinary appearance, having upon it a sort of grey shine. Andrew touched the surface gingerly, withdrew his fingers, which were now sticky and glistening, held them out for his wife's inspection and then, making a grimace of repulsion, put them to his lips.

He said, "Lard!"

Agnes said quickly, "Or pig. Andrew, this is getting nasty. I don't like it one little bit. What on earth shall we do?"

"Well, don't tell the old ladies yet. They're unlikely to leave the flat before the police get here, so they won't discover it. This is a police matter. For all we know it may have some connection with the late Coppenstall, if she's right in her identification. Pah! The funny man's smeared every inch of the door."

"I'm going round the flats to see who's in."

"You're not. You're coming to the police station."

"You go. Good heavens, Andrew, every minute counts!"

He said drily, "Does it?" but was content to follow at a more leisurely pace as she tore off down the two flights to the flat of Madame Charnet.

Agnes called up the staircase, "She's out." By the time Andrew, too interested to mend his pace, had drawn level with her black tricorne hat, she had found nobody at all at home. As they went through the main door, they met Madame Charnet coming in with a basket of shopping. She was a dried woman of middling height and indeterminate age. She wore rather thick glasses and, surprisingly, a lot of lipstick. Her coat had a paisley pattern, and frizzed brown hair of an indefinite shade showed beneath her brown and orange turban.

"*Bonjour, madame,*" Agnes said.

Madame nodded, smiled in the vague fashion of the very deaf, and said loudly in English: "Vairy cold!"

"Very. Been shopping?"

"Eh?"

"Shopping?"

"*Ah, oui! Oui.* It takes so long. The shops are so full. What do you say, so crowded?"

She passed on, nodding and smiling, dropped a lemon halfway up the first flight and thanked Andrew elaborately when he caught it on its third bounce and ran after her with it. *"Merci, monsieur, merci beaucoup!"*

He and Agnes bowed acknowledgment and set off for the police station at a good pace. "Counts her out, Andy. Why isn't Warrender in, or wouldn't he answer the door? He shouldn't be out, with a cold like that. Lang would be out anyway."

"Wrong on three points. Madame isn't counted out, because she could quite well have come in during her shopping, smeared the door with some nice new lard and made off again. I don't think she did, though. There's no need to make a mystery of Warrender, because he's probably gone to the early show at the Odeon. He's mad about the pictures, he told me once, and I suppose if he does get time off he likes to amuse himself, cold or no cold. Point three, you don't know Lang's out. He may not have gone to the hospital."

"I am outwitted," said Agnes, generously.

They went into the dingy police station and enquired of the sergeant if the Inspector was about.

They were asked to state their business.

"Well," Andrew said, "we think we've identified the corpse in the shelter."

The sergeant stared at him. "You Mr. Kinghof, sir?"

"I remember you. You ought to remember me."

"You came in last night. Your lady found the body."

"Helped by Clem Poplett. Clem did the real finding."

The sergeant turned abruptly to the constable, who during this exchange had been sitting as reservedly by the desk as the wax policeman in Madame Tussaud's. "Get the Inspector, Harris."

The Inspector appeared like the demon king before the constable was halfway across the room. "'Morning, madam, 'morning, sir. I was sending round to you this afternoon."

"They say they can identify the corpse, sir."

The Inspector, whose name, surprisingly, was Eggshell, glanced at them sharply and his eye brightened. "You can? Who is he?"

"Well, we can't actually identify him, because we don't know him, but we know someone who can. Mrs. Sibley of Flat 10, our block—that's the flat above us—says it may be her brother, Reginald Coppenstall. Oh, yes, and the most extraordinary things have been happening round there! Pigs' heads and lard on the front door."

"Get me Frankson!" snapped Eggshell.

Frankson was got.

"We'll go round to Number 10 now, sir, if you please," Eggshell said, and they all set off.

The door was opened, after the Inspector had duly inspected it, by the unsuspecting Mrs. Rowse.

"I should like to see Mrs. Sibley, please."

Vaguely she picked up an envelope from the mat.

"Inspector—er—Eggshell," he said diffidently. He had never become accustomed to the sound of his own name.

Mrs. Rowse, however, did not move. She was turning over the envelope, which was a hideous shade of pink, addressed in huge block letters to MA SIBLEY. It was not stuck down. "I'd better see this before I give it her," she said doubtfully, and her voice trembled. "If it's something nasty...especially coming after the pig..." She took out the folded sheet, of the same obstreperous pink, and as she read it she flushed.

"Give that to me," Eggshell said sharply.

Andrew and Agnes managed to read it over his shoulder.

It contained only seven words, printed in staggering capitals, "GREASY FELLOW AREN'T I? THE PIG-STICKER."

"Yes," said Eggshell. "Very well, madam, I'll take care of this."

Followed by the Kinghofs, the constable and Mrs. Rowse, he intruded himself upon Mrs. Sibley.

Chapter Three

MRS. SIBLEY, BROUGHT BACK HALF-FAINTING IN A policecar from her very positive identification of the corpse, was, after ministrations by Mrs. Rowse and Mrs. Kinghof lasting three-quarters of an hour, in a position to answer questions. First of all, however, she had her own question to ask. "How did he die?"

"Not to bother you with technicalities, madam, he was shot through the back," said Eggshell, "at close range." He gulped. "Death, I'm glad to say, must have been instantaneous. Now, madam, if it won't distress you too much—"

"She'll answer," said Mrs. Rowse defiantly, "she'll answer anything you have to put to her. She'll answer up like an Englishwoman, won't you, Addie dear? Courage. Courage."

Eggshell said drily, "If you'll please leave us, Mrs. Rowse—"

"No! No! Phyllada mustn't leave me. I only feel strong when she's here."

Andrew and Agnes, who, by virtue of their good offices, had been permitted to stay for the interrogation on condition they held their tongues, waited eagerly for a rebuke; but Eggshell merely said, "Very well, then, Mrs. Rowse. But you mustn't interrupt. Now then, Mrs. Sibley: When did you last see your brother?"

Agnes drew a delighted breath, visualizing Mrs. Sibley in a blue cavalier's suit.

"It must have been thirty years ago... Let me see...in 1912, when we were in Tunis."

"That would be twenty-nine years. Why Tunis?"

"My brother was an importer. Dates, it was. Desert Dates, Limited. I went abroad with him that year, the year before I married. He was lonely, because his wife had left him. She ran away with an actor called Steer."

"And how was it you lost touch with your brother after that?"

Mrs. Sibley appeared to hesitate. "After my marriage... There was trouble about money. We had an aunt who had always been fonder of me than of Reginald. When I returned to England I found her in very poor health, so it was natural for me to spend a great deal of time with her. Anyway, when she died, a year later, it was to me she left the greater part of her money."

"It was a large legacy?" Eggshell asked diffidently. "You must pardon me, madam."

"Seventy thousand pounds."

"And she left your brother—?"

Mrs. Sibley coloured faintly. "Seven hundred."

Andrew whistled. Agnes, anticipating Eggshell, shushed him.

"A great difference. And he resented this?"

"I'm afraid so. He wrote me a very cruel letter."

"You didn't offer to share your good fortune with him?"

Mrs. Sibley said sharply, "Certainly not, not after that letter. Besides, he was in an excellent way of business. He didn't need it, and I did. My husband had suffered considerable financial losses and I wanted to help him rebuild his business... He had become bankrupt. He had lost everything."

"His business was—?"

"Antiques."

"I see."

Eggshell, no less than Andrew and Agnes, thought that if the bric-a-brac in Mrs. Sibley's room were a fair sample of Mr. Sibley's stock, it was no wonder the man failed.

"What happened to your brother in those intervening years?"

"I don't know. I don't know whether he lived here or abroad. He never communicated with me, nor attempted to see me."

"You'd never set eyes on him from that day to—to this?"

"No." Mrs. Sibley dabbed her eyes and rolled up the wet handkerchief into a ball.

"Despite the separation, you were fond of your brother?"

"Of course she was!" Mrs. Rowse interposed excitably. "Isn't blood thicker than water? Isn't it natural that with all his faults, she—" It was Mrs. Sibley who stopped her. Staring from Eggshell to her friend with an odd and rather touching dignity, she said, "No, Phyllada. I'm going to tell them the truth. Inspector, I was so disgusted with my brother's reception of my good fortune that the affection I had for him died... I never cared to hear his name after that. What is affecting me now is shock, not grief."

"Thank you, ma'am. I take it—I take it that your brother suspected you of undue influence with your aunt?"

"I am not interested in what he may or may not have suspected. I only know how cruel he was."

"Yes. Thank you. Well, madam, I'm not going to trouble you further today, though I'm afraid I must call you at the inquest, but you'll be spared as much as possible. Oh, one minute. This practical joking. Have you any suggestions to make? Any suspicions?"

She coloured; opened her mouth, shut it tightly.

"No? Well, we'll keep an eye on the flats here, and I hope you won't be troubled again. I'll bid you good day. Mr. Kinghof, I'd like a further word with you and your wife. Will you come along, please?"

"Come to our flat," said Andrew, "we can talk there."

Mrs. Rowse saw them to the door. To Andrew and Agnes she said, "You've been so kind, so thoughtful! I hope, when my book is published, to be able to make a small return, if you'll honour me by accepting an autographed copy. Oh, I know my little effort may seem rather juvenile to you, but I flatter myself that it is written in good, pure English, and after all, I often have letters from quite elderly people... A bishop wrote to me once, saying how much pleasure and profit he had had from *Cuckoo Delahaye: Mischief of the Fifth*. And the year before that, when I wrote—"

Tactfully, they managed to clip the flow, and in a moment or so were in the blissful quiet of Number 8.

Eggshell refused a drink, but accepted a cigar. "Now, Mr. Kinghof. About this pig business."

"Will you let me tell it in my own way? I've got ideas on the subject."

The Inspector slowly nodded. "Fire away."

So Andrew and Agnes, in chiming duologue, related the grotesque tale, and told him the results of their minor investigations. "So you see," Agnes finished, "it must have been someone in the flats! It couldn't have been an outsider."

Eggshell shook his head. "Not certain. The constable said no one went into the shelter, but he may have been mistaken. It's not easy to see in the black-out, and that's a dark street anyway."

Agnes looked her disappointment.

"Oh, come, madam," he said kindly, "we can't be sure one way or the other. On the face of it, though, I don't fancy your suspects unless young Lang is playing games."

Andrew plunged boldly. "Look here, Eggshell, there's a link to this business—the pig and the body."

"You think so, sir? And what's your idea?"

"You've got an idea yourself?"

"Maybe yes, maybe no. Let's hear yours."

"Well, suppose Coppenstall thought her a pig for taking the money—which obviously he did. Don't you think someone connected with him might be impressing the fact on her?"

"Andrew," Agnes said simply, "I think you're wonderful."

Eggshell was not so sure. "Yes, I thought of that myself. But who is this someone?"

Agnes countered smartly, "Who stood to gain the money if anything happened to Mrs. Sibley? Coppenstall?"

"You're wonderful, too," murmured Andrew.

"That remains to be discovered, ma'am. Is Mrs. Rowse a relation?"

"I don't think so."

"When did Mr. Sibley die?"

"About four years ago, I believe. She came to the mansions on his death and took Mrs. Rowse to live with her."

Eggshell said slowly, "Let's suppose Coppenstall was the

heir. Now he's dead, who's next? Assuming she should die intestate?"

"Someone," Andrew suggested, "who is a funny man. The sort who puts on funny hats at parties, bursts balloons and frightens the children into fits. The sort who buys disgusting fancies from the practical joke shops—Whoopee Cushions, Spilling Glasses, Dirty Fidoes. Altogether, a vile piece of goods. And, of course, he's Mrs. S.'s next of kin."

"Maybe," said Eggshell, "maybe." He rose. "Well, I'll be pushing along. Inquest on Thursday, eleven-fifteen. See you there."

When he had gone, Andrew asked his wife how she would like to spend the evening.

"Pig," she said remotely.

"Now listen, haven't you had enough bacon for one day?"

"I meant our Pig. Lord Pig." She referred to Andrew's cousin, Lord Whitestone, who was someone of considerable importance at Scotland Yard. His sobriquet was the result of his strong facial resemblance to the animal, a resemblance that had led Andrew, as a small boy, to attempt the fastening of a ring through his cousin's nose. This incident had aroused some friction and a lifelong coldness only mitigated by Pig's dour affection for Andrew's wife, whom he had met in connection with a series of grotesque murders handled by Louis Chalon, now safely lodged in Broadmoor.[1] "Let's go up and see him, shall we? I'm sure he'd be very pleased to have visitors. It must be very dreary for him sitting all day in that dismal little room, even if he is swell enough to have a carpet on the floor."

But Andrew thought differently. "He wouldn't be in his room at this hour of the evening; he'd be at home, junketing

1 See *Tidy Death*.

respectably with Mary. But anyway, this is different from the Chalon affair. The police are in on this corpse already, so we can't butt in on their preserves. Besides, there's nothing to go on yet awhile."

"I only meant a social visit—not official. Let's ring Pig up now, and then we can go up immediately after dinner."

"Immediately after dinner we're going to see Garbo," her husband replied firmly.

———

The most maddening thing about Agnes was that, since her marriage, she had become jovial at breakfast. Before meeting Andrew she had behaved fairly reasonably at this meal, eating in comparative silence and reading her paper from the front-page splash to the Births, Marriages and Deaths. Now, behold her in tailored gown of black corduroy, her musical legs bare, her symphonic feet in cherry-coloured mules. Hear her singing a verse from *A Foxtrot for a Play*, by W. H. Auden (whom she much admires), as she butters her fourth slice of toast:

> "'Some are mad on Airedales
> And some on Pekinese,
> On tabby cats or parrots,
> Or guinea-pigs or geese.
> There are patients in asylums
> Who think that they're a tree;
> I had an aunt who loved a plant,
> But you're my cup of tea.'

"You are my cup of tea, Andrew. Have another?"

"Another what?"

"Cup of tea."

"No. Yes. Be quiet, darling. I want to read the P.M.'s speech—*Parapluie Munichoise*, in case you didn't know. When on earth is something going to happen? It always comforts me to think that I've been an anti-Fascist since Fascism was invented and anti-Hitler since 1933. I don't have to make the right-about-turn some chaps do."

"Andrew, do you think Mrs. Sibley will still hold her meeting?"

He mumbled through marmalade, "What meeting?"

"Well, last week she sent round letters asking us to go up to her flat tonight and discuss how we could work together to protect Block 3 against fire. If she is holding it, we'd get the full cast together, wouldn't we? It would be interesting to watch them all."

"What are you talking about?"

"The late Mr. Coppenstall."

Andrew's eyes lit with unexpected approval. "I see what you mean. Why not find out from Mrs. S. if she still means business?"

"I will. I'll go up this morning. There are one or two other little matters I'd like her to clear up," she added mysteriously.

"Now look here, don't you go butting in on the poor woman."

"I shall be the soul of tact," Agnes reproved him. *"To market, to market to buy a fat pig, Home again, home again, jiggety-jig,"* she trolled pleasantly, until her husband, leave or no leave, was forced to take his newspaper into the bedroom where it was quiet.

That morning she dressed herself in sympathetic black, put on rather less make-up than usual and went upstairs to call on Mrs. Sibley. Mrs. Rowse, to her relief, was out shopping in the West End.

"Do forgive me for intruding," said Agnes, "but I did want to know if you were still having the fire meeting."

Mrs. Sibley's eyes protruded. "But certainly! I hope I should always put patriotism before private troubles."

"That's the spirit!" Agnes smiled approval. "Well, we'll both be there. Is everyone else coming?"

"Everyone—or rather, Mr. Warrender will come if he's not working. Will you have a little sherry? I feel low this morning. Poor Phyllada had to go out, I know, to buy mourning-gloves and scarves for us both, but I don't mind confessing to you that after my recent shock I don't like being alone."

"I'd love some sherry," said Agnes, with a ghastly glance at the bottle which, despite her breakfast cheerfulness, was still having some effect upon her. She comforted herself with exploded saws about hairs of dogs.

As they sat together over a very small gas-fire that burned the insteps while the calves froze, Agnes manoeuvered the conversation in the direction she desired. Finding, however, that no manoeuvering would lead her to the information she most wanted, she risked a frontal attack.

"Mrs. Sibley, I know this may sound dreadfully impertinent, but I'm so anxious to have this horrible business cleared up, and one never knows what may hinge on apparently insignificant things, does one? Will you tell me if—" She blushed. "—If Mr. Coppenstall would ever have…have come into any of that legacy?"

Her hostess stared. "Yes, I'm afraid that does sound impertinent. Still, you're a nice girl, Mrs. Kinghof, and you've been very kind to me, so I don't mind telling you. Yes,

Reginald would have inherited. Having some conscience, I made my will in his favour and told him, when I replied to his brutal letter, that he must wait for his fortune."

"And now?"

"As my will stands… But I shall be making a new one, I expect. Naturally my next of kin will inherit."

"And that is—?"

"You're asking a lot of questions, aren't you?" said Mrs. Sibley acidly. "Well, I suppose there's no reason for conceal-ment. Maclagan Steer."

"Maclagan Steer?"

"Reginald's boy. When his wife left him, she lived with Steer for two years, then asked Reginald—impudent crea-ture—if he would allow her to divorce him. He had few good qualities, I fear, but chivalry was among them. He assented. She married Steer, and the boy, who was then five, lived with her till he reached his majority, when he changed his name to his mother's. Encouraged by Steer, he was act-ing in repertory from the age of seventeen; he had talent, I believe. At twenty-two he went out on a Canadian tour, and his mother lost track of him completely. She and Steer were killed in a railway accident a year later, and the boy, for all I know, has vanished off the face of the earth."

Agnes said, "Could he know that, failing his father, he would inherit?"

Mrs. Sibley grinned sourly. "I have had a reputation— perhaps exaggerated—for conscience in family matters. My conscience was a family tradition. Yes, I think Maclagan would have assumed it. But why all this, Mrs. Kinghof? I really can't see—"

"I'm sorry," Agnes said quickly. "You must be furious with me. I'm only asking questions in the hope of getting a lead, but there doesn't seem to be one. How old would Maclagan be now? What does he look like?"

"Thirty-two. Look like? How should I know? I've never set eyes on him since he was a squinny thing of ten. His mother brought him to tea once. We never got on well, though she did write to me occasionally."

"Thank you," Agnes said, "and please don't be angry with me." She rose. "Very nice sherry."

"Not at all," said Mrs. Sibley vaguely, and with unconscious truth. She was lost in thought, and her eyes were half-hidden by her heavy yellow lids.

Mrs. Rowse came in, her arms full of parcels. "Oh, Mrs. Kinghof! How nice of you to call! Such a morning, Addie dear, everything so hard to get, though I've got it now, and I've had to leave poor Fernia on the roof of the gym, and you know how difficult it is for me when I have to break my inspiration. Addie, are you feeling all right? You look white. It's her heart," she explained to Agnes, "it's been weak all her life, ever since she was a mere tot, and the doctor says she should always be protected from shocks. What, are you going? Well, we hope to see you tonight at our little meeting."

"Phyllada!" Mrs. Sibley said abruptly. "I want you to telephone my lawyer immediately after lunch. Oh, good-bye, Mrs. Kinghof."

Agnes made her farewells and went thoughtfully across to the "Green Doe," where Andrew was awaiting her report.

He looked sober. "Weak heart. Yes. Frightening tactics. Yes. Does she know, do you think? Does she connect up the pig-stuff with Coppenstall's murder?"

"I think she does, but she's ashamed to tell anyone. I imagine she was a bit greedy, and that she certainly did exert undue influence on her auntie."

Andrew patted her hand. "Smart work. I suppose you realize that when Eggshell goes over just the same ground with Ma Sibley, she'll burst with rage?"

"I don't give a damn if she does. Andrew, there's one big question in all this. Have you guessed it?"

He took a long drink, stubbed out his cigarette and lit another before he answered her.

"Yes, I have… Agnes, I like you in that suit. Did I pay for it, or did you?"

"You did. The pockets are quite new, aren't they? It's a Chaumière model. It may be a mite cold for this sort of weather, but I can't bear to squash it under a coat. Andy, don't fool. What's the question?"

He replied slowly, "Who is Maclagan Steer?"

Chapter Four

THAT NIGHT, ON THE STROKE OF EIGHT, THE KINGHOFS left their flat. They were greeted by Mr. Lang, who rose out of the depths below like a rosy hobgoblin, his curly fair hair flattened as much as was possible, his bow-tie, for once, neatly centred. "Hey! You two going to the Convention? Wait for me." He ran up to join them. "I say, Mr. Kinghof, I owe you an apology for playing sillyfools the night before last. I'd been on a bit of a whoop-up, I'm afraid."

"Glad to have been of service," said Andrew, looking curiously at him. "I must admit I was scared you'd break your neck on that pipe. You weren't in any state for athletics."

"I know. I'd been to about six parties, and I can't even remember where three of them were. I'll have to ask around a bit. Heard anything more about our corpse?"

"Nothing new."

Climbing the last flight together, they found Madame Charnet on the mat outside Number 10. "So seelly," she said, "I can't make them hear."

"Perhaps the bell's run down," Agnes suggested, and she

pressed it vigorously, afterwards putting her ear to the glass panel. "Doesn't seem to ring. Where's the knocker?"

Mr. Lang seized the brass dog's-head cunningly placed just where the eye did not readily observe it, and banged loudly.

Lights went up inside the flat, and in a moment Mrs. Rowse opened to them.

"Ah, here you all are! Welcome to our little gathering. I hope you've come simply full of practical suggestions. Mrs. Kinghof, Madame Charnet, may I take your wraps? And if the gentlemen will join Mrs. Sibley in the lounge—"

She waited while Agnes and the Frenchwoman took off their coats and hung them on the hooks behind the door.

"Half a minute," Agnes said, "my shoelace has come untied." They lingered for her, while she knelt to adjust it, then went into the lounge, where she followed them.

Mrs. Sibley, who had already appointed herself chairman, had made up her mind that the proceedings should be business-like. She was seated in the big armchair, and before her was a table on which were pencils and a pad of paper. Andrew, who liked to be warm at all costs, was sitting on the floor before the fire. Mr. Lang was perched in puckish fashion upon the stool, eager, attentive.

"Now, Mrs. Kinghof," said Mrs. Sibley, casting a disapproving glance at Andrew, whose informal posture was, she considered, jeopardizing the dignity of the meeting, "if you'll take the high-backed chair, perhaps Madame and Mrs. Rowse will make themselves comfortable on the sofa."

"Oh, I'd just as soon sit on the sofa," Agnes gaily interrupted, plumping herself upon it. She did not mean to sit in the bleak piece of faked Jacobean, with the cane broken in back and seat. Mrs. Rowse, having failed to move her by a stare of affront, was herself forced to take this instrument of torture. When all were seated, Mrs. Sibley reached for the shillelagh and knocked smartly on the table, clearing her throat to command attention.

"Ladies and gentlemen, we won't waste time."

"Hear, hear!" said Felix Lang.

"Mr. Warrender, I hope, will come, but we must begin without him and if he arrives later we will acquaint him with details of our discussion. Now, down to brass tacks."

"Brass—?" murmured Madame to Agnes, who hissed, "Figure of speech. Means 'get going.'"

"Ah. Ah, merci beaucoup."

The shillelagh sounded angrily.

Andrew said, "A moment, please, Madame Chairman. Ladies and gentlemen, I should like, before we begin, to express our appreciation to Mrs. Sibley for continuing this good work despite her—her recent strains and stresses."

"Hear!" yelped Mr. Lang. "Good show!"

Mrs. Sibley flushed with faint pleasure. "Thank you, Mr. Kinghof. Now then. The business before us tonight is to discuss how best we can protect these premises against possible incendiary bombs. The landlords have supplied us with a sand-bucket, kept on Floor 3, and a long-handled scoop. Some of us feel, however, that these precautions are insufficient. Has anyone any plans for further precautions, or ideas on how we should organize ourselves into a fire party?"

Madame Charnet said diffidently, "I 'ave 'eard, at A.R.P. lectures at the Town 'All, that eet is good to spread bran in the attic. The butcher is vairy good with letting me 'ave bran for my leetle cat, and I could easily spare some for putting under the roof—"

Five faces were constricted with emotion.

"It is *sand* one spreads in the attic," said Mrs. Sibley. "Bran would not be suitable, not suitable at all. But thank you very much."

"I am so sorry. My Eenglish is yet not good."

"But the idea," said Andrew, "is excellent. May I make the concrete suggestion that we approach the landlords for a supply of sand, and get Blake to put it up in the attic?"

"I second that," Mr. Lang enthused. "Oh, good show. Sound scheme."

"Blake can be very difficult," Mrs. Rowse said mournfully.

"Not if he's well tipped," Agnes answered. "I propose we make a collection for the purpose of tipping him."

"One motion at a time, please! Captain Kinghof has proposed that we approach Messrs. Carr and Co. for a supply of sand. Mr. Lang has seconded. Any amendment? No? Will all in favour signify in the usual fashion?"

All in favour said Ay.

"Phyllada, will you please enter that in the minutes? Now, Mrs. Kinghof has suggested that we open a common fund for a gratuity to Blake for services rendered."

"Services that may possibly, with any luck, be rendered," said Lang.

"Does anyone second?"

"I second," said Andrew.

"I don't think Carrs will give us any sand," Mrs. Rowse grieved, scribbling away at the minutes in a small note-book.

"We are acting on the assumption that they will," the chairman rebuked her. "I fear you are out of order. The motion has been put. Will all in favour—"

Again they said Ay.

At that moment the door-bell made a faint, but recognizable, chortling sound.

"Did I hear the bell?" Mrs. Sibley enquired.

"I think so," said Agnes. "It's a bit run down, so we used the knocker."

"Phyllada, will you please answer it? It will be Mr. Warrender."

"I'll go," said Andrew, bounding athletically upright from crossed ankles.

He went out into the hall and admitted George Warrender, a small thick man in his middle thirties or early forties, to whose flat face a big black moustache and a total lack of eyebrows gave an arresting appearance. "Oh, Kinghof. How are you? Meeting begun? Sorry I couldn't get along before. Had the devil of a job as it was, prising myself loose."

"We've passed two resolutions," said Andrew. "Mrs. Sibley is in the chair and Mrs. Rowse is writing an amazing number of minutes."

"Oh. Oppressive, eh?"

"I wouldn't say that. Business-like."

"Tomfoolery," said Mr. Warrender. "What do they know about fires? Well, where's the meeting? Lounge? All right. Lead on, Macduff."

Andrew led him on and, when Warrender had greeted and been greeted, went out to bring in a bedroom chair for him. He returned from this labour to find that Mrs. Sibley had lost no time. The Convention, as Lang had termed it, was once more in full swing, and Madame Charnet held the floor.

"It seems to me," she said, in her loud, deaf voice, "that we should all keep our bath-tubs fooll all the time, for the pirrup-pump."

"Stirrup," bawled Mrs. Rowse, smiling benignly to indicate that she bawled, not out of exasperation, but to make herself heard. "Yes, I think that is an excellent suggestion."

"But hell's bells, madam," Lang protested, "can't we wait till the raids start? We can't have permanent ponds in the flats. Besides, I have to leave the plug out of mine, because the tap drips so badly the bath would overflow in eight hours."

"Have you not," asked Mrs. Sibley, "a waste-pipe?"

"Choked."

"What with?" Agnes enquired interestedly.

"Oh, bits of hair, lumps off the sponge, gouts of old soap, fag-ends, I dare say—"

"My aunt, General Sidebotham, used to say you could tell a man's character by the state of his waste-pipe."

Andrew smothered a grin.

"Your—your aunt?" said Mrs. Rowse.

"Salvation Army. My aunt, General Sidebotham, used to say that if there was soap in a man's waste-pipe he might live to pick oakum; but that if there was hair, he would certainly be hanged."

"They're weaving the rope for me, then," said Mr. Lang, with the air of one who has surrendered all hope; but his eyes sparkled at her.

Mrs. Sibley used the shillelagh. "Very quaint, Mrs. Kinghof! Your aunt must have been a remarkable character. Nevertheless, I'm afraid she is not relevant to this discussion. Next, please?"

"Two yards of pink elastic," said Lang, but not quite softly enough, for the chairman banged, and glared at him.

"The baths, we were discussing baths," said Mr. Warrender wearily.

The subject was renewed with some bitterness, for the members of the Fire Committee were tired and were becoming increasingly apt to express boredom through spleen. Andrew, taking little part in the debate, looked from one to the other of three faces: Lang's, Madame Charnet's, Warrender's. But which? Seems idiotic. Must be Warrender or Lang. But surely Lang's too young. Not more than twenty-four, I shouldn't think. Warrender, then. But why?

The evening drew at last to a close, with agreement reached that the landlords should be approached for sand, a common fund should be opened, if need arose, for tipping Blake—Mrs. Sibley proposed sixpence each, which would be three and six, and was defeated on an amendment by Andrew, who suggested that the job would be worth a shilling a head, or seven bob—and a loose arrangement was reached by which those who wanted to keep their baths filled should do so, indicating this permanent water-supply by a big "B" marked in blue pencil on the front door. This method of indication, facetiously proposed by Felix Lang, was applauded in all seriousness by Mrs. Sibley and Mrs. Rowse, and out of sheer exhaustion by Warrender, Andrew, Agnes and Madame. At half-past ten Andrew suggested that the meeting be adjourned, and after thanking the owners of Flat 10 for their hospitality, the Fire Committee trailed out into the hall.

Agnes picked up from the mat a white envelope, addressed in typewriting to Mrs. Sibley, Flat 10, Block 3, Stewarts Court, S.W.

"Oh, thank you, Mrs. Kinghof. What's this, I wonder, a circular? What a lot of paper gets wasted these days!"

She took out the enclosed sheet, read it, and went ash-white. Without a word she passed it to Andrew, who glanced at it and handed it to Agnes. The characters were black, thick, staggering.

FIVE LITTLE PIGGIES WENT TO MEETING
BUT THIS LITTLE PIGGY STAYED AT HOME.

"THE PIG-STICKER."

Agnes said, "Then it was an outsider!"

Andrew turned to the three others, who, struck by the fear in Mrs. Sibley's face, were lingering on the doorstep. "Better go along now. Mrs. Sibley's not very well...a slight shock. Bad news."

"What did he say?" Madame asked, hand cupping her ear.

Mr. Warrender said, "All right, Kinghof. We'll clear. Come on, Madame. Come on, Lang. Good night, everyone."

When they had gone, the Kinghofs escorted Mrs. Sibley back to the lounge, while Mrs. Rowse, silent and appalled, went for sal volatile.

"Look here," Andrew said, "you're not to distress yourself. This is only silly clowning, and we'll catch the brute all right. Perhaps someone saw him come into the flats. Agnes, you're quite sure no one who came here tonight could have left it?"

"Well, I know it wasn't on the mat when I came in, because I had to tie up my shoelace, and I'd have seen it then. Besides, you went out afterwards."

"That's right. And it certainly wasn't there when I let Warrender in. I say, between the time he came and the close of the meeting, did anyone leave the room for any purpose whatsoever?"

Mrs. Rowse went red. "Only myself," she said rather stiffly, "and I assure you, I—"

"No, no, we know you didn't. But at what time did you go out?"

"Twenty-past nine," said Agnes quickly, "I know, because—" She was silent. She had, upon Mrs. Rowse's rising, looked at the clock in the faint hope that the old lady meant to make a cup of tea. The speed of her return had been self-explanatory, and Agnes had relapsed into hopelessness.

"So the letter was dropped in between twenty-past nine and half-past ten," Andrew mused.

His wife said, "I'll be back in a minute," and without further warning left the flat.

Outside the street door she found Constable Frankson. "Officer!"

"Yes, ma'am?"

"I'm Mrs. Kinghof."

"I remember, ma'am."

"Are you detailed to watch Block 3? Inspector Eggshell said he was putting a man on to prevent any more pig jokes."

"Why, anything happened?"

"Mrs. Sibley's had another letter. Who's been in the flats between twenty-past nine and half-past ten?"

Frankson looked apprehensive. "Only an air-raid warden."

"A warden?"

"Delivering circulars."

"Who was he? Did you know him?"

"Can't say I did. Youngish chap."

"Look here, constable, let's see if I've had a circular. Will you come up?"

He followed her. Agnes let him into her own flat and

found, sure enough, a white, typewritten envelope similar to the one received by Mrs. Sibley. In this, however, was a brief, cyclostyled appeal for recruits to the Warden, Fire-fighting and First Aid services.

"Come on. You'd better see Mrs. Sibley."

"I'd better," said Frankson grimly.

Andrew and Agnes were destined to broken nights. They sat up in bed, cigarettes at their elbows, hot-water bottles at their feet.

"Now we're lost. We're no further on than ever we were. The copper who said no one went into the well must have been mistaken after all."

"Yes, but anyone who went in must have come out again. That would be two people for him to see…or the same person twice, rather. Could he have been so blind as to miss that?"

"On the other hand, no one in the flats played tonight's joke, because we had our eye on them. The only alternative's an accomplice, and whereas I can believe in one madman, I refuse to believe in two."

"Steer's an air-raid warden. He must have taken our Mrs. S.'s circular and slipped the Pig-letter in. Surely a warden won't be difficult to trace?"

"I expect Eggshell will do the tracing. It's his from now on. Darling, we must get some sleep or you won't be fit for the inquest."

"And I must be fit for that," Agnes agreed. She slipped off her jacket and dropped it on the floor. Snuggling down in the sheets, she quickly finished her cigarette and gave it to her husband to extinguish. "All right, Andrew, I'm ready. Tuck down."

Darkness fell on them. He was just sliding into a mild,

sweet sleep when she said drowsily, "Pet, I don't think we ought to get into a groove, do you? I mean, we mustn't become obsessed by murder."

"Shut up, pet."

"I mean, we must have wider interests. Let's talk about the bombardier who got hit by the butter. Is he a really awful skunk? Can't you demote him, or aren't you powerful enough?"

Mr. Kinghof rolled over, presenting his back. He pretended to snore.

"You have such lovely shoulder-blades," his wife said dreamily, "just like two chickens' breasts. I should love to put bacon-fat on them and fry and fry and fry... No, not bacon. Enough pig as it is. Have them served with watercress and fried potatoes, hot, very hot, in a silver dish..." Falling asleep, she dreamed of food.

———

The inquest, held the following morning, passed off without incident, and the motley jury, rather like the jury in *Alice in Wonderland*, returned as directed the verdict of murder by person or persons unknown. They had all, Coroner and jury alike, been shaken by the sight of the body. Agnes gave her evidence in so subdued and precise a fashion that the Coroner complimented her upon it. When the proceedings were over she and Andrew hoped to have a word with Eggshell; but he was too busy to be bothered with either of them.

"Later, if you please. I expect we shall have a few talks yet. By the way, Mrs. Kinghof, it was smart of you to get Frankson so promptly on the scene last night. I think we've got a lead now."

"Would it help," Agnes said diffidently, "if I did a bit of snooping round the Town Hall? They know me pretty well there, and I don't think I'd arouse antagonisms—"

"I'll do the snooping, thank you kindly, ma'am," said Eggshell.

But Agnes smiled as she watched him walk away. "I think we're getting on better than we did in the Chalon affair, Andrew. Our hearts and Eggshell's are beating each to each, as it were. Even Pig couldn't complain."

Just after lunch they had a shock of a slightly different kind from previous shocks. The telephone rang, and Agnes, answering, heard a muffled, fierce voice addressing her.

"Mrs. Kinghof?"

"Speaking."

A long pause. Then—"This is The Pig."

"Who?"

"What's the matter?" asked Andrew, who had seen her jump.

"Shush, shush, pet. I'm listening. You, there? Who did you say you were?"

"The Pig. Listen, if you value your life! You and that military husband of yours had better keep your noses out of my affairs, or..."

"Or what?" said Agnes bravely. Perhaps she merely sounded brave. To Andrew she hissed: "We're being menaced."

Then the voice changed, and a fat chuckle rang over the wire, the self-conscious chuckle of a man not accustomed to chuckling. "Or Whitestone of the Yard will put you both under protective custody!"

She shouted at the voice, and giggled hysterically with relief. "Pig! You should be ashamed of yourself! I'd never have imagined in a thousand years that you could play a joke. You're ridiculous. How did you know about us?—Oh, I suppose Eggshell told you. Is the Yard going to be called in?—Andrew, it's our Pig. Lord Pig.—I say, Pig, do come and see us, will you? Will you lunch with us tomorrow and bring Mary?"

"One question at a time," replied her husband's cousin. "Regarding the Yard, maybe yes, maybe no. You'll find out. I'd like to come and see you, but I'm too busy at the moment. We both hope to get in touch a bit later on. How long will Andrew be home?"

"I don't know. Maybe a week, maybe a fortnight. Want to speak to him?"

The voice seemed to curl with disgust. "Speak to him? I've never wanted to speak to him in my life. It's been forced upon me. Oh, Agnes: you two keep out of this affair. I don't like the sound of it, and I don't want the time of my department wasted in hauling you out of trouble. Spend your leave like Christians. Go to night-clubs. Go to one of those dreary, disgusting leg-shows. Go to the Yellow Chicken before we're compelled to raid it. But don't mess about with Eggshell's murder. That's all. Good-bye."

Agnes retailed the gist of this to her husband. "Can you beat it? Old Pig, playing jokes. I always told you there was good in him somewhere."

"He's got a fine liver and one tooth stopped with gold," Andrew grumbled, "otherwise, I wouldn't say there was anything good in him anywhere. What shall we do this afternoon?"

"I thought, if I just looked in at the Town Hall—unobtrusively you know—and saw old Major Rafferty..."

"No, you don't. We're going to see the French painters

at Mayor's, then we'll have tea at Simpson's and I'll buy a couple of shirts, then we'll go and see Myrna Loy, then we'll have dinner at the Café Royal and a few drinks, and then, and about time too, we'll come home and go to bed. What hideous ideas of entertainment Pig has!"

"They're only his ideas of our ideas. His and Mary's notion of a real day out is a visit to the Royal College of Surgeons' museum, tea at an aunt's, and an evening with *Hiawatha* at the Albert Hall."

Dismissing him with contempt, they set out for the West End.

———

That afternoon, Eggshell went round to the Town Hall, where he solicited the help of the Controller, Major Rafferty.

"I want to know, sir, who was responsible for the sending-out of the recruiting circulars, who made up the bundles and who undertook delivery."

"You'd better come down to the basement and meet Hartlebrass. He'll know more than I do."

So the men went downstairs into a great, cold room opening with swing doors on to the blind alley at the back of the Town Hall. There were a good many people about, men and women in blue boiler suits, nearly all of them smoking, and all making a great deal of noise. It was tea-time, and trays of heavy white china were passing to and fro, as if by supernatural levitation, through the smoke-screen. Major Rafferty picked out a svelte, ginger-haired young man who was checking uniforms, tin helmets, and respirator bags.

"Hartlebrass, come here a moment, will you? This is

Inspector Eggshell. Eggshell, Mr. Hartlebrass, head of our stock-room. Now then, I want you to answer a few questions for the Inspector."

Eggshell explained what he wanted to know, and Mr. Hartlebrass scratched his head so energetically that a delicate flight of dandruff settled on the bright silk scarf that he wore tucked into the neck of his uniform. "Well, Inspector, it's all a bit tricky. One labours and sweats, and still one isn't properly organized. I had a team here addressing the envelopes and putting them into bundles for delivery. Some were regular wardens, and others were the *hoi polloi* that drift in here to give a hand from time to time."

"Here, here!" the Controller expostulated.

"Oh, sorry about the '*hoi polloi*', sir, but really, they're often more hindrance than help. They won't join the service right out, though we can badger them till we go simply mauve, but they just ooze in and out when they think they will and then tell their friends they're helping the war effort."

"But you do know the names of these people?" Eggshell asked anxiously.

"Oh, yes, we know that. Like a list, Inspector?"

"If you please."

"Larita!" Hartlebrass attracted the attention of a plump young woman who was managing to type with one finger and drink her tea simultaneously. A silver-blonde, she opened great blue eyes at him, after the fashion of a shy gazelle, and fluttered lashes doughy with navy mascara. "Derek, pet-lamb?"

"Do me out a list of last night's envelope team, will you? So grateful."

"But with delirious pleasure!" replied Larita, turning her smile upon Mr. Hartlebrass, the Inspector, and the Controller, whipping out the sheet of paper from her machine, inserting another and rattling away at top speed.

"Oh, and just put 'R' beside the regular wardens, will you?" Mr. Hartlebrass was nothing if not efficient.

"Certes, O Knight," Larita answered him, her eyelashes beating her cheeks.

Eggshell, who had patiently endured this exchange, said, "Can you tell me who delivered the envelopes, Mr. Hartlebrass?"

"Oh, that's easy. Only the Carlyle district envelopes went out last night, and four regulars took them. I think they're all here now, because we've just changed over shifts." He leaped sprightlily on to a chair, cupped his hands to his mouth and said, "Tantivy, everyone." A flattering silence fell. "I say, who delivered the recruiting circulars in Carlyle Street last night?"

"I did the West side," said a tough girl, swallowing a mouthful of biscuit in a hurry and choking on it.

"No, I meant the East. Who delivered to Stewarts Court?"

A young man, of pleasant, solid countenance, spoke up. "Me. I did."

"Who are you? I can't see you for all this ghastly miasma."

"Dennison."

"Oh, Dennison!—Come along here a minute, will you?"

Hartlebrass jumped down, and the noise was resumed.

"Have to get you into the force, sir," said the Inspector, faintly ironic. He turned to greet Dennison. "You a regular warden?"

"Since October '38."

"Our oldest inhabitant, stout fellow," Hartlebrass commented.

"Ah. You delivered Stewarts Court?"

"Yes, sir. Anything wrong?"

"No, no. Only a matter of routine. You remember dropping a circular in on Number 10, Block 3?"

Dennison pondered. "Can't say for sure, sir—I mean, I didn't notice particularly—but I did every flat in the Court except the ones I knew were vacant, so I must've."

"I see. Yes, thanks. That's all."

When the young man had gone, Eggshell said, "He looks a sound sort of chap."

"Mattera fact, I know he is," Major Rafferty confirmed him. "His father was my chauffeur for eleven years, and I've known young Ted since he was a schoolboy. Father means the boy to go up in the world. Had him well educated. He's studying accountancy now."

Eggshell said, "Good. Thank you, sir. I think that's all."

The Controller remembered something. "Hartlebrass! I hope you've made arrangements for storing the uniforms safely now." The young man flushed. He had had a bout with one of Eggshell's men on that score shortly before the inquest on Mr. Coppenstall, and had hoped, in vain, that the matter would not be referred to the Controller. *"Oui, mon capitaine."*

"What? Express yourself properly."

"Yes, sir."

"It was a revelation to me that it should have been so simple to walk off with equipment from the stock-room. I'm told a uniform was missing about a month ago."

"Yes, sir. Sorry, sir. I can only suppose whoever was in charge here at the time might have just—er—slipped down the passage, I suppose, and it wouldn't have been difficult for someone to pop in from the alley, especially if—"

"If they were fairly familiar?" said Eggshell. "Quite, sir.

One of the 'Irregulars,' perhaps. Well, Major, as far as we're concerned the incident's closed. I'm sure Mr. Hartlebrass here will see to it that nothing of the kind happens again."

"Oh, it won't! All taped now. Everything under lock and key." Hartlebrass was unhappy. To work off his embarrassment, he shouted at Larita. "I say, are you going to be all night, dear? Hurry, hurry, hurry, there's a good girl."

"Nearly finished," she responded; "just one more weeny little name."

"Look here," said Rafferty, "I hope you certainly do mean to tighten things up here in future. I don't want any more missing uniforms."

"Oh, they're already tightened, sir.—Thank you, Larita. Give it to the Inspector, please, pretty, please."

She handed it to Eggshell.

There were seventeen names, twelve marked with Rs. These he decided for the moment to discount: but he said, "Miss, I'd be obliged if you'd do one more little job for me. Will you list the five itinerant helpers—the ones who are not regular wardens—on a separate sheet, with their addresses?"

"Like a flash of lightning," she smiled, and within five minutes had supplied him with his requirements.

Eggshell glanced down at the sheet.

"Miss Cecilia Morrow, 3 Haig Square.

"Robert van Ryden, 84a Wilde Mansions.

"Mrs. Hazlerigg, The Studio, Blandings Street.

"Gilbert Smith, 12 Cooley Street."

But it was the last name that arrested his attention and sent the blood to his cheeks: or not so much the name as the address.

"Henry Race, Flat 8, Block 3, Stewarts Court."

Chapter Five

WHILE EGGSHELL WAS PONDERING THE IMPUDENCE of a criminal who had dared use the respectable address of Captain and Mrs. Andrew Kinghof, and while he was eliciting from vague wardens that Henry Race had been putting in an hour or two a week for three months past and that he was a dim sort of little man with black whiskers—opinions differed as to the degree of blackness—Mrs. Sibley was resting on Mrs. Rowse's bed in the smaller backroom of her flat.[1]

Mrs. Rowse was in town bullyragging her publisher, who had that morning announced his shameful intent to remainder *Cuckoo Delahaye* at fourpence a copy. She had set off in what Mr. and Mrs. Kinghof had often termed her battle-hat, a savage structure of maroon velvet, a cross between a biretta and a rowing-boat, leaving her friend as comfortable as possible with a box of Turkish Delight and the latest chapters concerning Fernia Prideaux.

Mrs. Sibley, who, though weak-hearted, was on the whole strong-minded, had determined that with the inquest

---

1 See plan 2.

behind her, she would put the entire ugly affair out of her mind. Violently she suppressed the gnawing anxiety for which the practical jokes were responsible. After all, they might be the work of some lunatic, some person with a grudge, though she knew of no one who might have cause. As for Maclagan, for all she knew he might be at the ends of the earth; for all she knew, buried under six feet of it. Danger to me? she thought. Ridiculous. I'm not going to be frightened by turnip-ghosts. I must keep very calm, not allow myself to be upset. The doctor said I must watch my heart.

It was a mild day, and a soft, apricot sunlight gilded the walls. Mrs. Sibley had chosen her friend's room instead of her own because it was smaller, and therefore warmer; also, because the latter had disagreeable associations. From the square at the back of Stewarts Court, bounded on one side by the flats, on another by the walls of the Polytechnic, on a third by the higher wall of the Theological College grounds and on the fourth by the backs of Welwyn Studios, came the fragile laughter of small children at play. They ought to be evacuated, thought Mrs. Sibley, but less because she cared for their welfare than because the noise had always irritated her. The square, having two entrances only, one an alley-way down the side of Welwyn Studios, the other a passage between the College and the Polytechnic, was inaccessible to traffic and was therefore marked down by a beneficent Borough Council as an ideal playground for the children. It was a rectangular court, asphalted, with a few plane trees absurdly fenced about in iron. When the children were at school, or in bed, it was a quiet place.

She thought, and she smiled to herself, Well, if it was Maclagan, there's a shock coming to him.

Mrs. Sibley picked up Fernia, rejected her. She liked

Mrs. Rowse, but could not honestly admire her work, nor see in it that pure English style which, its creator considered, compensated for the juvenility of the matter. Sighing, she returned it to the file and took *Sparkenbroke* from the shelf. She became so engrossed in the spiritual adventures of the funereal peer that for the first time in two days her fear melted away and she began to sink into comfortable languor.

She was, in fact, on the point of dozing when the children's voices sharpened, their laughter grew more shrill and there arose a sound from the asphalt of trundling wheels. Mrs. Sibley raised her lids with an effort similar to that required of a strong man who must lift from the stage two iron bars with hundred-pound weights on them, and she said aloud, "Disgraceful, disturbing the residents! I shall write to the Council. Why do we pay rates?"

Then came a new sound, rising above the children's laughter and applause, a sound that touched a chord in her heart. It was a cackling voice crying—"Shallabalah! Shallabalah!" and there followed a clattering of wood on wood, a creaking and a thumping, an eldritch scream, "Judy! Judy!"

Now all her life Mrs. Sibley had loved a Punch-and-Judy show. All her friends knew it. She had told them all many times, and her acquaintances too—"It's the child in me. I can't resist the old play—can't resist it!" So, languor forgotten, she rose from her couch, opened the window and leaned out into the mild air.

It was a sorry enough show that met her eyes, a tottery box mounted on wooden wheels, the paint smudged by the dirt of ages and blistered by the suns of half a century, the curtains ragged and filthy; and Punch, who sat mooning in repulsive fashion on the ledge, was a featureless blob in clothes that had faded from red to a sickly brown.

But the children loved it. As the play proceeded, as Punch laid about him and Judy squawked, as the measly Toby lurched on his string, fell from the stage and was jerked back as savagely as if the Hangman himself held the cord, they clapped their hands, jumped up and down in delight; and their chiming voices were like the rise and fall of bells.

Mrs. Sibley, though disappointed by the meanness of the apparatus, was charmed almost to tears. It seemed to her that the showman was inexpert, for the incidents were out of order and some, indeed, were entirely strange. Still the voice went on: "Shallabalah! Judy, Judy, Judy!" and then, suddenly: "Addie! Addie!"

The shock ran through her like lightning. She thought wildly, I'm going mad. I'm fancying things. It's all that's happened lately, all these horrors. I must take a grip on myself.

Then it rose slowly out of darkness to grin at her from the stage: a pig's head, white and shining, the dead eyes closed, the snout purplish-white, a red Punch's cap set between the ears.

Mrs. Sibley knew no more.

———

The children, whose first show this was, were delighted by the pig. Those more experienced, for whom the pig was an innovation, welcomed it no less eagerly; so it was a great disappointment to them all when the curtains clashed together, a man dodged out from the box, took up the handles and trundled it away as fast as he could go, down the passage between the Polytechnic and the College, towards the waste lot marked down for the site of a super cinema.

———

Oddly enough, it was the Kinghofs who were the first to discover Mrs. Sibley. At ten to six they were returning to their flat by way of the square, for Agnes had developed a slight headache and had suggested that perhaps it might be best to cut Myrna Loy and have a quiet evening at home. As they entered the square from the passage Andrew said, "Let's look in on Ma Sibley, shall we? It's rotten for her being alone today." They had met Mrs. Rowse on the bus, on their way to town.

"If you like. The Most Famous Girl in Stewarts Court said poor Addie was going to rest in the small bedroom, with her feet up and Fernia Prideaux to read. Poor thing. I say, Andy! Her window's wide open, and it's turned freezing cold. Would you think she liked fresh air?"

"Some people have odd tastes. Come on, darling, don't loiter."

But Agnes was thoughtful as they went into Block 3 and climbed the stairs to the top landing. Having experience of the Sibley bell, they thundered at the knocker.

"I *don't* like that window," Agnes mused. "I mean, it was lovely this afternoon and anyone might have opened it; but why leave it open, now it's so bleak? Besides, she's not blacked-out yet, and she should be."

"I don't suppose she's in that room at all. Knock again."

They knocked.

"Perhaps she's gone out," said Andrew.

"No. She'd have blacked-out first. She always does. Andy, I've got such an odd feeling about her! We've got to get in."

"Don't be ridiculous. We can't. Let's knock again." But the third knocking yielded no result.

Andrew said suddenly, "All right. I'll take a chance on your hunch. Come on downstairs—I want to change my clothes."

"Why on earth—?"

"For climbing."

He changed from his uniform to slacks and sweater and then, with Agnes excited and curious at his heels, went into the bedroom that lay immediately below the one in which Mrs. Sibley had spent so painful an afternoon.

Opening the window, he leaned out, fumbled at the stack-pipe that ran down the side of the house and said, "It'll hold."

"What are you going to do?"

"Enter her flat. God help me and my career if I'm seen, but we must hope for the best."

"Andrew, you Lochinvar!" cried Agnes inappropriately, but she did not deter him. "Be careful. It's a long way to fall."

Happily there was no moon that night. The sky was overcast, and there was no one in the square.

Andrew stood on the sill, gripped the pipe and began to swing himself cautiously upwards. His wife craned out to watch him, and when she saw his shoes disappearing through the Sibley window, drew a long breath of relief.

Then she heard him call down to her through the darkness. "Agnes! Something's happened. Come up as fast as you can and I'll let you in."

She raced upstairs to find him standing at the door of Number 10, his face grim.

"You were right. I found her flat out on the floor and I can't bring her to. She must have fainted and given her head a smack on the table-leg when she went down. Be a good girl and black-out in there at once, while I get her on to the bed."

"Lord Pig can't keep us out of this," Agnes murmured, as she followed him down the passage.

They had only just pulled the double blinds and hoisted Mrs. Sibley from the floor when Mrs. Rowse came in. They heard her shouting from the hall as she took off her coat and her rubbers. "So sorry I'm late, Addie dear, but Mr. Spiker was so difficult, and anyway he was half an hour late, but I've beaten him, dear, I've beaten him, and they won't remainder *Cuckoo* until…"

Agnes came out to meet her.

"Why, Mrs. Kinghof, how very nice—"

"Mrs. Rowse, please be prepared for a shock. Mrs. Sibley's been taken ill. My husband and I called but couldn't make anyone hear, so he broke into your flat by the back window. She—"

"Is she… She's not dead?"

"No, but she's unconscious. Who's your doctor? We've got to 'phone him."

Mrs. Rowse said uncertainly, "Why…why, Doctor Rowbotham, of course—" and burst into tears.

Agnes said, "Pull yourself together, she'll need you," and went into Mrs. Rowse's study, where the telephone was concealed beneath the wide skirts of a large Dutch doll.

In the meantime, Mrs. Rowse sat down on the umbrella stand and wept. "I can't bear it. It's too much. The strain's killing me."

"All right," said Agnes, re-emerging, "cry; because I can't do anything for you now. Take some Sal V."

She rejoined Andrew, who had succeeded in bringing Mrs. Sibley to life by burning under her nose one of the feathers from an Indian headdress that decorated the wall. "Sal V.," he said.

"Mrs. Rowse has it."

"Then take it away from her. She must sweat."

So Agnes pounced on the weeping woman, snatched the bottle from her trembling hand and marched back to administer a stiff dose to Mrs. Sibley.

She looked at them glassily, in her eyes a look of such intense, cringing terror that Agnes felt suddenly ashamed of every small flippancy of an idle life.

"Come on," said Andrew, "sit up, like a good girl. Doctor's coming soon. Sit up and take it easy. You're with friends. Know me?"

She murmured, "The Punch-and-Judy. It came up at me, that head…it was horrible. I want to die. If I were dead they couldn't frighten me like this."

"Be quiet now," he said gently, patting her hands. "You can tell me about it later. How's your head feeling? You've got a bump, you know. Nasty table hit you."

"It hurts… There it was, coming right up with a cap on it, and the snout all purple…" Suddenly, and rather piteously, she leaned forward and buried her face in his shoulder.

Andrew said to his wife, "Maybe you'd better get Eggshell."

Leaving him with Mrs. Sibley in his consoling embrace, she returned to pick the telephone from the Dutch doll's inside.

"Mrs. Kinghof speaking. Is the Inspector there?"

"Hold on a moment, madam. I'll tell him."

He came promptly upon the wire, his voice anxious. "Inspector Eggshell speaking. Anything wrong?"

"I'm in Mrs. Sibley's flat. We found her unconscious, but we got her round and now she's talking wildly about pigs and Punch-and-Judy shows. I've called the doctor, but I do think there's something up."

"Punch-and-Judy? Good lord—yes, I know." She heard him muttering rapidly to someone at his side.

"Mrs. Kinghof. You still there?"

"Still here."

"I'm coming up right away. Lord Whitestone is with me—he tells me he's your husband's cousin, ma'am—and he'll be along too. Good-bye."

He hung up.

"Well!" Agnes breathed, "what a brute Pig is, what a cagey brute! He didn't tell me he was going to see Egg." She went back to Mrs. Sibley, pausing for a moment on her way to adjure Mrs. Rowse, in the latter's own literary metaphor, to brace herself up and keep a straight bat.

Eggshell, Pig, and the doctor arrived simultaneously.

"Hullo, you," said Pig, snorting at Andrew, who by this time had succeeded in quieting Mrs. Sibley considerably.

"Hullo. How nice!"

"Very nice. Move over, please." Pushing his cousin aside, he sat down on the bed beside Mrs. Sibley and stared at her. Eggshell introduced them.

"Doctor!" Pig roared, "you go ahead. We'll stand by. And I don't think we want Mr. and Mrs. Kinghof in here."

Agnes flushed, but when she answered her voice was sweet. "Of course you don't, Lord Whitestone! Come on, Andrew dear." As she led her husband from the room she whispered, "The beast! But we'll punish him. Don't be surprised later at anything I do."

They went into the kitchen, thus by-passing Mrs. Rowse, and in a moment or so Eggshell joined them.

"I'd like to hear your story, please, Mr. Kinghof. I'd better tell you first that Mrs. Sibley's not light-headed so far as her Punch-and-Judy tale goes. You know we don't allow street music or entertainments in war-time? Well, I had a report that a Punch-and-Judy had been seen coming from the theatrical costumier's in Regent's Road, and that some sort of show had been given to the children in the square behind these flats. Harris spoke to one of the kids and heard that a pig's head had been used as a puppet. Of course he tried to follow the thing up, but by that time the men who worked the show had disappeared, and all Harris found was the box, the dolls and the animal's head abandoned on the waste ground behind Woolley Street. I tell you," he continued frankly, "it made us look fools, especially with Lord Whitestone coming down suddenly, like that; but it was all done so simply, and so quick… Of course, I sent a man round to Baggot, the costumier, and he said it had been hired by a smart-looking young man, thirty or so, he thought, small and middling-coloured, who said it was for a private party just along the street. Paid two pounds for it, too. Well, there's your comedian again, Mr. Kinghof, as bold as brass and with the devil's own luck. Now you tell your yarn. I'm listening."

They told him. Eggshell said something rude under his breath. "And if I did get him, all I could charge him with is…" He fell into a miserable stupor. After a moment he added, "I could charge him with precious little. Well, thank you, sir. And about bursting into here, you did your duty as a citizen and it was lucky you did; only please try to be careful, Mr. Kinghof, and don't do it again if you can help it, because Lord Whitestone is so particular about you and Mrs. Kinghof not getting involved in these—er—unpleasant cases."

The doctor came out. "Inspector?"

"Here."

"Mrs. Sibley is suffering from shock, and her heart's in

a poor way. Head bruises, fortunately, are negligible. I've told her she must get away first thing tomorrow, somewhere quiet, and I don't think she should sleep alone tonight."

"I'll sit up with her," said Agnes; "Mrs. Rowse is by no means herself."

"You will? Good. Well, if you're going to be nurse I'd better instruct you. Will you step into the lounge, please, madam?"

In the meantime Andrew was set upon by Pig, who, the moment Eggshell had repeated the former's account of the affair, charged out of the bedroom like a wild boar.

"Look here, didn't I tell you to keep clear of this?"

"If I had, she'd have been lying there till Mrs. Rowse came in. Ever read her work, Pig? She's Phyllada Rounders, the growing girl's friend. Ever read *Cuckoo Delahaye: Mischief of the Fifth*? I'll send you a copy for Christmas."

"Andrew, if I catch you breaking into anyone else's house, legally or illegally, for good or ill, I'll have you taken up. Nothing personal, mind. But I'll do it."

Then Agnes, who had speeded Doctor Rowbotham on his way downstairs, came smiling towards her cousin-by-marriage and, as diffidently as a little girl, touched his sleeve. "Pig, dear, don't be angry. I know we've interfered again, but after all, we did more good than harm this time, didn't we? Forgive?"

She was so dainty, so feminine, so prettily arch, that Andrew went sour in the stomach.

Pig bridled, flushed, looked at his boots. "Well, Agnes, after all, it wasn't exactly you who—"

"Listen; Andrew and I are retiring. We're out of this. From henceforth—or rather, after we've sat up tonight with Mrs. Sibley."

"We!" Andrew exclaimed, in a voice between a scream and a death-rattle.

"Yes, we, pet. After we've sat up tonight with Mrs. Sibley we're going to give crime the go-by and just have a wonderful time. Now then, as a token of forgiveness, will you and Mary come to a show with us tomorrow night?"

"Well, Mary can't, because she's dining with her mother; but maybe I—"

"Splendid! Now I want to take you somewhere very special and very 'surprise,' so you must meet us here at—No; come and have dinner with us here first, seven sharp. And don't dress." She was thinking of a poster she had noticed from the bus-top that afternoon on the wall of Haig Square.

Andrew, who had been on the point of explosion, remembered his wife's earlier warning and so controlled himself. He said weakly, "Yes, do, Pig. It'll be something out of the way for you."

"Legal, I hope?" asked his cousin sternly. "Nothing shady?"

"*Shady?*" Andrew whispered. "Can you imagine either of us being shady? I'm ashamed of you, Pig."

"I can imagine you being shady. Yes. Without the slightest difficulty. As for Agnes, anything wrong she ever did would be the result of your influence. Eggshell!" Pig became official. "Come along now. I've some work for your men."

"Seven sharp tomorrow!" Agnes cooed, standing unnecessarily upon tiptoe to wave good-bye.

"What the hell?" Andrew burst out, when they had gone.

Whispering, she told him; and over his face there spread a beautiful balmy smile, like the sun shining out over a field of asphodel.

———

The fourth night of leave found them in worse sort than the other three, for Agnes bunked herself up on two chairs in Mrs. Sibley's bedroom and Andrew, rather more lucky but not surpassingly so, made himself a bed on the springless sofa in the lounge.

Mrs. Sibley, well drugged and consoled by the thought that tomorrow she would go to stay with Mrs. Rowse at the river-side bungalow owned by them jointly, slept fairly well, though once or twice during that interminable night she awoke sweating, her eyes searching the windowed space which, for once, Agnes had insisted upon screening. For Frankson, sta-tioned in the lower hall, there were only two incidents of any interest: at twelve-thirty, when Mr. Warrender let a lady in, and at two-fifteen, when Mr. Lang let one out.

Andrew slumbered evilly, maintaining his position on the couch only by hooking one leg around the carved end, and one arm over the back; and he was not too pleased when, on the only two occasions when sleep took him utterly, his wife tiptoed in to kiss him, thereby awaking him instantly to the realization of physical woe.

Agnes herself, who might have snatched an hour or two of rest, was deprived of the solace by the loud snores that, penetrating through the wall, indicated that Mrs. Rowse, at least, was comfortable.

When eight o'clock came and Mrs. Sibley awoke, Andrew and Agnes flexed their cramped limbs, refused Mrs. Rowse's offer of breakfast and crawled like arthritic sufferers down-stairs to their own flat. There they brewed tea, bathed, and then, overcome by weariness, sank down upon the bed and slept till noon.

When they awoke they completed their dressing, drank some whisky and went out to lunch. Mrs. Sibley and her friend had left for "Osokozee," Hooham-on-Thames, their address a secret to all save the Kinghofs and the police; and the world smiled again.

Agnes, bobbing to her husband over the rim of a Manhattan, said "*Bon santé*, my dear, and damnation to Pig."

"*A la lanterne* with Pig! My love, we have him on the hip. Do you think he'll enjoy himself?"

"Like a child," said Agnes softly, "like a lit-tle, gay-hearted child."

Chapter Six

ON THEIR WAY HOME FROM LUNCH THEY MET Eggshell, who said, by way of a *pourboire* for past assistance, in however unlawful a shape it had come, "Traced the pig's head to a West End butcher. Described the fellow who bought it as small, middling-coloured. No whiskers. Oh, and we're getting a little forrader with the business of Coppenstall. Old lady gone?"

"Went off this morning on the 11.15."

"Good. Well, Mr. Kinghof, I hope there will be no more bother for you and your wife."

"Surely not!" said Agnes.

"Positively not," said Eggshell, and left them.

They spent a pleasant afternoon in the kitchen, where Agnes prepared the foundations of an agreeable dinner and Andrew, putting the portable gramophone on the dresser, played his favourite records. Thoughts of Pig turned him to songs of martial mood: he played *The Campbells Are Coming*, *The Song of the Steppes Cavalry* and the *Mars* movement from *The Planets*. By a quarter to seven they were sitting around, in their best clothes, awaiting the guest.

Prompt to the hour Pig arrived, hearty, determined to be sociable, and slightly condescending. They gave him a meal of divine contriving, some of their best sherry and a bottle of Nuits St. Georges that Andrew had been saving for a special occasion, an occasion such as this. Pig mellowed. He became bluff. He told three very clean jokes and told Agnes that his mother would have liked her. They parried his questions concerning the evening's entertainment until he was wild with curiosity.

"Oh no," said Agnes playfully, "you must wait and see. If I told you it would be like saying what we mean to buy you for Christmas!" They meant to buy him nothing for Christmas.

Andrew glanced at the clock. "Better be going, I think. Shall I call a cab, Agnes?"

"No, it's only a step. It would be nice to walk, don't you think so, Pig?"

They had mackintoshes. He had none, and it was a cold, drizzling night. "As you please," he said dubiously.

They took him through back streets and alleys, through interminable short cuts.

"Nearly there!" said Agnes cheerfully.

Let no one say that Pig is not stout-hearted.

Though his shoes made a sucking sound as the water spurted from them, though the brim of his *chapeau melon* was filled with rain, he made no complaint. "I know where we're going!" he said. "You're taking me to one of your Bohemian clubs. I warn you, Andy"—the 'Andy' was jocularly said—"if it's anything shady I shall go home."

Ahead of them, at the end of a cobbled passage, a low, pointed roof reared against the lesser darkness of the sky.

"Ah, *here's* the drill-hall!" Agnes cried gaily.

Pig stopped dead. "The what?"

"The drill-hall. Didn't you guess? And you a detective. We're taking you to the New Year Concert of the Milmanscroft Road Division Guides and Scouts."

Taking his arms, they pulled him up a flight of wooden stairs and pushed him through a sopping blackout curtain into dazzling light. A clergyman, blandly smiling, asked for their tickets, which Agnes gave him. "Miss Hobson, of the draper's, is Guide Captain. If it hadn't been for her we'd never have got seats in the front row, would we, Andy?"

Still speechless, Pig was prodded up the aisle between two blocks of forms, on which sat a steaming crowd in mackintoshes, to the three rows of chairs at one-and-six. The platform was veiled by a red plush curtain in which the moth had campaigned for many a year. Below it a row of ferns shuddered in one of the several draughts. Above it were two Union Jacks tied in the middle with pink ribbon. Already, two adolescents, with piano and violin, were competing as to which should finish the overture first.

Pig, sitting on a very small chair between Agnes and Andrew, was deep-red in the face. Comment still being beyond him, he dragged out a cigarette and lit it, puffing out his rage in fat grey cornucopias of smoke. A bright woman in Guide's uniform came up to him and said, in a whisper that drowned even the noise of the overture, "Sorry! No smoking!"

"That's Miss Hobson," Agnes said with enthusiasm. "We think she's charming, don't we, Andrew?"

Pig's foot stamped furiously on the offending cigarette.

Just then, the overture came to an end and the lights dimmed. The clatter of the audience ceased, hushed by parents who wished their children to be heard to the best advantage. The curtain drew back in a series of nervous jumps, revealing an uneven line of girls dancing on, and a distraught stage manager tiptoeing off. The girls sang:

> *"We are the Guides of Milmanscroft,*
> *We always hold our flags aloft.*
> *We're glad you've come to see our play,*
> *We hope you have a happy day."*

Miss Hobson, who had taken the seat behind Pig and for the past few minutes had been breathing down his neck, touched him on the shoulder and whispered—"The girls wrote the words themselves. The fourth from the left, Bessie Milton, is quite a poet."

"Like her namesake," said Agnes politely, and a little too loudly; for she was unanimously and venomously shushed by the first six rows.

After a few more couplets and a dance, the girls disappeared, only to reappear a few moments later to receive the thunderous applause of their fathers and mothers. When they had disappeared for good, the last three tripping over Bessie Milton, who was trying to get more than her fair share of the reception, a stringy young woman with glasses and pale-blue false teeth announced that Scout Percy Fiddle would give an impersonation of Mae West. This was so embarrassing that Pig took out his season ticket and read it carefully front and back until Percy had bowed his way off the stage.

Next, Scout Aubrey Bottomley recited *Vitae Lampada*. "'Plup, plup and play the game,'" Andrew whispered to Pig, in case he should not recognize Aubrey's pronunciation of the title. Although the lad's poem ended in a stutter he was clapped with goodwill, for the audience ranked staying-power and hard work above genius. He was followed by the choir, who sang secular songs in a classical manner, and brought Part I of the entertainment to a rousing *finale* with *Simon the Cellarer*.

"There!" Agnes exclaimed as the curtain fell, or, more precisely, collapsed, for two Scouts had to bring up ladders to mend it; "doesn't it make you feel young again?"

"Genuine talent," said Andrew, "brilliant youngsters. Don't you think so, Pig?"

Pig swallowed, and made a gobbling sound.

"Dry?" Agnes enquired solicitously. "Yes, it is hot in here." She beckoned a little girl who was hawking glasses of pale-green lemonade. "Come here, darling! This gentleman would like to buy a nice, cool drink. Sixpence, Pig," she added *sotto voce*, "and all for the good of the cause."

"I don't want—" he began.

"Of course you do." Agnes ordered lemonades for the three of them and saw that he paid. She and Andrew bravely swallowed theirs, knowing that Pig could scarcely fail to follow the example.

The curtain rose prematurely, showing the scene-shifters in wild transit. Miss Hobson leaped to her feet. "Lower it! Overture, please."

Violin and piano played *In a Persian Market*, the pianist supplying the "Backsheesh, Allah, Allah."

Then the clergyman stepped on to the stage, thanked the audience for coming, and murmured that at the exits those who wanted to make a little extra token of appreciation would find collecting-boxes for the Jamboree fund. He then announced the *clou* of the evening, the pantomime

Red Riding Hood, with Bessie Milton as the heroine, Percy Fiddle as the Grandmother, and Scoutmaster John Truelove as the Wolf.

It wound its weary way. Bessie packed her basket with pottles of jam and pats of butter, Percy Fiddle was a scream, and a little fat child performed a toe-dance in the character of Will-o'-the-Wisp. But then the Wolf came in, with pelt of rags and brown wool, and papier-mâché head.

At the sight of this last, Andrew thumped Pig on the knee. "Right. We'll go now. Come on, Agnes."

Fighting their way through an audience bitterly hurt and mutely hostile, they gained the refuge of the porch.

"Jamboree box," Agnes said to Pig. She was as yet unforgiving.

He had no change.

"They don't mind paper."

He stuffed a ten-shilling note through the slot, said something under his breath and stumbled down the steps into the rainy night. "I'm so sorry to spoil the fun," Andrew said, "but I had an idea. Agnes! Know where they got that wolf's head?"

"Where?"

"Baggot's. Costumiers. I remember now, he had a whole stock of animals' heads just before Christmas, and there was a pig's head among them!"

"Well?"

"I bet the comedian bought the first head there. What do you think, Pig?"

"Look here, Andrew—"

"You know the cane that was stuck through the bucket? Well, it was much too thin to bear the weight of a real pig's head."

"And where," said his cousin, "does that get us? We know he bought the Punch-and-Judy at Baggot's. It doesn't much matter whether or not he got the other object from him."

"I suppose not." Andrew was despondent.

"We shall look into it," Pig told him shortly.

"I suppose," Agnes said cautiously, "that you wouldn't be seen with us in the 'Green Doe'?"

"That," Pig replied in a voice harsh with rage and exhaustion, "is where you're wrong. Where is the place?"

After his third double whisky, he began to look more pleasant. After his fifth, he said shortly: "Right, Agnes; one round to you. The concert, I mean."

After her fourth double whisky, she was remorseful. "We'll take you to a real show soon, Pig. No hard feelings?"

"Say there are no hard feelings," Andrew echoed her.

"No hard feelings," Pig replied, "but you will reimburse me for the lemonade."

Andrew complied.

"And for the Jamboree donation."

Andrew was meek.

———

By two o'clock on the afternoon of the same day, some eight hours before Pig took his fifth whisky, Mrs. Sibley and Mrs. Rowse were at Hooham-on-Thames, engaged in the arduous business of opening up, "Osokozee" having been sealed like a vault since the previous August. It was a brick-built bungalow, set back from the river by a lawn some fifty feet deep. The roof was green-tiled, the paintwork orange. The whole building was permeated by that curious river-damp which can seep into the best airing-cupboard and set the linen steaming like a cauldron the moment it is placed within range of a fire. The furniture was cottagey—that is, liable to unstick at the joints—and the curtains, carpets, and cushions bore respectively the print of rhododendrons, roses, and apple blossom. Every drop of water had to be pumped from the river, and there was a rather unprepossessing water-closet of the type that is usually at the end of the vegetable garden, and was in this case adjacent to the scullery.

By four, both ladies had violent headaches and were utterly miserable. The alders on the lawn's edge were sodden with rain, and a dismal drizzle poured unceasingly down the window-panes. The lawn was long and yellow, the flower-beds by the steps full of rank and blackened plants, where the yellow slug crawled at ease.

"You'd better fix up a double blanket over the bathroom window," said Mrs. Sibley faintly. "Thank heavens we've blackouts for the rest."

"Smells sweet here," Mrs. Rowse said hopefully. "Nice to be out of dear old London, really. Don't you feel the better for it, Addie?"

"I'll tell you tomorrow. I'm too tired to think now." Rising with an effort, she crossed the room to peer through the bay window, through which she could just see the bungalows on the other side, "Weetu" and "Kum-Ry-Tyn," both unoccupied. "How are we off for food?"

"We'll be all right when they send the order from the village, and they promised it at six."

"It's a pity not to have company, don't you think? We'd both feel better with company. What about asking the Kinghofs down for the week-end? Mary Hobday's promised to do for us as long as we want her, so it shouldn't make much work."

"If they'd come," Mrs. Rowse murmured, "but I don't think they would."

"Well, try, dear, try! Run along to the village and send a telegram. The post-office doesn't shut till half-past five."

Mrs. Rowse did not fancy a ten-minute walk through the sopping gloom. "Don't you think it would be more restful, for a few days, to be just we two?"

"No, I don't. I want company. I want to see bright, cheerful faces."

Sighing, Mrs. Rowse put down her cup and went to find her mackintosh.

"Ask them to come down for lunch tomorrow," Mrs. Sibley shouted after her.

That evening, as the ladies sat by lamplight trying to hear an "In Town Tonight" through the frying noises made habitually by their wireless, Mrs. Rowse said suddenly, "You don't suppose he'd know where to find you?"

It was not tactful, and Mrs. Sibley visibly greened.

"Of course not," she snapped, "and I don't want to talk about it."

"He seems to know so much," Mrs. Rowse murmured; but mercifully her words were drowned by a vicious crackle from the radio, and by the sudden emergence of the broadcast voices into tremendous volume. "Here is our next visitor, Herbert Wool, who has been a dustman for sixty-five years. Isn't that right, Herbert?"

"That's right, sir, and me father before me."

"Splendid! It must be a fascinating life. Won't you tell the listeners some of your experiences?"

"Well, sir, I don't rightly know as if—"

"Turn that thing off!" Mrs. Sibley snapped.

As silence fell, Mrs. Rowse thought, That wire. It couldn't

get into the hands of the wrong person, could it? No, surely it couldn't!

——

Coincidence plays a large part in life; but in the drama of Mr. Coppenstall and the pigs it played a very small one.

The only coincidence, indeed, lay in the fact that at this moment the Wrong Person was reading the telegram.

"Name of Kinghof?" the boy had said, meeting the Wrong Person on the stairs.

"That's right," said the Wrong Person, putting out a hand, and returning with the envelope to seclusion and a steaming kettle. Handed in at Hooham, 4.45. Good enough. The Wrong Person re-sealed the envelope and stole out to slip it into the Kinghofs' letter-box.

——

Andrew and Agnes, returning from the "Green Doe" after having assisted Pig discreetly into a taxi, let themselves into their flat, took up the wire and read it.

"Good heavens!" Andrew said. "Soak down there, in this weather? I know Hooham well, and it's a hell's spot. Lies in a valley, rotten drainage, population both stinking rich and semi-literate. Scene of countless famous scandals, sex and finance. Grandmothers with purple lips in trousers."

"You can't wear lips in trousers."

"Graveyard packed with cirrhosis cases. Beer poor. Communications intermittent."

"Rainfall .004, pop. 1,202, typhus cases .24, tomb of First Baron Hooham in chancel, fine reredos," Agnes added crossly.

"What do you mean, 'point 00 four'?"

"Oh, I don't know. Just adding to your Baedecker. Let's go, shall we?"

He stared at her. "Did you say *go*? My dear girl, you're tight."

"No, honestly; why not? It's a breath of air."

"Foul, damp, cesspool air!"

"And something might happen."

"What?"

"Oh, anything. Andrew, do you really suppose the comedian will give Mrs. Sibley up so easily?"

"Now listen—"

"Besides," she argued speciously, "we did promise poor Pig we'd keep out of trouble, didn't we? So if we went away, we'd be keeping out properly?"

"No. I'm damned if I will."

"Just till Sunday night."

"No."

"I'll send a wire on the 'phone. We can catch the 11.15 train."

"I will not go!"

"Funny."

"What is?"

She sighed deeply, and with an air of utter dejection crossed the room to the chimney-piece, where she bowed her head on her hands. "You're not the man I married. You used to be so ready for adventure… So…so vital, somehow. And now, you're set, stolid, a pipe-by-the-fire man—"

"Hey! Who climbed in Mrs. S.'s window?"

"A flash in the pan," said Agnes, "a final flicker before the fires burn low and fall to grey, grey ash."

"Agnes! I will not be bullied!"

Slowly she swivelled on lovely legs, legs covered by smoke-grey silk so fine that it gave to them the bloom of grapes. Her eyes were large and mournful. "Would you like some hot milk before you go to bed, Andy dear? And I think, now the nights are so cold, that you ought to wear a vest under your pyjamas. Is that a grey hair I see?"

"You see correctly," said Andrew, whose hair had been slightly greyed since his fifteenth year, "and I am not galumphing down to Hooham."

"Very well, dear. Andrew, you really are looking tired! What you need is real, undisturbed rest. Now you go to sleep in the spare room—I'll put a hot-water bottle in the bed, and I won't wake you till ten tomorrow, and then—"

"Oh, send your repulsive telegram," said Andrew savagely.

On the following day he said, "Look here, suppose I get a wire recalling me? They won't know where to send it. I can't go down to that place, I tell you."

But even this excuse was denied him, for a telegram came within ten minutes, extending his leave until further notice.

He was not in the best of spirits at the start of the expedition, but the sun came out as the train drew out of London, gilding the chilly fields and melting the webs of frost over grass and hedge, and by the time they reached Windsor Andrew was whistling *Franklin D. Roosevelt Jones*.

Agnes, who, in grey and lemon tweeds, with tangerine turban, sweater, socks, and gloves, reminded her husband of the house-party scene in a well-dressed revue, was extremely pleased with herself. "You know, Andrew, I'm sure we're going to have a wonderful time! There's danger in the air. I know it."

"If you mean that rather disagreeable smell entering by the windows, my dear, that is not danger. It's influenza." But he was not himself displeased.

When they left the train they took the station cab to Hooham, and were not cheered to learn that to get to the bungalows they must walk an eighth of a mile down an unmade road. This walk did violence to Agnes's brown suède brogues. Andrew slipped on some mushy grass and fell on his face. They arrived very dirty, very damp, and aggressively cheerful. Had they not been cheerful they would have greeted with lumps of mud the appearance of Mesdames Rowse and Sibley on the verandah.

"How sweet of you to come out to the wilds!" the latter cried. "I hope you haven't had too bad a journey?"

"No, no," said Andrew gently, "we welcomed the breath of air."

"That's right," Mrs. Rowse applauded him, "that's capital. That's the spirit. Come in and sit ye doon."

Before lunch there was Sunnymaloo sherry. After lunch there was the alternative of taking a nice walk or being quiet as a mouse indoors while Mrs. Sibley slept. "She sleeps so lightly," Mrs. Rowse explained, "that she can hear even the turning of a page."

But there were no pages, either of book or newspaper, to turn. Andrew and Agnes wandered about in the rain for half an hour and spent the remaining two hours in the lounge playing a very quiet game of dominoes.

"Thank you, Agnes darling," Andrew whispered viciously, "for a lovely week-end. I only hope you're enjoying it as much as I am."

Chapter Seven

AFTER A CHILLING SUPPER OF PICNIC ROLL AND POTATO salad Agnes retired to the bedroom on pretext of fetching a handkerchief, and she signalled to Andrew that he should follow her. Comparative seclusion reached, she said, "I say, do you think we could get out for a drink? I shall die. That awful meat loaf lies as heavy as triplets; I can hardly move for it."

"There's a good pub across the river," Andrew replied thoughtfully. "The 'Walrus and Carpenter.' I used to go there in my wild young days."

"How could we get there? I don't fancy ploughing back the way we came and taking the ferry."

"Osokozee" was approached, on leaving the unmade road, through a wooden gate, down a track through a small, dense thicket, along a flagged path bisecting the vegetable garden and round to the front of the bungalow, which, of course, faced the river.

"No," he agreed, "I'm not feeling my way through that wretched copse in the dark, or floundering through the vegetables. Hasn't Mrs. S. got a boat?"

"No, but there's a dinghy tied up outside 'Kum-Ry-Tyn,' next door. We could pinch that."

"What excuse can we make?"

"I know," said Agnes craftily; "we'll ask them both to come. They won't, of course, and then we can say, 'Well, would you mind terribly if we did?' It would look rude, of course, but does that matter?"

"I was well brought up," said Andrew, "and taught that such things do matter. Think of something else."

"Well…oh, I know. We'll say it's your birthday, and we want to go to the 'Walrus' to buy something for a little celebration. Then we can bring back a bottle of gin; they look as if they'd like that."

"Gin," said Andrew fiercely, "is a drink for the very debauched and the permanently adolescent. If I caught a daughter of mine drinking disgusting 'gimlets' I should hit her till she signed the pledge… Yes, we could do that, though it's pretty weak. Come on, then."

Their suggestion was fairly well received; evidently Mrs. Sibley did not dislike the thought of the celebration. "You could take Madame du Jardin's dinghy, I suppose. I know her very well, and I'm sure she'd never mind. She should have put it under cover, of course, but she went to America the moment war broke out and left the place just as it was. Can you get across all right, though? It's pretty dark tonight."

"We can manage, thank you. Come on, Agnes—we won't be above half an hour, Mrs. Sibley, or not much above it."

The clock on the mantelshelf, a cunning affair designed to represent a windmill standing in a tulip garden, announced that it was eight-thirty.

"Anyhow, we shan't be a minute more than three-quarters

of an hour," Agnes beamed, tucking her hand into her husband's arm.

Mrs. Rowse and Mrs. Sibley stood on the verandah, watching their guests as they went down the lawns and climbed the fence separating "Osokozee" from "Kum-Ry-Tyn." Oddly enough, this departure was watched, in all, not by two pairs of eyes, but by three.

———

Mrs. Sibley returned to the lounge, where she took up her knitting, Mrs. Rowse went into the back kitchen to wash up. The latter had been so engaged for about fifteen minutes when a tap on the window arrested her attention. She went to the side door, opened it and saw, on the crazy paving at the foot of the three wooden steps, a police constable, dim starlight shining on his uniform.

"Oh, dear, officer! Is it the lights?"

A youngish chap, he replied hesitantly in soft country burr. "No, ma'am, but I'm afraid… are you the householder, ma'am?"

"No, my friend Mrs. Sibley is."

"Is she here?"

"Yes, but why—?"

He said rather diffidently, "Well, I'd be obliged if she'd step out down the garden with me as far as the road and tell me if she knows what's happened to the gate. It's been tied right back, and would cause a serious obstruction, if anyone came along in a car after blackout—"

"The gate's tied back? How?"

"Well, someone seems to have druv' a stump in, and lashed the bolt to it with wire. Would Mrs. Sibley come, please?"

"Oh, dear, she's so tired! Won't I do?"

"Seeing as it's her gate," he murmured, swinging the beam from his torch aimlessly over the rotted cabbage stalks.

"All right, I'll get her, then; but it does seem so much red tape."

Mrs. Rowse, annoyed, went to annoy Mrs. Sibley with the constable's information.

"The gate? How ridiculous! I suppose it's some silly trick of the local boys. Still, it's as well to know the police do keep a watch on the bungalows. Give me my heavy coat."

"Shall I come, dear?"

"Oh, no, no. I'll be back in a minute." Mrs. Sibley stumped through the kitchen and went down the back steps to join the policeman. "All right, constable, go along. I'll follow. You might shine your torch ahead, please."

"Right you are, ma'am." He threw a lean pencil of light down the path, and set off cautiously. "Rain's made it slippy, hasn't it? Sorry to get you out on a night like this, but since war was started we have to take notice of irregularities and such. Maybe it's only some kid playing silly, but I have to carry out my orders. Funny sort of war, ain't it, ma'am? Ought to hear the sergeant on it. 'The last war,' he says, 'was comic opera played in a slaughter-house, but this one's dumb crambo played in a loony-bin.' He's a wit, the sergeant is."

"I'm sure of it," Mrs. Sibley snapped. She was very cold, and had trodden twice in puddles.

Reaching the end of the vegetable garden, the constable stepped into the thicket; but for a moment he stopped, and seemed to put his hands to his face. Then he stepped briskly on, torch lowered, and Mrs. Sibley followed, her gaze on his broad back.

"Really," she said, "this is quite absurd. Why you couldn't have untied the gate yourself without dragging me out I can't think." Angrily she brushed aside the damp twigs that struck her face and caught in her hair. "I shan't let this pass unnoticed, constable, and I can't help thinking you're exceeding your duties. Why, what on earth are you talking about? There's nothing wrong with the gate. There's—"

She looked at him, and her heart died in her. He had stepped into the shadowy starlight of the road, and his back was no longer towards her. He was holding the torch steadily, the beam directed upwards; and beneath the helmet shone yellow flesh, a glistening snout, and small eyes that shifted and sparkled through immovable sockets.

Mrs. Sibley would have screamed, but the sound froze in her throat; for the torch went out, a sharp point pierced her clothes, searing the fat above her ribs, and the Pig said, "Pleased to meet you, Aunt…"

Mrs. Sibley knew the frozen ecstasy of steel slid home. Her knees crumbled like rotten masonry, and she fell with her face in the sucking mud of the unmade road.

———

Mrs. Rowse, as she dried the dishes, was pondering the future adventures of Fernia Prideaux. Would it be too daring, too adult for her readers, if in the holidays Fernia were to meet a jolly young naval cousin who admired her pluck and consoled her in her sufferings? It was understood that no young man should sully the maiden whiteness of Miss Rounders's books for girls; yet surely, introduction of a platonic comradeship between the sexes could do no harm, and might do much to prepare readers for the Life beyond the Upper Sixth? And yet—perhaps not. Better to make Miss Valaine, the gym mistress, guide, counsellor, and friend. Fernia, shunned by the school, should rescue Miss Valaine from shipwreck… How to get them on a boat? Yes, that would take some doing… should rescue Miss Valaine from shipwreck and haul her up the cliff face to safety by means of her handkerchief, both stockings and a guide-belt… Mrs. Rowse saw the kitchen clock. Five to nine already? Good heavens, what a time the policeman was keeping poor Addie! She went out about half-past eight… Twenty-five minutes! Mrs. Rowse jumped. "Better go and fetch her," she muttered, "see what's wrong." Feverishly she bundled herself into a mackintosh.

Just then the Kinghofs came back, very merry and rosy, each bearing a bottle.

"Hulloa!" Andrew shouted. "Sorry if we're late. What, going out, Mrs. Rowse? Let me go for you. What is it, coal?"

"Oh, Mr. Kinghof, I'm worried! A policeman came round at about twenty-five past eight and said he wanted Mrs. Sibley to come with him and inspect the thicket gate, as someone had tied it back, and it was causing an obstruction in the road. She went out with him at half-past and hasn't come back—"

The Kinghofs, acting in concert, dumped the bottles on the draining-board and made for the door. "Don't you come," Andrew called back to Mrs. Rowse, "you stay here."

He and Agnes plunged down the steps, through the cabbages, and smashed neck and neck through the thicket. Just beyond the gate they found the body of Mrs. Sibley, lying in a puddle, face pressed downwards into mud, a thin steel dagger, of the kind sold as a paper-knife, protruding from her ribs.

———

A night of police inquisition was followed by a chilly morning that brought Lord Whitestone, Inspector Eggshell, and Inspector Corcoran from the Yard down to the bungalow at Hooham.

"Damn it," said Pig to Andrew, privately and bitterly, "if you have to stick your noses into murder, can't you see it doesn't happen on a level with your blasted upper lip?"

"Oh, don't," Agnes begged, "we feel wretched. As if it were our fault. Don't go on at us, Pig. Please, please don't."

So he snorted and did not rebuke them further. Eggshell knocked and was admitted. "We've found a pig's mask, stiffened muslin thing, hanging on a bush. It's your comedian all right, Mr. Kinghof. Lord Whitestone, sir, doctor reports death from shock. The knife hadn't penetrated more than half an inch."

"Thought so. Eggshell, I'll leave Corcoran down here with the local man. You'd better come back to town with me. I want to know where the occupants of Block 3, Stewarts Court, spent the night. By the way, does Baggot confirm selling that pig's head?"

"Says he sold it just before Christmas to a young chap, middling-coloured, tallish. Says he doesn't think it's the same as hired the Punch-and-Judy."

"Elevators," said Pig. "Must have used them as the police constable, too. Find out if he got that rig-out from Baggot."

A local constable came in to report that a policeman's helmet and tunic had been found in Hooham reservoir. "Must've 'ad 'is own clothes underneath, sir."

"Yes. All right, Wilson. That's all."

Pig turned to Agnes. "You'd better stay here; Andrew

too. The local men will want to talk to you again, and Mrs. Rowse can't be left alone."

"All right," she agreed, much subdued. She and Andrew spent a miserable day suffering from bad conscience. They were too miserable even to broach the bottles they had brought back from the "Walrus and Carpenter."

Agnes said despairingly, "If I'd been here, do you imagine I'd have let her go out alone on that crazy wild-goose chase?"

"Do you imagine I should, either? That gate story shouldn't have deceived a child of three."

"Poor Mrs. Sibley! How ghastly it must have been for her! What a ghastly death! What do you suppose he did? Put the mask on and looked at her?"

"Something like that."

"And it would never have happened if we hadn't gone to the 'Walrus.' Oh, Andrew, it sounds like the punishment for wrongdoing, in a child's book! If Matilda hadn't been so fond of matches she wouldn't have been burned. If the children hadn't laughed at Elijah's—or was it Elisha's?—bald head they wouldn't have been eaten. If we hadn't liked Irish whisky Mrs. Sibley wouldn't have been murdered. Oh, dear, that sounds like a syllogism!" Agnes giggled feebly, then began to cry.

"My darling, don't beat yourself like that," her husband protested, "because after all, it wasn't our fault. How were we to know anything would happen? We had no idea the comedian would know where to find the old lady."

"I hope Eggshell follows up that line," Agnes said, brightening, "finds out how the secret leaked out. Do you think I ought to ring up and remind him?"

"I think we've done quite enough," Andrew answered, rather grimly.

———

Agnes need not have worried. The first thing Eggshell did on returning from Hooham to town was to trace and interview a telegraph-boy.

"Why didn't you put the wire through Mr. Kinghof's door?"

"Because they weren't in when I knocked, and while I was half way downstairs looking for the porter, a person met me and said they was Kinghof."

"A person? Man or woman?"

"Man."

"What was he like?"

"Well," the boy fumbled, "I'm not much hand at descriptions, and anyway, it was dark and there's no light on them stairs. Youngish, I thought from the voice."

"Colouring?"

"Couldn't see."

"Height?"

"Well, sir, it's hard to say, as he was several steps up while we was talking. Tallish, I thought."

"How tall? My height?"

"Couldn't say for sure. About."

"On what flight did the man meet you?"

The boy pondered arduously, scratching his cap with hands roughened to brick colour by the winds and rains of winter. "I wish I could say, sir!" he burst out despairingly, "but I truly couldn't take my oath whether it was the second or third."

"Where did he go to after you'd given him the wire?"

"Couldn't say.—Oh, you must think me an orful mug, but I just went on down, and didn't see."

"All right," said Eggshell shortly, and dismissed him. He went into a small office where Pig was scowling at a sheaf of records.

"Charnet, Jeanne-Louise. Widow. Aged 41. Café proprietress at Puteaux till 1937, when she retired on coming into small legacy. Shut up café, but would sometimes put up commercial travellers for a night or so. Believed to have protectors since early 1938. Came over here August 25th, 1939. Passport in order. Some trouble at Dover customs, where she didn't declare two bottles of scent. Protested ignorance of law, was fined. That's all about her. George Wilshin Warrender, bachelor, 32. Born London. Believed to have worked as commission agent in Manchester, 1933–35. Became temporary Civil Servant 1936, entered Circumlocution Office 1937. On war-work there connected with foreign propaganda. Highly thought of. Oh, here's something, Eggshell. In February 1937 joined Free British Mussolites, but resigned in following June, and apparently no connection with this body since. Might look into that a bit. Lastly, Felix Lang, 24, born London, educated privately, became medical student at St. Patrick's 1936; that's what he says, Eggshell; he's no father or mother, and no means of identification. Check up on education. Report from Pat's says he's a brilliant student but not very steady and too fond of the ladies. Squares up with what Frankson told us about him letting a woman out of his flat."

"Warrender let one in, sir."

"I'd like to hear more about her, and about Lang's girl. See what you can do. Well, Eggshell, what do you think?"

"Not much there, is there? Warrender's age squares with Steer's, and it seems his correct age; but Lang's more suspicious. Could he be thirty-two?"

"You've seen him. I haven't. What do you say?"

"Just possible. You never know with some chaps. He's the right temperament, though. People at Circumlocution Office think Warrender's a bit of a stick-in-the-mud. He looks older than he is."

"If the Maclagan Steer theory's correct, either Lang or Warrender is: one, Henry Race, the Town Hall irregular—"

"Sounds like Sherlock," Eggshell grinned, and was rewarded by a hard stare from his superior.

"Two, the middling-coloured young man who bought the Punch-and-Judy, three, the young, tallish, and middling-coloured purchaser of the pig's head, four, the tallish person on the stairs, five, the tallish constable. That is, if you believe in the Steer story. Do you believe it, Eggshell?"

Eggshell blushed. "Well, sir—yes, sir."

"Ah. Hum. So do I."

The men mused separately, silently. Then Pig said, "Come on; we'll go round to Stewarts Court and see what we can find out. Might catch 'em in on a Sunday. Damn it, I wish I could question them officially!"

"Grill them, as the films say."

"But we must be careful. Careful as walking on eggshells."

"Yes, sir," the Inspector agreed, pretending not to notice the gaffe. Pig had not noticed it; he never noticed such things.

They went first to Madame Charnet, whom they found in the middle of tea, her wireless at full blast, a ginger and a tortoiseshell cat sleeping on the settee.

She looked rather scared to see Eggshell, whom she knew as a policeman, and she could not at first catch Pig's name. "I must turn off the raddio," she shouted, "I 'ave to 'ave it loud because I do not 'ear well. Will you come in?"

They went into her pleasant room, furnished a little flor-
idly in the French style, with ribboned wallpaper and bright
yellow curtains to match the roses in the carpet. Madame
herself was in a purple housecoat, a grey chiffon scarf about
her hair.

She turned off the wireless and sat timidly down, motion-
ing them to do likewise. "What is there I can do?"

Pig said, very slowly and clearly, "You might just possibly be able to give us some help. Madame, I have some sad
news. Mrs. Sibley, your neighbour in Number 10, has died
in very tragic circumstances."

"Oh, no! But only the other day, 'er poor brother—"

"Yes. And now, madame, for purely routine purposes I
want you to tell me where you spent last night."

"I? I was 'ere, monsieur, all the evening. I spent the late
afternoon at the Classic *cinéma* in the 'Igh Street, seeing a
French film, and then I came back 'ere and was reading till
bed-time."

"What film was that?"

"*L'Ordonnance.* It was vairy interesting."

"You haven't the half of your ticket?"

She looked surprised. "No. I always drop it on the floor,
don't you?"

Smiling, Pig admitted that he did.

"But I sink the girl would know me, the one at the desk.
Monsieur, what 'ave I to do—"

"All I wanted to know," said Pig quickly, "was whether
you'd noticed anything amiss in the flats last night. Nothing?
Nobody coming in late, for example?"

She smiled. "No, but then I would not. My 'earing is so
poor. And besides, till about eleven I 'ad the raddio turned
on."

"I see. Thank you, madame. You've been most kind."

They left her. "Might check up at the cinema," Pig said moodily. The porter came upstairs with a refilled sand-bucket. "Dom lot," he grumbled to no one, "always 'alf-inching the sand. Old girl in Number 5 pinches it for 'er cats 'alf the time."

"You Blake?" Eggshell snapped.

He stood to attention. "Yes, sir. Sorry, sir. Didn't see 'oo you was. Black as your 'at in 'ere."

"You don't set foot in the flats after 6 p.m., do you, Blake?"

"Not as a rule, sir. I was 'ere last night, though—"

"Why?"

"Mr. Lang wanted me to get 'im a chicken. My brother was killing some of 'is own, and when I told Mr. Lang so 'e said, 'Get one for me, Blake, there's a good chap,' so as I 'ad it last night I popped in on my way 'ome from Ted's—that's my brother's—and took it up."

"What time?"

"About 'alf-past ten. Mr. Lang keeps late hours. Still, 'e wasn't in, so I put it down in Flat 2, wot is empty, knowing it was so cold the fowl would keep."

"Why didn't you send it up on the lift?"

"Ruddy thing's jammed," said Blake crossly, "and a fine lot of work it makes, 'eaving an' 'auling."

"Was Lang expecting you?"

"No, sir, because I said I wouldn't be able to get it till today."

"Think carefully. You didn't notice anything out of the way last night? Any of the residents going in or out?"

"Why? Wot's up?"

"Never mind. Did you?"

"Nope. Not a soul."

"You don't know if anyone was in?"

"Nope. Except Madame Charnay, with 'er wireless blaring fit to wake the dead. Don't know 'ow the others stand it. She didn't 'ave it on long, though, not last night."

"All right. Well, Blake, Mrs. Sibley's been found murdered down at Hooham, in Surrey. So if you think of anything else, come and tell us, will you?"

"I'll do that, sir." Blake saluted. "But there's nothing more to think. Cor, poor ole lady—though she was a bit mingy, and could be a tartar. First 'er brother in our shelter, and then 'er. Getting quite a necro-polis, sir, ain't we?" He passed on to deposit the bucket in its war station.

Chapter Eight

MR. WARRENDER WAS OUT. MR. LANG, HOWEVER, WAS in, and he invited them into a welter of books and papers. His rooms were warm and scruffy. Ink spattered the wall near the writing-desk, a portable typewriter was balanced precariously on one end of the sofa. Hanging over the fireplace was the one concession to decoration: a large and excellent reproduction of *The Rape of Helen*, by Benozzo Gozzoli.

"Bit of colour," Lang explained, seeing Pig's eye upon it; "not my taste really; had it for Christmas. You get fond of it, though. What's up, Inspector? Here, move over the ticker and you'll find a cosy spot."

Eggshell introduced Pig, and Lang seemed impressed. "Excited to meet you, sir. Don't get much fun in a dull life. I haven't been doing anything, have I?"

"Someone has." Pig, who did not like being described as "fun," replied not too agreeably, and he asked Lang where he had spent the previous evening.

The young man squinted down at his nails. "I was here, working."

"I'm afraid you weren't," said Pig, "according to the porter, who called to bring you a fowl."

Lang folded his rather thick lips and said nothing.

"Now look, Lang, this is only a routine matter, but we'd like to have your co-operation. Where were you?"

"As a matter of fact, I spent the night with a friend. I was worried about something in my work, so I went for a walk over Hampstead Heath."

"Unpleasant weather for a walk," Pig suggested.

"I don't mind rain."

"And a good deal of mud out there."

"And I don't mind mud," Lang retorted, rather savagely. "You've only got to look at my brown shoes, if you don't believe me. What's all this about, anyway?"

"With whom did you spend the night, sir?"

Lang said, "I told you. A friend."

"What friend?"

"Have I got to answer?"

"No, Lang. Not yet. But I should, in your place."

"Well… I left it too late for my last bus, so I called in on a—a young lady I know who has a studio in Hampstead and she let me sleep on her bath. It's one of those with a cover on."

"Her name and address?"

"Look here, Lord Whitestone, I'm not going to give it. I mean—well, it was quite all right, if you know what I mean, but it might look queer, and I couldn't tell you without consulting her. I mean, it might get her a bad name, which would be ridiculous, because—"

"Anything you say will be treated in confidence. I shall merely ask for the lady's confirmation, and that will be the end of it."

The young man rose and walked up and down the room, his face flushed, head cast down. Suddenly he stopped. "Right you are. Miss Kathleen Smith, 4 Herring Studios, Ferncroft Hill, N.W.3."

"Thank you, Lang. That's all for today."

"And quite enough too," said Felix Lang rudely, banging the door behind his departing visitors.

"Well, Eggshell?" Pig demanded, as they walked back towards the station in a stained and luminous twilight. The evening sky was mirrored bluely in the wet pavements. The shopkeepers were pulling down the blinds over their bright windows.

"Seems a shame to black-out any bit of cheer we get," the Inspector murmured, watching regretfully as the greengrocer faded out a glowing picture of oranges, tomatoes, and good green apples.

"Eggshell!" Pig had no romance in his soul. "What about them?"

"Them? Well, we know nothing about Warrender. Madame seems O.K. Lang's the sticky one. Do you really think he went for a walk in that weather? Sounds a crazy story."

"You have to bear in mind," Pig remarked tolerantly, "that some people are mad enough to enjoy mud… Is that the cinema Madame Charnet visited? May as well make that query."

Eggshell crossed the road and spoke to the girl in the box-office.

"French lady? Yes, I remember her. She asked me for some cigarettes and said had I got any French ones. Course I hadn't, and I told her so, too. Took a shilling ticket."

"What time was that?"

"Five o'clock, more or less."

"Did you see her come out?"

"No, can't say I did."

"Good girl. Thanks."

Eggshell returned to retail this to Pig, who said, "It seems to me this lady is eager to arrest attention. She must know a cinema like that wouldn't sell foreign cigarettes. Wonder if she's got an independent game of any kind? Keep track on her, Eggshell. Wonder why she left France?"

They walked on. "Well," Pig said, "I can't stay here much longer. Must be getting back. But before I go, we'll see if Miss Kathleen Smith confirms Lang's statement."

Back at the station, Eggshell rang up the Hampstead police and asked them to make immediate enquiry. While they were awaiting a report he said, "I must say, sir, I do appreciate your—your personal interest in this case. All of us here are honoured."

"Don't be," Pig said. "My interest is very personal. I've had my cousin in trouble like this before."

"But Lord Whitestone, Mr. and Mrs. Kinghof are only indirectly connected with this case."

Pig pointed a bulging red finger at his subordinate. "If you knew my cousin, Eggshell, you'd know that without supervision Mr. Kinghof might easily appear in so conspicuous a role as that of corpse. And Mrs. Kinghof, if a good influence on him, is not a profound one."

He was so moved by the thought of Andrew on a slab—though less out of affection than out of fear that his own reputation might be compromised—that he drank without protest the horrible cup of tea Frankson brought in for him.

Twenty minutes later, the Hampstead Inspector telephoned.

"I'll take it," Pig said, and announced himself.

"Miss Smith categorically denies that Mr. Felix Lang spent last night at her flat," said the Inspector. "She was very angry when I told her of his statement and said she hardly knew him. She had met him only once, at a party."

Pig sucked his teeth. "Ah, yes. Yes. What sort of a girl is she?"

"Very quiet, I should say, very steady sort of girl. Twenty-five or -six, roundabout. Fashion artist."

"Pretty?" Pig snapped.

"More pleasant-looking, if you know what I mean, sir. Fair hair, worn in a bun, tweed costume, blue wool jumper, grey shoes. Sort of parson's daughter type. Good figure. Wears an engagement ring, very fine sapphire with pearl and diamond shoulders."

"Thank you. Good. Very well, Inspector, that's all I want to know. Good night." To Eggshell he said, "That girl denies Lang's story. Says she hardly knows him." He gave details of the telephone conversation. "Better go round to Lang and tell him. And by the way, will you call on Warrender? I must go now. Keep in close touch with us."

Pig assumed his *chapeau melon*, a new one, since Andrew and Agnes had between them ruined the old, and went his way.

———

Behold Lord Whitestone at home in his flat in Regent's Park. Dinner is over, coffee on the fireside table. Mary, his wife, in lamé blouse and black satin skirt, is reading *The Queen*. She is a big, colourless woman, healthy, white-toothed; she has the great, high-bridged nose, the great, long, narrow feet of the well-bred. Shoes made for such feet are very ugly and very expensive. It is only the cheaper variety that commit the solecism of being alluring. Well-bred women should not expect to allure.

"Mary," Pig says thoughtfully, "you wouldn't, I imagine, call me a revengeful man?"

She studies a portrait of herself, toothy in white satin. "Of course not, dear."

"And yet I hardly feel I can let the Kinghofs go unscathed."

"Are you still thinking of that silly Scout concert? My dear Herbert, it would be most lowering to take any action."

"Nevertheless," he replied, "I am only human, Mary, only human. I think I must arrange an evening for them."

"You wouldn't want to descend to their level, Herbert."

"But perhaps I would," he muses. "Mary, what do you suppose would be their idea of entertainment?"

She considers. "A risqué revue, I should think, followed by a 'bottle society,' or party, or whatever they're called."

"Yes, that's about it. Well, I shall ask them out next week and take them to see the revival of *My Uncle Polovtsnai* at the Avant-Garde Club."

"But, my dear, that's a terribly highbrow play! Susan Charteris told me she's never been so puzzled in her life. All the actors wear chromium masks and talk baby-talk. How will you endure it yourself?"

"I can endure anything in a good cause," Pig says darkly. "Thursday, I think, Mary. Yes, Thursday. We'll give them a good dinner; they certainly gave me one, and fair's fair. After *My Uncle Polovtsnai* we shall go to a poetry-reading by old Jane Valery. Some fool sent me a card. Yes. Condign punishment, Mary. I shall enjoy it."

He rings the bell for some of his most prized brandy.

———

Mrs. Rowse was a woman of resilient spirits. After dinner on Sunday night—she had cried herself red-eyed all the afternoon—she said suddenly, "Well, doesn't do to let oneself go. I have my work to consider," and she sat down with pad and pencil to write about Fernia's rescue of Miss Valaine from the wild Cornish seas. Her example revived the Kinghofs, who got out the bottles and the late Mrs. Sibley's Snakes and Ladders board, with which diversions they amused themselves drearily until bed-time.

On the following day Mrs. Sibley's body was brought home to London, and Mrs. Rowse and the Kinghofs returned to their flat. They found on the mat an invitation from Pig, winningly worded, for dinner and a show on Thursday.

"Better go, I suppose," Agnes sighed. "We'd better give the poor little thing his little revenge. I wonder what horror he's planned for us?"

"Lord knows," said Andrew despondently. "Pity we've got to waste an evening indulging Pig. I wanted to see *My Uncle Polovtsnai* at the Avant-Garde before I went back. They say it's quite extraordinary."

"Well, we may be able to fit it in. Better write and accept poor Pig's silly invitation."

Tuesday morning saw the inquest on Mrs. Sibley's death. Seven fascinated jurors returned, as directed, another verdict of murder against person or persons unknown.

On the same afternoon, just as Agnes and Andrew were thinking of going out to see Cary Grant at the Odeon, Felix Lang called upon them.

"I say, I wonder if I could talk to you for a tick? I'm in a mess and I don't know which way to turn. No excuse for bothering you, but may I?"

Andrew regarded the young man steadily, noticing his heightened colour, his trembling hands. "O.K. Come in. Don't mind talking before my wife, do you?"

"No," said Lang, "if she'll listen." He collapsed miserably on top of Agnes's felt hat, which she had left on the settee. He looked at her legs and seemed to draw courage from them. "The police have been asking me questions. That lump Eggshell and a bigwig from the Yard came round on Sunday afternoon, wanting to know where I spent Saturday night."

"Well?" Agnes encouraged him. "And where did you spend it?"

"I was worried about my work, so I went to walk on Hampstead Heath. It sounds nuts, I know, on a wet night in the black-out, but it's God's own truth. I left it too late for my bus, so I went to the flat of a girl I know, on Ferncroft Hill, and she let me sleep on the lid of her bath. I told this big-stone Whiteshot—I mean big-shot Whitestone—about it in confidence, and he called up Kathleen to confirm it. Grim thing is that she denies it flatly. Only met me once, she says. Never set eyes on me Saturday night. Heaven knows what's got into her! I called her up this morning, and she just went on denying it—to me! I tell you, I'm desperate. What the devil shall I do? She always seemed such a nice kid."

"Look here, if you're innocent, nothing on earth can prove you guilty," said Andrew, rather stuffily.

Not thinking the remark in the best of taste, Agnes hastily interposed, "Though of course we know you didn't do it."

"Good lord!" Lang said in a despairing squeak. "I didn't even know till I saw the papers yesterday what I was supposed to have done! Can't they prove I wasn't at Hooham? What about the ticket-collectors? Or the Green Line conductors?"

Andrew suggested that Mr. Lang might well have cycled down.

"Now look here, Kinghof—"

"All right, Lang! I was only exploring every avenue."

"Leaving no stone unturned," Agnes added.

"Dotting all the i's," Andrew grinned at her.

"Examining every possibility."

"Leaving nothing to the imagination."

"No, Andrew!—That's not a good one.—Pinning every winkle."

"You made that up. That's cheating."

"Well, I—"

"I won't intrude on you further," Mr. Lang said icily, "as you seem to be having such damn' fine fun." He made for the door.

"Oh, do stop and have some tea or sherry!" Agnes shouted repentantly after him.

"No, thank you, ma'am. Mr. Kinghof! I hope you get Night Starvation."

"Rancid Hair to you," said Agnes, defending her mate.

The door slammed.

The next visitor was Eggshell.

"Thought you might like to hear the latest, sir." He was sweaty and beaming, plainly under the intoxicating influence of good news.

"We surely would," Agnes replied.

"Not, mind you, ma'am, that it's official; but knowing you've been upset, and knowing that Lord Whitestone… You understand, Mrs. Kinghof."

She said she understood. "Look here, Inspector, we're on the point of having tea. Will you join us in a cup?"

He hesitated, cocked an eye at Andrew. "Well, Mrs. Kinghof, seeing that this is unofficial—"

"Splendid. Come on in and sit down."

"I suppose," said Andrew curiously, "that you cleared my wife and myself of—of Saturday night? I only ask because it's nice to know."

Eggshell regarded his clean, square fingernails. "Well, sir, as a matter of routine we did check up with the 'Walrus and Carpenter.'" He grinned engagingly. "All right, sir; we've nothing on you."

"Now don't you dare tell my husband any news till I come back," Agnes said, going out to bring the tray. Heroically he held his fire until she returned with tea, toasted crumpets, and Dundee cake. She supplied Eggshell with food. "And now? We're all ears."

He drew a long breath, sucked up a trail of butter from his chin, beamed about him and said very slowly and clearly, "At seven forty-five p.m. on Saturday last, George Warrender was seen by the ticket-collector at Coldersbrook, the next station on the line to Hooham."

They received this information in tributary silence. Then Andrew said, "Oh, Eggshell, this is great! Congratulations. As the little boy said, taking up the sugar-bowl after enquiring if God was everywhere, and slamming it down on the table—'Got 'Im!'"

Agnes deprecated this chestnut by a sneer.

"Well, sir, may look like it; but we can't be sure. He admits being there, but won't say what he was doing. Flatly refuses. Not that we've finished with him."

"What about Lang? He told me his girl refused to back his statement."

"We're going further into that… Oh, did he tell you? What's he up to?"

"I may be innocent," said Agnes, "but I fancied he wanted a little human sympathy."

"Perhaps you're right, ma'am. I don't say you're not."

Andrew said slowly, "Inspector, if the question I'm going to ask you is improper, tick me off. But I still mean to ask it. Or two questions."

"Fire away, sir."

"Do you believe that the name of the murderer is Maclagan Steer?"

"Yes, sir."

"And that he lives in Block 3, Stewarts Court?"

Eggshell hesitated. Then he said, "Yes."

Agnes rapped out, "Who is he?"

He turned on her his blue eyes, guileless as a child's, opaque as turquoise. "You tell me, ma'am."

"We're left with two runners, aren't we? Warrender or Lang. Have you found out anything about Warrender's early days?"

"Not much, ma'am; says he was born in London, and we've traced his name to Clapham Parish Register. Educated at a private school now disappeared. Burned down about twelve years ago. We're trying to find someone who remembers him. No information on him till 1933, when he worked for two years in Manchester. We checked that."

"Could he have been Steer?"

"Possibly, unless he is the Warrender of the parish register."

"Could Lang?"

"Age difficulty there. But still possible." Eggshell rose suddenly. "That's all, sir. Oh—one more news item for you. Reginald Coppenstall came to London from Algiers on the nineteenth of July, 1939. Traced to Bayswater Hotel, where he spent a week. Then lost sight of completely. I say, Mr. Kinghof—" His eyes twinkled. "Hasn't your good lady forgotten someone?"

"Who?" Agnes exclaimed.

"What about poor Madame Charnet?"

"Jumping cats, you don't mean—"

Eggshell smiled. "Well, she does seem to have kept her own bed Saturday night, I'll admit; but we think she may be involved in another little affair."

"What's that?"

"All in good time, Mrs. Kinghof."

"Inspector! I think that's disgraceful of you, to whet my appetite and then refuse to talk. You're a regular—what would you call him, Andrew?"

Mr. Kinghof looked speculative. "A regular tease," he suggested coyly.

"A little rogue."

"A slyboots."

"A Puss in the Corner."

"A male hussy," Andrew contributed triumphantly.

"No! I've got it. A larrikin!"

"That, madam," Eggshell protested, "is an Australian hooligan, if I am not mistaken. We'll settle on 'rascal,' if you don't mind."

They grinned at him.

"Well, must be going back to the grind. Thank you for your hospitality. Good evening."

"Thank you for telling us so much," Agnes said. "We appreciate it."

At the door he paused, and turned back. "Will you be at the funeral tomorrow, Mrs. Kinghof?"

"We both shall. Old Mrs. Rowse seemed anxious for us to attend, so we said we would. Why?"

"Only you'd be doing me a service if you'd let me know who turns up. Will you do that? Can I count on you?"

"My aunt, General Sidebotham," Agnes began, "always used to say, 'What I like about Agnes is that you can count on her: I call her Auntie's little Abacus.'"

Andrew said, "Be quiet, pet. No time for funniments. Yes. Inspector, we'll do that. Right away afterwards."

When the door had closed behind Eggshell, Agnes kissed her husband. "How lovely it is," she said dreamily, "to be cousin to a Pig! It opens all doors to one."

Chapter Nine

IT WAS EXCELLENT FUNERAL WEATHER, GREY AND mild, with a thin mist lying over the grass and sifting between the cypresses. If poor Mrs. Sibley's friends had been few, they had achieved a lavish display of flowers; mauve and white chrysanthemums from Mrs. Rowse, red roses from the Kinghofs, a chaplet of immortelles from a former maid, and a mass of pink carnations bearing the card, 'In affectionate memory of Aunt Addie from Bubbles.' At the funeral there were but six mourners: Mrs. Rowse, Andrew, Agnes, Mr. Cole, who was Mrs. Sibley's solicitor, a good-looking, horsey young woman in hasty black who proclaimed herself, to everyone's surprise, the daughter of Mrs. Sibley's sister, Mrs. Ashton, some years deceased, and lastly, a gloomy, soft-moving man who talked to nobody, stood apart at the graveside and afterwards disappeared into the rising mist with the disagreeable facility of Count Dracula.

When the ceremony was over, Mrs. Rowse asked the Kinghofs if they would please come back for sherry and biscuits. "We shall be reading the will," she told them, "and I believe dear Addie didn't forget people who were kind to her." She, Mr. Cole, and Miss Ashton went in the first coach, and the Kinghofs followed in an unnecessary second vehicle. "Who's the man who left us a few minutes ago?" Agnes whispered to Mrs. Rowse.

"I don't know, but he has the most abrupt manners. I suppose he's some sort of relation."

Agnes said to Andrew, as they drove back to Stewarts Court at a pace reasonably brisk in comparison with the outward journey, "I say, do you think we ought to have stuck to him? Suppose he's—"

"Oh, rot! He's six feet two if he's an inch."

"He could build himself up."

"Not about half a foot, he couldn't."

"Why not? He could do anything."

"But he was big-built. You could see that. Anyhow, we'll tell Eggshell about him."

"When? Shall I pop in home, on the way upstairs?"

"We'll both pop in."

On alighting, Andrew said to Mrs. Rowse, "We'll be along in a moment. I have to make an important 'phone call."

They rang up Eggshell.

"We've just come back from the funeral," Andrew announced.

"Ah, yes, sir. Very sad," the Inspector said mechanically. "Who was there?"

"Mrs. Rowse, Cole, Mrs. Sibley's solicitor, a niece, Miss Ashton—I think she calls herself Bubbles—and a very queer chap, who wouldn't talk to anyone and hared off just as soon as it was over."

Pushing him aside, Agnes snatched the telephone from his hand. "Inspector? Mrs. Kinghof speaking. I thought I'd better talk to you about this man, as, after all, women *are* better at descriptions, aren't they? He was tall, about six foot two, heavily built, with rather a bovine expression: 'looby,' one might say. He was mid-fair and had a small moustache that didn't look quite genuine. A dried sort of moustache, the sort you buy in toy-shops with a bit of wire to stick up your nose so that it stays on. He wore a navy-blue serge suit, not well cut, a navy overcoat with mourning-band, and a black felt hat. He didn't seem at all moved by the funeral, and if you ask me—"

"Madam," said Eggshell, cutting into the flow, "I don't think Henderson would be flattered by your remarks about his face or the cut of his clothes. He is wearing the mourning-band for his grandfather, and his moustache, I assure you, is a natural phenomenon. Henderson—"

"Who is Henderson?"

"Our representative. We have to send one, naturally, in such a case, and—"

Agnes roared at him, loudly enough to smother the echoes of her husband's mirth. "I think that's too bad! Why did you ask us to keep a watch for you, if your beastly Henderson was going?"

"It's nice to have an independent eye kept on things," he answered pacifically. He had given Andrew and Agnes a job out of simple desire to satisfy their urge for interference.

"I don't love you," said Agnes very sorrowfully and very emphatically; and she hung up.

The Kinghofs, more or less chastened, went upstairs to drink Sunnymaloo sherry.

In Number 10 they became better acquainted with Miss

Ashton. She was a pleasant-looking girl, blonde and bonny; but she had no idea how to make the best of herself. Her front hair was yanked up above her round face into a mass of flat, doughnut-like curls and was allowed to cascade behind after the style of a horse's mane. Her face was patchily adorned with white powder, but none of it had touched her handsome, but large, nose. Fortunately her mouth was large, sweet and full of natural colour. It was the mouth of a girl with many unrealized possibilities.

"Mrs. Rowse says you were both ripping to poor Auntie, and I want to thank you. I haven't seen her for years because she and my mother, I'm sorry to say, didn't get on too well, but she was always good to me when I was a child, and she's never once forgotten my birthday." Miss Ashton cried a little.

"We did nothing," Andrew murmured, with some justification.

"She had faithful friends," Mr. Cole droned, "she was rich in them. Her friends were her treasure on earth."

Agnes thought it odd that their numbers were so few; but she recollected that Mrs. Sibley's personality had not been lovable. She said to Miss Ashton, for want of a subject that did not deal with death: "Do you live in London?"

The girl looked as though she had stepped on a frog. "Live here? Oh, no! I like the fresh air, and the fields and the trees. I wouldn't live in a fuggy old town for anything. What can you do in town?"

"You can go to the pictures," Andrew suggested anxiously, not liking to find persons in this frame of mind.

"But I hate the pictures! All those nasty American accents."

"There's a foreign film on sometimes," Agnes pleaded.

"Oh, but one doesn't want to hear a lot of foreigners talking away in silly languages. I don't mind a decent English picture sometimes, but there aren't very many."

"They seem a lot," Agnes said. "Where do you live, then?"

"Oh, a girl friend and I run a stunning kennels in Warwickshire, near a wonderful old-world village. Shakespeare is said to have slept in the local inn."

"Well, if it's a good inn, that's something," said Andrew.

"It's nice to look at. Of course, only the rough people go into it, and fast crowds from London, sometimes."

"Oh. What do you do in the evenings?"

"Knit, or sew, and then go to bed!" Miss Ashton pealed gaily, showing very pretty teeth. "Have to, if you're going to be up bright and early at five."

Andrew suppressed a shiver but was sure he must have blenched. "Do the dogs need feeding at five?"

She laughed. "Oh, no, but one likes to be about early in the country. If you lie in bed you miss the best part of the day. Don't you like seeing the dawn come up, Mrs. Kinghof?"

Agnes was saved from reply by the intervention of Mr. Cole, who, by his manner deploring so much brightness over baked meats, begged attention for the reading of the will.

It was not a long one, and was dated the day prior to Mrs. Sibley's death. After the usual preliminaries it read: "'To my faithful friend Mrs. Phyllada Rowse, I leave my bungalow-house, "Osokozee," Hooham-on-Thames, Surrey, with contents complete; and in addition the sum of £500 free of death duties.'" Mrs. Rowse, overcome, began to cry intently and silently.

"'To Mr. and Mrs. Andrew Kinghof, of 8, Block 3, Stewarts Court, I leave the sum of £50, in gratitude for recent kindnesses during a time of trouble.'"

"That's damned nice of her," Andrew whispered, and was reproved by a glassy stare from Mr. Cole.

He wiped his glasses carefully, coughed, and seemed a little agitated. "'Finally, I leave the residue of my estate, after payment of my debts and of death duties, to my niece, Miss Joan Averil Ashton, Setters Croft, Beanscot, Warwickshire.'"

After the dead silence that followed, Miss Ashton gave a faint, strangled cry. "Me? But it's fantastic! I haven't seen her for years—"

"There are two further sentences," said Mr. Cole. "I may add that I had no hand in drawing up this will, to which the deceased merely requested my opinion as to its validity, and my consent to act as executor." He read, "'To my nephew, Maclagan Steer, I leave nothing. He will know why.'" He folded the will and sat gazing into the fire, his face troubled.

"I can't bear it," Miss Ashton moaned, "I don't want to take it. I've hardly ever done a thing for her. Is it very much?"

He answered shortly, "Mrs. Sibley has been fortunate in her investments. At a conservative estimate, after taxation and the discharge of a few minor debts, the residue would amount to £95,000. Permit me to offer you my congratulations."

Miss Ashton rose and groped for nothing. Abruptly she sat down again. "But we all thought Maclagan would inherit if anything happened to Uncle Reg! I expected a few hundreds, but this—this—'He will know why.' What is Maclagan supposed to know?"

The solicitor replied awkwardly, "I was not authorized... am hardly authorized to pass on assumptions."

She turned to Mrs. Rowse. "Will you tell me?"...But that lady was too far gone in tears to do more than reply, in broken fashion, that she never wanted to talk about the horrible affair again.

"You can't treat me like this!" said Miss Ashton, looking for a moment very like Fernia Prideaux. "I've a right to be told."

Andrew came to her aid. "If Mrs. Rowse permits, my wife and I will tell you, as best we can, what Mrs. Sibley had in her mind."

Mrs. Rowse said, "Yes, yes. You tell her. Not before me, though. I can't stand any more."

So when the solicitor had gone, Andrew and Agnes took Miss Ashton out to lunch at "The Amber Witch," the quietest, if hardly the best, restaurant in the vicinity, and after she had eaten, told her the tale from the beginning.

She listened without comment, and though, at its conclusion, looked rather pale, she was quick to seize on vital points.

"Suppose Maclagan had inherited? How could he have got the money, with the police believing he murdered my aunt?"

Andrew said, "That would have been the trickiest part of the business; but it seems to me that after a reasonable time, one of the residents of Block 3 would have gone quietly away to disappear into the *ewigkeit*; and that after another tactful time-lag, a young man called Maclagan Steer would have walked in, bold as brass, to collect his inheritance. Suspicion can't hang a man, and he isn't the kind of man to supply proof."

She said unsteadily, "Yes, I realize that. But there's something else."

"Here," Agnes pressed her, "do have another brandy, Miss Ashton. You've had a day of shocks."

The girl looked suddenly childish and uncertain. "Will you call me Bubbles?" she said awkwardly. "You've been nice, and I don't like being formal with people who are decent."

"Of course we will. My name's Agnes, and this is Andrew; but I expect you know that by now. Bubbles—brandy?"

"No, really I won't. I'm not used to drinking."

"A tiny drop won't hurt you. Now then, what's on your mind?"

"Only," said Bubbles, in an abrupt, schoolgirl bark, "that I suppose I'm next on the list."

They looked at her staggered.

"If he's murdered two people," she continued, "he won't stop at a third. If I died today, he'd inherit. I've made no will, and he's my only living relation."

Andrew brought his hand down on the table. "I'm not going to fool about saying 'no, no.' or 'you're imagining things.' You've got a head on your shoulders, Bubbles, and you can take it. Listen: I don't know your immediate plans, but I want you to come and spend a few days with us."

"Oh, but I can't do that! I—"

"Were you planning to stay in town?"

"I was at Dean's Hotel last night and meant to be there one night more, going back to Warwickshire tomorrow, but—"

"Is your suitcase there?"

"Yes, but I can't impose—"

"We'll take a cab there right away and bring it back. Have you got a solicitor, Bubbles?"

"No. I've never needed one."

"Well, you're seeing ours tonight, and you're going to leave the bulk of your estate to a hospital, or some other deserving charity. Not to an individual. Individuals are vulnerable and institutions aren't. You can always make a new will later on, if you don't want the bequest to stand. Then we're going to let Block 3 know immediately, and I don't care how obviously we do it, that Maclagan Steer wouldn't stand to get a penny by your death. What do you say?"

"What can I? I think you're both marvellous."

"No, we're not. We…if you don't think it's in bad taste… we enjoy ourselves."

They took Bubbles to the West End, and before they collected her suitcase did a little shopping. "I want to buy some stockings," she said. The brandy had obliterated much of her initial distress. "You know, I think I shall buy a really expensive pair for once. Mine have never been expensive," she added wistfully. "I'm going to buy beige ones, of really heavy silk—"

"Now, why not," said Agnes persuasively, "buy three pairs of Van Dingen's *Couleur de Rose*, which are practically invisible, and *so* flattering?"

Bubbles looked startled. "Oh, but—"

"And darling, we've got oceans of time, so why not have your hair styled by 'Marquise'? She's marvellous, and I'm going to have mine done, anyhow. You'd look so nice with the new shingle; since the war hair's got so much smarter and less sloppy. Andrew can go and have tea at his terrible woolly club—it smells of very old men's cardigans—and we'll join him afterwards."

Whether Bubbles was too dazed to know what was being done to her, or whether she had, for many years among the red setters, hankered for just such sissy chic as was part and parcel of women like Agnes, no one ever knew; but after a surprisingly brief tussle she was swept away into Bond

Street, and Andrew retired to the "Four Swords," his club in St. James's.

Bubbles, on money advanced by Mrs. Kinghof, bought three pairs of *Couleur de Rose*, a black dress adorned with gilt cartridge-cases, in Russian style, and a round fur hat that Agnes would not permit her to wear until Marquise had been at work. Her funeral frock and hat were parcelled up, and the shop instructed to send them back to Warwickshire. In the beauty parlour Marquise snipped and polished Bubbles' hair till it lay short and bright as floss silk around her head, after which an assistant properly known as *Petit Miracle* "styled" her make-up, leaving the girl with a dewiness, a Turkish-bath freshness, no amount of country and air and home-grown spinach had ever succeeded in achieving.

When she and Agnes went to meet Andrew, he was silent before the transformation.

"Well," Agnes demanded.

He said to Bubbles, "You look smashing. I've never seen such a change in anyone—not that you weren't nice before."

"I do feel a bit effeminate," she muttered, scraping one shoe against the other, "but I suppose I'll get used to it."

As they went into Stewarts Court they were met by Mr. Lang, who was on the point of exit. Seeing Andrew and Agnes, he looked angry, and seemed about to pass them without a word. Then his eye fell on Bubbles, on Bubbles who was looking like Juno and feeling like Jezebel. His expression changed to one of extreme cordiality. "Hullo, Kinghof! How are you?"

"We're very well," said Agnes sternly.

"Oh, good. Yes, so am I. I mean, as well as can be expected, only still worried. Will you come in and have a drink with me tonight? Oh, and bring Miss—Miss—your friend."

"Miss Ashton, Mr. Lang." Agnes made a brief introduction. "No, I'm sorry, but I'm afraid we've another engagement."

"Perhaps another night?"

"Yes, perhaps." She swept on, bearing Bubbles with her, and Andrew followed majestically behind.

"Who was it we met on the stairs?" Bubbles asked rather shyly, as she watched Agnes preparing the spare room.

"Suspect Number 1. Or possibly Number 2. Felix Lang, the medical student."

"Well, I'm sure it's not he."

"No? So sure?"

"He looked nice," Bubbles murmured.

"So does Warrender."

"But Lang can't be Maclagan."

"Why not?"

"Oh—Maclagan could never have been nice."

Agnes sat down on the bed and lit a cigarette. "Do you remember him?"

"Hardly at all. I only saw him once, when he was about twelve, and as I was only six at the time I can't remember much. His mother brought him down to see Mummy and me, when we lived in Sussex."

"Can't you tell me what he was like?"

"Oh, rather a squinny child, mid-fair, very quiet. Cruel little beast. All I can call to mind sharply about him was that he deliberately trod on the cat's tail and tried to kick Tinker, my dog."

"There wasn't anything outstanding about his appearance?"

Bubbles considered. "No," she said reluctantly, "I don't think so. He's only a blur in my mind."

"All right. I won't bother you any more." Andrew knocked at the door.

"Come in."

"Oh, I say, Agnes! Gladwin says he'll come along to dinner. He's doing nothing. And he'll bring a will-form."

"Splendid. He likes sweetbreads, doesn't he? Darling, *do* see if you can run any to earth. The shops are still open."

"Damn his sweetbreads! All right. But I'm not going to more than one place for them."

Agnes said complacently, hearing the front door close behind him, "He's a wonderful shopper. We don't keep a regular servant because we have nearly all meals out and can manage with a daily woman; but Andrew's superb in an emergency."

Gladwin came at eight, a tough little man of near-albino colouring, who was thought a shyster by many, and acknowledged by all to be a first-rate solicitor. On Bubbles' instructions, he drew up a will for her leaving every penny to a children's hospital, and Andrew and Agnes witnessed it.

"And now," said Gladwin, who had heard the story and been fascinated by it, "how are you going to pass this good news around? No, thanks, Kinghof. I'd prefer port."

"Got white port, if you like." Andrew always catered for the hideous tastes of others.

"Hip, hip. Many thanks. Here's to us all, and congratulations to you, Miss Ashton."

Meanwhile, Agnes had seated herself at the desk and was writing on little strips of paper. This task completed, she put the three strips in respective envelopes and sealed them. "Going out," she stated, and before anyone could question her, had left the flat. She was back within five minutes, wearing the smile of the cat who has just stolen the rabbit meant for his next meal.

"They know now," she said.

"Mrs. K.!" protested Gladwin. "What on earth have you done!"

She giggled. "I wrote on the papers, 'Miss Ashton has made her will in favour of the Sargent Street Children's Hospital', and put them in unaddressed envelopes through three letter-boxes."

"Oh, ye gods *et petits poissons!*" said Gladwin.

"Why three?" Andrew demanded.

"I like an odd number."

"Why unaddressed envelopes?"

"So that if anyone puzzled by them rushes in here demanding an explanation—I forgot to tell you I signed them 'A. Kinghof'—I can say the envelope was delivered there by mistake. Now we just sit back and watch developments. Andrew, I should like some whisky. Some for you, Bubbles?"

"I think," the girl said faintly, "that I'd rather like to go to bed. If you don't mind. I've had rather an exciting day."

Benignly, they all excused her, and sat down to a fascinating vigil.

Chapter Ten

LET US RETREAT A FEW HOURS IN TIME AND HEAR about the unfortunate experience of Mr. Lang at the police-station.

On the afternoon of the day that saw Mrs. Sibley's funeral, Eggshell sent word to the young student that Miss Kathleen Smith was with him. "She is quite willing to make her denials in front of you, sir, if you'd like to step down here."

"Oh, she is, is she?" Mr. Lang bellowed. "Yes, I'd certainly like to step down."

He found Eggshell closeted with a tall, fair girl of open countenance; the sort of girl invariably described as "a lady."

"Look here, Kathleen," Lang said at once, "I don't know if this is your idea of fun, or whether it's some kind of revenge on me for telling the police I slept on your bath, but please, please don't do it! You'll get me into an awful mess!"

She flushed slightly and looked down at her grey-gloved hands. "Don't, Felix. You know it's not true, and I don't know why you should want me to tell a lie. I'd like to help you, but I can't admit anything so fantastically silly!"

"Kathleen! You don't understand. Now, listen quietly. I'm in a jam. A bad jam. All I want you to do is to tell the Inspector I spent Saturday night tucked up on your bath. Don't fool, please. You mustn't."

She turned abruptly to Eggshell. "Inspector, this is ridiculous. I've met Mr. Lang once, or twice, rather, once at a party given by a pianist friend, Moya Gabain—you may know of her—and once after another of Moya's evenings, when he came back to my flat, with three or four other people, for sherry. On that occasion he wasn't there more than half an hour."

"You are on Christian-names terms, I see," said Eggshell, "if you'll excuse me, Miss Smith."

She smiled ruefully. "Oh, that's just a habit in artistic circles. No one even mentions a surname, unless you specifically ask for it."

Felix Lang turned to her a face distraught with rage. "Is that your story? All right, I'll tell the rest. I know Miss Smith well. After the sherry party I rang her up next morning, and we got in the habit of seeing each other regularly. We went walking together at Richmond and Ken Wood, we've played gramophone records at her flat, been to the pictures and the ballet, and she's been to see me three or four times. Mind you—understand me—it was platonic. Yes, Kay, I'm admitting that. I could pretend you were my mistress, couldn't I? It wouldn't make much odds. But I'm telling the truth. I've been 'walking out' with Miss Smith, Inspector, as the lower classes term it, on and off for about two months."

She looked directly at him and smiled. "I've never been called 'Kay' in my life. Inspector, I'd like you to check that, and ask my friends whether, to their knowledge, I have ever been out with Mr. Lang."

"No, because you kept it hidden! Lord knows why. I didn't then, and I don't now, and sometimes it used to get in my hair: but you always said, 'Don't you think it's nice to have a secret?'"

She turned to Eggshell. She seemed now on the point of tears, and her hands were trembling. "Please, I can't stand much more. All this is untrue. Heaven knows I wouldn't try to get anyone into trouble, but—but—Felix, you must be mad! How *can* you stand there making up such nonsense?"

"How can you stand there lying at me, when I've told you I'm in trouble?"

She said slowly, "If you'd asked me in advance to lie, I think… I think I'd have done it. But I can't back you now—I can't, I can't!" She tugged so hard at her small pearl necklace that the clasp broke.

"Yes," Lang shouted, "and who gave you that?"

"How dare you? My mother gave it me."

"Ask her mother," said Lang to Eggshell.

Miss Smith stood up, and for a moment it looked as if she might strike him. Then she said quietly to the Inspector, "My mother is dead. He knows that perfectly well, because, for some reason or other, she came into the conversation at our first meeting."

"You bitch!"

"Sir! I won't have that. Moderate your language, please." Eggshell's sense of chivalry was outraged.

"Kay! I bought it for you the week before last, when we were in town to see that Soviet film. You were talking about jewellery, and you said 'I like pearls because they go with everything, but I've lost the only string I had'; so I said, 'Well, I can't give you real ones but you shall have a makeshift,' and I went into Lee and Adams and bought you that string! Inspector Eggshell. Will you check that?"

The girl said bitterly, "I hope you will. I don't think the assistants will remember him."

"I dare say they won't, as it was just on six and there was a howling mob round the damned jewellery counter: but I'd like you to try." Gratuitously he supplied Eggshell with the date.

"Please can I go now?" Miss Smith said rather wearily.

"Yes, madam. Thank you very much."

Gathering up umbrella and handbag, she went towards the door. Then she came back and touched the student's arm. "Felix, I don't know what trouble you're in, but I'm sure you've done nothing wrong. You know I'd shield you if I could, but it's not possible. Don't lie. Tell them the truth, however hard, because it's always best in the end." Quickly, before he could frame a reply, she went away.

"And now, Mr. Lang," said Eggshell, "it will save time if you will please give me an account of your whereabouts from 8 p.m. on Saturday last until the following morning."

"I—told—you! I left here at six, had some food at a Lyons up West—you'll check that too, will you?—walked on the Heath from about eight till eleven, went to Kay Smith's, had a drink there and *slept—on—the—lid—of—that—hypocritical—bitch's—bath!*"

"Sir! I've warned you about language."

"Sorry, but—oh, I think I must be going mad!"

Eggshell was writing busily. "Which Lyons?"

"Coventry Street."

"Floor?"

"Second, I think—no, third. One with a band."

"Where were you sitting?"

"Under one of the windows, not far from the door."

"Time?"

"Oh, hell! Six thirty-ish. I suppose I was there about an hour. Didn't keep count of time."

"Saturday night. It was crowded, sir?"

"Of course. Isn't it always?"

"Pity. And the store where you bought the pearls was crowded, too. Could you identify the waitress? Would you know her if you saw her again?"

Lang said defiantly, "Not from hell. Oh, wait a tick. Yes, I might. I think she had carroty hair."

"Right. Very well, sir. That's all. Thank you."

"That girl's a liar," the student said earnestly. "I don't know why she's lying, but she is. Check up on me, won't you? I'm not afraid."

"No, sir," Eggshell remarked expressionlessly.

When Lang had gone the Inspector, accompanied by Frankson, called on George Wilshin Warrender, who had intimated that he would not be working that afternoon.

"But it's no good your badgering me. I've told you all I'm going to tell. I've my private reasons—"

"You've told me nothing, Mr. Warrender. I'm hoping you'll amend the omission today. What were you doing at Coldersbrook last Saturday night?"

"Visiting a friend."

"Their name and address, please?"

No answer.

"Better tell me, sir."

"I'm not obliged to answer, am I?"

"Not yet, sir. But sometimes it's wiser to speak."

"I might," said Warrender, "have chivalric reasons."

"Better not to have them. I'd best tell you, sir, that if you persist in silence, I may be compelled—"

Warrender spoke loudly. "To arrest me, eh?"

Eggshell was silent. Then he said, "Taken your moustache off, sir?"

"What the hell's my moustache to do with you?"

"When?"

"When? Last night, if you want to know."

"Why?"

"Why! Go to the devil. None of your business." Mr. Warrender moved about the room, scowling at nothing, kicking at the fender. He said suddenly, "Makes me look a fool, I know, but—"

"Oh, I shouldn't say that, sir."

"The explanation, I mean, not the moustache! I took it off because a lady didn't like it."

"The lady," Eggshell suggested, "whom you let into your flat at 12.30 a.m. last Thursday night?"

Warrender flushed scarlet. "What do you know about that? Yes, if you must have it."

"Her name, please?"

Warrender turned like a tiger at bay. "That's enough! You get out of here and take that—that Charlie MacCarthy with you!" This was a cruel cut at Frankson's physiognomy.

"Very well, Mr. Warrender. But I warn you to use a better tone in addressing the police, and I hope you'll change your mind about giving information. I'll be seeing you again, sir."

As the policemen walked back to the station Eggshell said: "That woman who visited Warrender. Can't you give me any further description?"

"Well, it's as black as pitch in the hall, sir, and I only got a brief dekko at her as he opened his door. Tallish, and a lot of dark hair all over her shoulders. Wore a mac. I didn't see her face."

"And the one Lang let out?"

"Saw even less of her, I'm afraid, because she had on one of those hood things that cover up the hair. Middling height, and she struck me as younger than the other. She left at such a lick, though, I couldn't even see what colours she'd got on, and besides, he didn't put his hall light on: let her out with a torch."

"All right," said Eggshell, "all right. 'Even the weariest river,' etc., etc. But I'll be damned glad when we get to the sea. Morning papers are passing nasty remarks already. As the people who read those silly, inaccurate crime novels say, 'Whodunit?' Well, Frankson, who did?"

"I'd bet on Madame Charnet, myself," was the romantic reply.

Eggshell grinned. "Well, be careful you bet on her for the right crime." He added that a soft-boiled egg wouldn't come amiss for his tea.

———

The Kinghofs and Mr. Gladwin waited, and the latter drank a great deal of white port.

At ten, there came a timid knock at the front door.

"One!" said Agnes gleefully, and went to admit the visitor.

"Oh, I'm so vairy sorry," said Madame Charnet timidly, "to disturb you so late, but I theenk—"

"Do come in, won't you?"

"No, I theenk not. I just came to return this envelope, which I am afraid must 'ave been put by meestake in my door. I would not 'ave opened eet 'ad I thought—"

"My dear, I'm so sorry! I *am* a, blundering ass.—And, good lord, I haven't even addressed it! How silly! I suppose what I did was to put it into a plain envelope by mistake and leave the addressed one on the desk. So nice of you to bring it up."

"Not at all. Good night, Mrs. Kinghof."

"Thank you *so* much. Good night, madame."

The next caller was Mr. Lang, who bounced in as if he had not a care in the world, accepted the invitation to a drink, and, the moment he got inside the lounge, looked round for Bubbles. Recalled to attention by Agnes's cheerful voice introducing Mr. Gladwin, he said, "Oh, I say! Found this on the mat. What on earth does it mean?"

She gave him, word for word, the explanation she had given the Frenchwoman.

"I see. Gave me a turn at first! Never mind, no bones broken, I hope. Wouldn't have read the thing if I'd known."

Agnes said archly, "If you're looking around for Miss Ashton, we've sent her to bed."

"Me? Who? Oh, no, no, I was only staring around. Rude habit, but there you are. Can hardly keep from reading other people's letters if they're left lying about. Not out of nosiness, you understand, but pure interest."

"I," said Andrew, "*can't* keep from reading other people's letters. No 'hardly' about it, where I'm concerned. Sit down, Lang, and let me fill up that glass."

"Lots of people have nasty habits," Gladwin remarked, "only they don't like shouting the odds. I, for example, tear up the *Radio Times* to light my cigarettes, and it's nearly always tomorrow's programme."

The door-bell rang again. "My turn," Andrew said, beating Agnes to the hall by a short neck; but it was only the warden, asking them if they could just pull their curtains over a bit to the left of the window. Mr. Warrender put in no appearance that night.

———

Bubbles had so much difficulty in going to sleep that, after an hour's hopeless struggle, she took two compound aspirin and within fifteen minutes was sleeping like a baby gorged with milk.

At 1 a.m., when all in Flat Number 8 were asleep, there came a little, urgent tap on the window of the spare room. Tap, tap. Silence. And again repeated. In the well the moon was full; but the walls cast deep shadows, and in the blackest shade of all someone stood, holding a cane long enough to reach to a third-floor window. Tap. Tap. Something soft as a baby's foot, but glowing bluely, bumped against the pane, leaving a smear of fat. Someone waited for the curtains to part, for a white face, lined with horror, to appear between them; but Bubbles Ashton slept soundly. Disappointed, someone lowered the cane, removed the pig's trotter treated with phosphorus, and hid the stick behind a waterpipe.

Someone, this time daring even more, was in the well again at ten past six, in the black fog of a foul January morning. The milk bottles stood on the lift. Someone nipped the lid from one of the Kinghofs' bottles, slipped in a paper, and put the cardboard ring back into position.

———

The Kinghofs' daily woman came at eight, in good time to make up the fires and get breakfast. When Agnes, sleepy-eyed, walked into the kitchen to say that sausages for three would be nice, Mrs. Hooker said, "Oh, ma'am! Something mucky's got into the milk."

Agnes frowned, and held the bottle up to the light. The

milk had turned to a not unpleasing mauve, and, more strangely, refused to flow from the neck of the glass. "Why, Mrs. Hooker, how very repulsive! Wait a minute, let's see. Oh! There's some paper wedged in it."

Gingerly she extracted the slip, wiped it as best she could and spread it out on the dresser. It was still legible, though the indelible pencil had badly run.

"CLEVER GIRL, ASHTON. SO YOU'RE SAFE? DON'T YOU KNOW I SHALL FINISH YOU AS CHEERFULLY FOR YOUR 'BEAUX YEUX'? THE PIG-STICKER."

Mrs. Hooker, who had been peering over her mistress's shoulder, gave a long grunt of awful pleasure. "Cor! Another of 'em." Andrew himself had acquainted her with the drama to date, supplying new details by way of daily *feuilleton*.

"Look here," said Agnes, "it's Miss Ashton who's staying here now, and I needn't tell you that she's not to know a word about this thing."

"Cor!" Mrs. Hooker repeated. "Well, now, that's funny; wouldn't 'ave mentioned it if this 'adn't come up, but do you suppose that pig's trotter I found 'ad anything to do with it?"

Agnes whipped round in a chilly glory of magenta chiffon négligé. It was a ridiculous garment and she was frozen stiff in it, but Andrew callously favoured the thing. "What pig's trotter?"

"Found one in the well this morning."

"What on earth were you doing out there?"

"Dropped your duster out of the window, mum, so I 'ad to go all the way round to fish it up."

"You needn't have got it," Agnes interrupted sympathetically, "I'm sure we've got two dusters."

"—And there I found the 'orrid thing, on the ground, all greasy like a bit of dead 'uman!" Mrs. Hooker, in retrospect, found her discovery dramatic. It had not impressed her at the time.

"What did you do with it?"

"Slung it in the dust-bin."

"Oh. Well, the Inspector can fish that out. All right, Mrs. Hooker, go ahead with breakfast and I'll 'phone the police-station."

But first she aroused Andrew, who arose from the sheets like a Venus not liking her first glimpse of the world above sea-level.

"Whatsamarrer? S'the crack of dawn."

"Now, Andy, please unstick yourself quickly, because I've no time to waste watching you do it bit by bit. The Pig," she added, with a drama borrowed from Mrs. Hooker, "has struck again!" And she wagged beneath his dim eyes the damp purple communication.

He said, "All right, all right, give me a chance. Ach! Gladwin always makes me drink."

"Think how much worse you'd have felt if he'd had your whisky and you'd had his white port."

"That's true," he admitted generously. "Well, give me the thing." Having read it, he whistled. "What do we do?"

"'Phone Eggshell."

"Yes. Look here, we must get Bubbles out of this."

"Where?"

"Well, look here, why don't we go down to Warwickshire with her for a week, if she'd have us?"

"Why? You idiot, have you forgotten you're in the Army?"

It was just what he had forgotten.

"Well, I'll go when you've gone back," Agnes suggested comfortingly.

"You won't. Do you think I'd have a moment's rest if I

knew you were putting yourself in the path of some damned maniac with a knife?"

"Oh, Andrew," said Agnes, embracing him, "you *do* love me, then!"

"You don't have to love anyone so much not to want them to get a knife in their guts," was the complicated and disappointing answer. "Anyway, what does Bubbles pay rates for? So the police can see she doesn't get murdered."

Lean legs, in striped grey and rose, swung gingerly out of bed, followed by the rest of Andrew. "Here, give me my dressing-gown.—All right. Now let's go and 'phone Egg. Anyway, we can stick to Bubbles like limpets while we've got her here."

"Oh, lord! I'd forgotten. We promised to go out with Pig tonight. We can hardly take her, if he means to play some simple-minded joke on us."

"We'll have to ask him, anyhow," said Andrew.

When they had communicated the morning's news to Eggshell, who agreed that it was better not to alarm Miss Ashton, Agnes telephoned Pig and asked if it would be possible for them to bring a guest. She explained who the guest was, and what were the circumstances. As she had expected, he replied cautiously, "Well, my dear, it's not possible for her to come with us as—as I could only get three seats, but we'd be delighted if she'd join us at dinner and perhaps...perhaps sit with Mary till we get back."

"That would be marvellous," said Agnes. Hanging up the receiver, she turned to Andrew. "Yes, he's planning something horrible. So horrible that he's quite awkward about it. Still, he says Bubbles can come to dinner and sit with Mary while we're out. That will serve her right, poor girl."

"Nonsense. They'll get on like a house on fire."

They went to rouse Bubbles to breakfast.

The morning passed without incident, save that policemen were seen lingering about the halls and peering in at the street door.

————

In the afternoon, however, Andrew received a wire telling him to report to Aldershot before midnight on the following day.

"Well," he said, "that finishes murder for me. Coming to see me off? I'll get the ten-fifteen train."

"Yes, if you like."

"You may as well."

"But what shall I do with Bubbles? Shall she come too?"

"Certainly not! I will not be seen off by Bubbles. No. You must arrange for Eggshell to keep an eye on her till I get back."

————

They had a lovely evening. Agnes and Andrew, having had an enthralling time at *My Uncle Polovtsnai*, were given, by Pig, the rare privilege of entering the Edwardian house of old Jane Valery, last of the great *salonnières*, and of hearing her recite, for no apparent reason, in her voice that was like an underground river flowing between walls of amber, the verse of Ebenezer Elliott, the Corn Law poet. Miss Valery wore a ruby gown covered with sequins, most of which were hanging loose, and over her still magnificent shoulders a cape of moulting marabout. Her eyes flashed marvellously, her gestures were those of a queen. About her, on the floor, on window-ledges, even on the broad marble mantelpiece, sat all the advanced youth of London, youths in checks and corduroys, sweaters, and silken ties of many colours. Afterwards Miss Valery regaled the guests with claret-cup and macaroons.

As the Kinghofs and Pig stepped out of this warm past into a night full of stars, Agnes took her host by his elbow and said, "Look here, Pig, Andrew and I owe you an apology. We thought you meant to play a joke on us, to give us as dreadful an evening as we'd given you, and now we're ashamed of ourselves. You couldn't have chosen any entertainment we'd have enjoyed more, and we think you're a sportsman."

"You're a sportsman, Pig," said Andrew warmly.

His cousin, who all that evening had been haunted by the uneasy feeling that perhaps his guests' enthusiasm was not, as he had first imagined, feigned, recovered himself manfully.

"Oh, I don't bear you a grudge," he said.

They returned to collect Bubbles, who, looking handsome in a black velvet dress lent her by Agnes (who had hastily let out the side-seams), had thoroughly enjoyed herself with Mary. They had discussed dogs from eight till nine-thirty, the Government from nine-thirty till eleven. Mary had given Bubbles a new idea for making a *petit-point* fire-screen, Bubbles had given Mary, for the cook's benefit, a recipe for vegetable pie.

Agnes said, "We've got to go now, dear. Mary, Pig's been wonderful and we've so misjudged him! He'll tell you all about it."

Lady Whitestone, with years of self-control behind her, only just prevented herself from giving her husband a single, astounded glance.

Chapter Eleven

By happy fortune, Andrew and Agnes, on their way back from the "Green Doe" the following morning, met with Colonel Eckersley Plumpfield, the noisiest War Reserve of all; and leading him back to Number 8 introduced him to Bubbles, whereupon, taken by her Junoesque appearance, he offered her hospitality for the night at his house in Carlyle Street. Needless to say, Mrs. Plumpfield would be present also.

Having thus disposed of the guest, whom she meant—Andrew willing or unwilling—to accompany next day to Beanscot, Warwickshire, Agnes went with lightened conscience to see her husband off to Aldershot.

Waterloo presented its usual appearance of war-time excitement. Tired men in khaki and blue trailed their kit towards the platforms, wives and sweethearts roamed in search of their lovers through the bands of fog. In the buffets glasses and thick china rattled and clattered. The smoke from a thousand cigarettes rose to the vaultings above. Porters swung their trolleys wild just in time to miss the heedless lounger. Men and women kissed and clung, oblivious to the sifting crowds. Mothers, with nodding, wailing babies awake too late, sought their menfolk.

Agnes, always moved by the fact of Andrew's departure, whether it might be to Seringapatam or the British Museum, gripped his arm and walked closely at his side.

"Awful moment, Pet. I dread going back and finding Number 8 empty, without you."

"My dear, don't get upset, because they may pack me back again in a few days and then this will seem such an anticlimax."

"I can't help it, Andy. Leaving you always makes me feel tatty inside."

For once he did not rebuke the shortening of his name. "Leave this murder stuff alone. I shall go crazy if I think you're sticking your little nose out to be shot at."

"I'm finished," Agnes said, "except for seeing Bubbles home and delivering her to her girl-friend."

"I don't like you doing that."

"Darling, in the *broadest* daylight!"

Andrew saw the clock. "Come on, or I'll miss my train." They moved quickly, still knee to knee, and passed through the barrier on to the platform, where the train awaited them.

"Only just time," Andrew gasped. "Hey, porter! Find me a corner in a smoker!"

He was found such a seat only two seconds before the train drew out. Kissing his wife quickly, but with considerable vigour, he pushed her back, tore open the compartment door and leaped inside, landing, rather ungracefully, on one knee. He was so busy picking himself up, dusting himself off, that Agnes was cheated of a farewell wave.

Feeling flat and spiritless as the dregs of ginger beer left on the pub counter on a hot day, she walked slowly from the platform. With her walked a few score of equally spirit-less sweethearts and wives. Waterloo now seemed stale and dingy. The colour was out of it. The crowds, that had at first seemed to her in violent, excited motion, now drifted like bogged figures in a dream. Agnes visualized the empty flat full of his memories, his pyjamas left in a heap on the linen-basket, his cigarette-ends in the grate, the telephone pad scrawled with a message in his hand, on the gramophone the last record he had played. She shivered. It was chilly, and the fog seemed thicker than before. If it were bad in the streets, even a taxi would take the devil of a time to get her home.

She bumped into someone, apologized dreamily and was about to go on when some strange mental prod made her swing round to gaze at the man with whom she had collided. Agnes stood still. Warrender! Yes, she'd know him anywhere, moustache or no moustache. She'd know that stocky figure, that very black hair, that remarkable absence of eyebrow. Andrew, the empty flat, Bubbles, the fog, the taxi, her promise to keep out of trouble, all these faded from her mind. Agnes sprinted after the retreating Warrender and, having caught up with him, followed discreetly on his heels. She stalked him to Platform 20. The Coldersbrook train goes from there, she thought, and she watched him pass through the barrier on to the platform.

With Agnes, luckily or unluckily, to think is always to act. She noted that there was a considerable crowd forcing its way past the ticket-collector, soldiers forming the greater part of it, for there was a big military camp at the terminus of the line. Catlike she watched, until she saw a fat civilian, his wife close behind him, rout out two tickets in preparation for presenting them. Quick as lightning, Agnes inserted herself between him and his lady, and got safely past the collector. She did not wait to hear the squeal of rage from the lady who found herself ticketless, husbandless and her story discredited by authority; she flashed up the platform on strong, lovely legs and leaped into a third-class carriage. Standing in the corridor, panting, elated, she saw the fat civilian run to rescue his wife, rip her through the barrier and drag her into the train. Tactfully, Agnes retreated into the lavatory and locked the door. It might be well to remain there until Waterloo had been left behind. Coldersbrook, as she well knew, was the first stop, and she did not choose to risk apprehension at the outset of the journey.

The whistle blew. Agnes, peering with interest through the hole in the floor, saw the flash of rails. "We're off!" she shrieked joyously all to herself, and to celebrate the occasion had a nice wash with the company's liquid soap.

Clapham Junction passed, she ventured gingerly out and was relieved to see that nobody in that crowded corridor looked at her with interest. There were soldiers standing two deep, arms folded on the wooden rail, eyes staring blankly out on to the blank night, and between groups of them kit-bags, coats, and rifles were piled high as small mountains.

Agnes, who had decided that she had better make a search for Mr. Warrender, began a perilous journey up-train. She had never been so close to real mountaineering. The soldier who saw her face helped her out of politeness; the soldier who saw the rest of her gave her his arm or shoulder with real *éclat*. For all that, it was tiring work.

She had made this nightmare journey through three coaches before she found Warrender, sitting in the corner of a third-class carriage, holding a newspaper somewhat ostentatiously to his face. Cautiously she backed away from the compartment and took up a stance between a soldier and a very young and glowing airman, both of whom, within five minutes, had offered her cigarettes and were competing to tell her their life-stories.

The trip, despite these diversions, seemed interminable. It had not seemed nearly so long on that day when she and Andrew had gone to spend the fatal week-end at Hooham. There was, of course, no hope of a drink and no hope of a seat, though she did take a few minutes' rest on the soldier's kitbag.

At last the train, roaring out of a tunnel, began to slow down.

"Are we at Coldersbrook," Agnes asked plaintively, "or have we just stopped to uncouple—which is, I believe, what trains do?"

Her friends in the forces took this as a delightful joke. "Yes, this is Coldersbrook."

"Oh, good. I should hate to trip out on to the line. Isn't it queer that more people don't?"

"Got any bags?" said the airman. "I'll root for them if you have."

"No, thank you, nothing. Well, good night!"

And to their surprise she did not leave by the door they had gallantly opened for her, but instead made a chamois-like rush down the corridor, taking soldiers, rifles, and kitbags in her stride. She left the train by the door of the next compartment.

Out on the freezing platform, the white fog rising thick about her, she waited patiently until she discerned dimly the form of George Wilshin Warrender. He was making towards the exit.

Agnes thought quickly. It was one thing to get on to a platform in a crowd; another to get through the barrier of a station empty save for the ticket-collector. She was an observant woman; and now a picture flashed into her mind, the picture of Coldersbrook station by daylight. She had noticed it last week, when she was with Andrew, and she realized the value of a comprehensive eye. Ducking into greater shadow, she crept to the platform's end, felt her way down the slight ramp and found herself, as she had expected, on a strip of gravel, a low hedge behind her.

It is not easy, in the foggy dark, to get through a hedge. How difficult the feat was she did not know until she arrived, damp, scratched, draggled, both stockings torn, favourite hat gone for ever, in the shaggy field on its far side. There was no time for repining. She hurled herself forward over the grass, swearing as her feet stuck in mud and came out with a noise of suction, thanking her stars that her shoes were of the bootee type that are laced up to the ankles. At last she gained the road, and stood there panting, her arm about a lamp-post.

And here, if Mr. Warrender had chosen to turn left on his exit from the station, she would have been lost, have had all her efforts in vain: but he had turned right. Indeed, he cannoned into her, muttered an apology and strode on.

The ticklish business began. Agnes knew well enough that following feet are far more noticeable in a fog, by night, than in the clear daytime; and so she trailed him at a decent distance, again returning thanks to supernatural powers that her shoes were crêpe-soled.

Damn Mr. Warrender! He would choose a night like this for a long walk. On he went, down a muddy avenue, a quarter of a mile along the river, back along an unmade road and then—final torment—across a ploughed field.

To Agnes's horror, the fog was lifting and the steely moonlight was forcing its way through the sky. The thin frost on the earthy ridges gleamed faintly. Warrender was clearly visible, even at a distance of sixty or seventy yards, his dark figure outlined on space. And I? Agnes thought in panic: If he turns round he'll see me at once. There's no refuge anywhere.

Once he stopped dead, and seemed to listen. He looked sharply from left to right as if he smelled danger, but happily, did not look back. Again the single-file procession of two went on its way, and at last there loomed up in the distance a tall shape, like a high, broad house with high pediment. Its sugar-loaf shadow fell across the brightening moonlight, and of a sudden Mr. Warrender was swallowed up in it. Agnes, her heart beating, waited for several moments before proceeding. Suppose, in the shadow, he had turned and was gazing at her, as the spectator in the darkened auditorium gazes at the actor exposed upon the brilliant stage?

She summoned her courage. Impossible now to draw back. She crept forward, and found herself before a sizeable barn, plainly in disuse. Stealing to the door, she listened intently; and heard a soft babble of voices. No word was audible.

Agnes went round to the side of the building and, in her agitation, nearly smacked her head against a ladder that leaned drunkenly against the barn, its head reared against the sky. "Now where does that one go to, 'Erbert?" she whispered aloud, reassuring herself by the familiar sound of her own voice. "Better find out."

Workmanlike as ever, she doubled over the waistband of her skirt, thus shortening it by a couple of inches, bloused her coat over the broad belt and started upwards. It was a terrifying business, this climbing into nowhere like Jack on the Beanstalk; and Agnes had a moment's frightful fancy that she might step out on to a cloud and into the arms of an ogre with a pig's face.

Just then the fog lifted from the moon and the splendid silver light flooded the flat and dreary landscape, throwing the hedges and the ragged trees into bold relief. The barn was lit as brightly as by day, and Agnes, pausing on the ladder to catch breath, saw that immediately beneath her was a trap-door giving on to a hayloft. She took two steps down, and said, "Here goes!" and, leaving the half-rotten rungs, which now seemed to her separate havens of refuge, crawled into the loft.

Light showed through an open square in the floor, and voices rose clearly. Shutting her mind against the thought of great barn spiders spreadeagled on the floor, she crawled forward on hands and knees until she could look down upon the scene below.

She saw a trestle table set about with candles in enamel sticks, these supplying the sole light of the place. About the table sat an odd company, four men and one woman, this last a tall, sullen-looking creature with heavy black hair curling upon her shoulders. All wore extraordinary capes made of some dark stuff—Agnes thought it might be black-out material—with a Union Jack some seven or eight inches square sewn in the centre back. The girl sat at the far end. Facing her, standing upright, was a blond, pimpled young man who seemed to be the leader. To his left sat Mr. Warrender and an elderly man with a broken nose; to his right were two youngsters of nondescript appearance, each with writing-pad and ink-bottle before him.

Agnes listened. The Leader was speaking. "Trooper Jones, we are ready to hear your suggestion."

Broken-nose got to his feet. "Well, Group Leader, I don't think we should begin our meetings with 'Eil, Doosey!' After all, we're the Free British Mussolites, so being free, we don't 'ave to follow our foreign brothers slavishly, if I might so put it. I move that from 'enceforward we say 'Ail."

"I second that," said one of the youngsters languorously, when he had scribbled what was apparently the motion upon his pad, "but I would add, in support of Trooper Jones, that 'Heil, Duce' is not even correct. 'Heil' is a German word. Our Italian brothers express their allegiance, I believe, by the cry of 'Duce, Duce'; I fancy that 'Ave, Duce', which might possibly be a correct form—"

"I don't think it is," Mr. Warrender interrupted.

"—is not used. 'Heil' would be reserved for the German Fuehrer—"

"And we don't want no truck with them Narzees," said Broken-nose.

"Not," the Group Leader commented smoothly, "at this present time, anyway. There is much, of course, admirable in the Nazi system; we all admit that without reserve; but as Germany is unfortunately the enemy of our country, she must needs, however regrettable this may seem, be our enemy also. After the war is over, we shall reconsider our attitude."

This was greeted with approval.

"And now, I will ask our Propaganda Trooper to give us her report. Trooper Cottenham."

The woman rose, sweeping her comrades with a steely glance. She was well built and handsome, though her brown eyes tended seriously to protrude. It's glandular, Agnes thought sympathetically. She added to herself, I've never known before just what "deep-bosomed" meant. Now I do. It means bosom on the waistline.

"Fellow Troopers!" Miss, or Mrs., Cottenham's voice was loud and incisive. "I am not pleased with the pace at which our message is reaching the masses. Only too frequently, when I ask my neighbours—casually, you understand—if they have heard of an influential organization called the F.B.M., they say they have 'never heard of it'!"

A murmur of shocked disapprobation ran round the table, and one of the young men, whose name was Figgis, said that this just went to show the imbecility of the blind masses.

"Now this won't do. We may be forced underground by necessity, but that is no reason why the single, thrilling fact of our existence should be unknown. Brothers, I charge you with lethargy!" She indicted them with outflung arm. "Trooper Warrender, how many have you distributed of our 'Trust Mussolini' pamphlet? And you, Jones? You, Figgis? You, Trooper Mabane!" She pointed to the second of the secretarial nonentities. "Have I seen our stickybacks prominently displayed on public buildings? I have not! And believe me, I am far from unobservant."

"I did put a couple on the Featherstone Mews convenience," said Mr. Warrender, apologetically.

"A drop in the ocean. I want results! Now then, I have to hand over our new leaflet—'Hands Across the Mediterranean,' and I propose to give each one of you district leaders two hundred copies for distribution. Can I count on you?"

"'Ail Doosey. You can count on me," said Jones.

"Oh, damn it," murmured Figgis. "I got rid of three hundred 'Trust Musso's' last week-end."

"Must 'ave more time on your 'ands than wot I 'ave."

"I put them in plain envelopes and had them handled by District Messenger."

"Trooper Figgis!" the Leader rapped out. "You must not use your more happy financial position to score advantage over your brothers. You will deliver the new batch yourself."

"I say," said Mabane, "we still haven't voted on Trooper Jones's motion."

They repaired the omission.

"I've a point to raise." Mr. Warrender rose, shaking his cloak about him. "It's about our meeting-place. It's all very well for most of you, because you live in suburban districts, but I have an hour's journey from Waterloo and a beastly, wet half-hour's walk to get here. It's not so bad when we start early, as we did last Saturday night—"

"Twentieth inst.," said Trooper Mabane, for no particular reason writing it down.

"—but unless someone can put me up tonight, I'm stranded."

So am I, Agnes thought bitterly.

"You can come to me, darling," said Trooper Cottenham, speaking out of character.

The Group Leader rose. Mr. Warrender sank back into his seat looking awed but hopeful.

"Trooper Warrender raises a personal issue. At a time when the F.B.M.s form the vanguard of order in a world mad with war, when F.B.M.s are suffering persecution and oppression, Trooper Warrender wishes us to consider a matter of his personal comfort."

Very crushing, Agnes thought. Almost enough to make Andrew wilt, if not me.

"Would you not have thought that to be allowed to serve as a humble soldier of our great Cause would have been sufficient? Would you not have thought—"

Now Agnes had been too interested in the Leader's

discourse to keep her mind steeled against hayloft spiders; and at this moment a large one, dry, grey, and delicately furred, ran over her hand. So she screamed.

It was not a big scream—was, in fact, little more than a squeak. To call it a squeak would not, indeed, have been a ludicrous example of meiosis. But it was enough.

She withdrew her head only a split second before five faces were tilted upwards and the Leader shouted, "My God, there's a spy up there!"

Leaving the conference table, they crowded below the hole, arguing, shouting, bullying the unknown observer.

"All right, you can show your dirty face! We've seen you!"

No, you haven't, she thought. It was too dark.

"Come on down, or we'll fetch you. It'll be worse for you if you hide!"

Trooper Cottenham said, "Let's get him. Masks on, everyone!"

"Him," Agnes said to herself, much relieved. Then they most certainly didn't see me. But the next moment fear flashed through her, for she saw herself trapped. The company, belatedly and rather self-consciously, took black hoods from their pockets and put them over their heads.

"Where's the blurry ladder?" Jones shouted.

"Outside." This was Warrender. "We'll have to go up that way. Quick, after him, or he'll escape."

"Figgis and I will climb up," said the Troop Leader. "Follow me, all of you!"

Why he wanted them to follow is not clear, unless he thought his capture of the spy would show him in heroic light and wanted no one to miss it: but it was his mistake. In another minute, the great room was empty.

Agnes crouched in the dark, too scared to breathe,

knowing that in another moment she would hear feet on the ladder. The hayloft was high above ground level, and there seemed no means of descent.

The ladder creaked and groaned.

She began to grope around her, hardly knowing what she sought: but the first thing she encountered—painfully—was an iron spike sticking up between the floorboards.

"We're coming to get you!" a voice roared. "We'll give it you, you spy! Your own mother won't know you when we've finished." And the voice was rising higher and higher. Frantic, she sought for her handbag in the capacious pocket of her tweed coat, where she had stowed it, and routed out a box of matches. She flashed the meagre light round the loft and saw, not a foot away from where she stood, a coil of fairly thick rope.

Now Agnes has never been a Girl Guide, and so, knows nothing about tying knots; but she will try anything once. As quickly, but as securely as she knew how, she knotted one end of the rope to the spike and threw the coil down through the hole into the candle-lit barn. In another second she was shinning down, the cord tearing away the last of her stockings and grazing her hands.

She could hear them now, scrambling through the trap door; and she realized suddenly that the rope swung full twelve feet clear of the ground. Happily she had read handbooks on how to escape from burning houses. She swung her feet free, wriggled down so that she was grasping the extreme end of the rope, jerked herself outwards and let go. She landed on all fours, filthy, grazed, and trembling: but safe.

All the Free British Mussolites saw when they peered down through the ceiling was the slender back-view of a woman who was making excellent time to the door.

She resisted an impulse to cock a snook at the treed troopers, or to see how many of them were up there. The essential thing now was to dodge those who might lie in wait outside. Agnes, having gained the fresh air, bolted round the right side of the barn; the ladder was on the left.

The next thing she knew was that Trooper Cottenham had brought her down with a rugby tackle.

Agnes's behaviour was not maidenly, but it was sound. Struggling to her feet, she evaded a further clutch and back-heeled at the Trooper's head. There was a stifled grunt, a gurgle of pain. Agnes had planted a crêpe-rubber heel squarely in her antagonist's mouth and had, temporarily at least, imposed silence.

The advantage with her, she made good time over the field, which now was luckily in darkness, for the moon was swallowed up in cloud. As she tore across the furrows, even now taking pride in her own nimbleness, she heard the sounds of pursuit, sounds that grew fainter and fainter until they died away altogether. Agnes, alone in a misty bitter night, miles, apparently, from any manner of civilization, thought she deserved a cigarette, so she crouched in the shadow of a hedge, lit a Goldflake and smoked it down to a quarter of an inch. Then she went in search of the main road, where she hoped to cadge a lift homewards.

Chapter Twelve

WE MUST NOT, HOWEVER DULL THEY MAY BE, HOWEVER dreary their interminable enquiries, neglect the police. After all, we pay rates for them.

On the afternoon of that Friday, while Andrew and Agnes were having a farewell tea at Simpson's preparatory to the former's return to Army life, Eggshell was hearing an odd tale from the youngest of his constables, a smooth-looking youth with a Hendon manner. He had never, in fact, been near Hendon; but no one would have guessed it.

"Yes, sir. I know a good bit about the Pretty Pictures Club, because a girl I know around here used to pose for the chap who runs it." Constable Jeffries flushed a little at being compelled to reveal the nature of his acquaintances.

"Go ahead," said Eggshell, smiling a little.

"Well, she's really a very decent sort of girl, though she does pose for artists—"

"That, in itself, doesn't damn her."

"No, sir—but she did get taken in a bit by Currie and his mob. He's a toad, that chap, rolling in money and just paints a bit to be in the swim. Well, he started this club in Welwyn Studios about two years ago. Private membership, and all very hush-hush. Anna—that's the young lady—says nearly all the films are foreign, made by amateurs, and they're all filthy ones. Just about awful, she says, and I don't think she'd set foot in the place if it wasn't for Currie—she's nuts about him."

"Obscene films. I see."

"Awful, sir. Nude people, doing all sorts of things: not what you like to talk about."

"No, Jeffries. Well? Let's hear about Madame Charnet."

"Well, Anna says she's been coming practically every week since she came to the district. She slips in and sits at the back, never talks to anyone. On Saturday 20th she got in there about 5.30 p.m.—Currie has 'em early, with cocktails after—and sat down at the back as usual. I say, sir, if anything happens… I mean, when we shut up the club, I hope Anna won't get into trouble."

"You can see she's not there that night," said Eggshell. "Did she see Madame Charnet leave?"

"Says not. It's as dark as pitch in there. But anyhow, Madame Sharney wasn't there at seven, when the cocktails went round."

"Who pays for the drinks?"

"Currie affords that out of the subs. It's seven guineas a year, for fortnightly shows. He doesn't open up July or August, but otherwise they're all the year round."

Eggshell scowled and drew a nude woman on the pad before him. Such things had been recently put into his usually virgin mind. "Yes. So Madame Charnet goes into the High Street Picture House at five, makes a fuss about French cigarettes so the girl in the box-office shall notice her, and manages to slip out unnoticed in time to be at Welwyn Studios by 5.30." He laughed suddenly. "Dirty old thing! The most ridiculous part of it, Jeffries, is the attempt to lay a false trail. Who did she think was watching her?"

Jeffries said diffidently, "Don't you think it's rather pathetic, sir? I mean, it's only people with two-year-old minds who go in for that kind of thing. They haven't lost their sense of shame, either, because most of them take it terribly hard when they're caught. I almost hope we don't catch her when we raid."

Eggshell nodded appreciation. Young Jeffries had a head on his shoulders; if he developed Frankson's stolidity he would become a very fine policeman. "Well, I can't guarantee that; but so far as your Anna goes, we'll be raiding—When's the next show?"

"Fortnight from the last. Saturday week, the third of February."

"Well, you can tip Anna off; but on the morning of that day, remember, and not before; and if the news leaks through to Currie I'll hold you personally responsible. Think you can manage it without messing up our plans?"

"I'm sure I can, sir."

"Good. That's all. Good work, Jeffries."

The boy glowed. "Thank you, sir."

He had just left when there was a telephone call from Scotland Yard. Lord Whitestone was enquiring whether there was any further line on Felix Lang. Eggshell replied that he would get in touch with the Yard later in the day, and taking up his soft hat, he went round to Flat 3, Stewarts Court.

He found the young medico in, struggling with a thesis he was, with great difficulty, writing. Lang looked tired and worried; he seemed too despondent to offer any sort of fight.

"Oh, come in, Inspector. Got the handcuffs?"

"Not today, sir."

"Sorry. Tawdry sort of crack. Tell you the truth, I'm all in."

"Busy?"

"Yes. Busy and worried. Hard to work when you're worried."

Eggshell said, "Had your tea?"

"No. Why?"

"You look as if you could do with it, if I may say so, and it's long past the hour."

Lang wandered about the room, vaguely attempting to tidy it. Putting up a hand, he wiped his brow, which was smudged with ink and cigarette ash. "Not a bad idea, I suppose. I imagine you wouldn't have a cup of tea with me? Don't eat with suspects, do you?"

"I'll have a cup of tea," Eggshell said, quite without expression.

"All right. Come in the kitchen while I make it and you can badger me there."

The kitchen was in as foul a state of muddle as the rest of the flat. "Do you have a daily woman?"

"Oh, sometimes," said Lang. "When things get too bad. That is, she's not daily."

"I should have thought this a big flat for a single chap like yourself, sir."

"It is, isn't it? I thought I was going to live with two other blokes when I took it, but that fell through."

"Big upkeep?"

"Oh, yes; or rather, the rent's high. I don't bother to upkeep the damn' place much, as I suppose you can see."

"Wouldn't a cheaper place suit you better?"

"I suppose so, but I never seem to find time to move. Anyway, I'm not hard up, thank the lord. Got a private income. Even if I do make a mess of doctoring, which wouldn't surprise me, I shan't find myself in the gutter. Come on, tea's made. It's warmer in the front room."

They returned to it, and Eggshell, wandering around cup and saucer in hand, paused to admire the picture that hung above the mantelpiece.

"Like it, Inspector?"

"Why, yes, I think I do. I've only the man-in-the-street's taste for art, but that takes my fancy somehow."

"Know what you like, eh?"

"Yes," Eggshell replied simply, "I do; but I don't imagine a picture's great art because it happens to please me." He stepped back a few paces. "That is pretty, sir. I like the sort of dolls' faces everyone's got, and that tree sticking up in the middle, and all the bright colour. What's it represent?"

"The Rape of Helen."

"Looks as though she isn't minding it much."

"I don't suppose she did mind."

"Who's it by?"

"Oh, damn, I always forget. 'Ben' something. Look on the back, won't you? You'll find it there."

Idly Eggshell swung the picture over; then as he saw what was written on the back of the frame, he whistled.

"What's up?" Lang asked lazily, lighting one cigarette from another.

"'To Felix, with love from Kathleen. Christmas 1940.' Lang, who gave you this?"

"Kay Smith. Oh!" The student jumped up as if he had

sat on a wasp. "Yes, she gave it me! Said my taste needed educating. Now tell me I don't know her!"

Eggshell said, "Kathleen's a fairly common name, sir."

"So it may be, but she's the only one I know. I say, you'll ask her about it, won't you?"

The Inspector put down his cup, reached for his hat. "Thanks for the tea, Mr. Lang. Yes, we'll make a check."

"If you prove she knows me well enough to make me a Christmas present—"

"I've still got to prove whether or not you slept on her bath. Good day, sir."

When Eggshell returned to the station he telephoned Miss Smith. She was out; but a girl's answering voice said that her friend would call him back the moment she got in. In about twenty minutes, Miss Smith rang up the Inspector.

"Forgive me troubling you, ma'am, but—"

"Not a bit. What can I do to help?"

"Regarding that picture you gave to Mr. Lang for a Christmas present—"

"Yes?" said Miss Smith encouragingly. Then she seemed to realize what she had said, for her gasp sounded over the wire, light as the flutter of wings. She added hastily, "A picture, did you say?"

"Thank you, ma'am," Eggshell said slowly. "I won't take up your leisure. I've just found out that what I wanted to know has been under my nose all the time. Sorry for having bothered you." Ignoring her agitated voice, he hung up.

"Frankson!" he called. "If Miss Kathleen Smith should ring back, tell her I've gone out and won't be back till tomorrow."

———

One-thirty a.m. the following morning, a morning of black frost, saw Mrs. Kinghof sitting on the tailboard of a lorry singing *Ah! si vous connaissiez ma poule* to a group of delighted but uncomprehending militia men who were also enjoying a lift. At the crossroads she jumped down, thanked everyone for the ride, and turning right where the lorry turned left, thumbed another lift. This process, three times repeated, brought her back, sore-eyed, to Stewarts Court at three-forty-five. Letting herself in, she poured a stiff drink, turned on the bath, stripped off her damp and filthy clothes, and descended luxuriously into the hot water, where she steamed gently for half an hour. Then she wrapped herself in a blanket, filled a hot-water bottle, and falling into bed slept until ten-thirty, when she was roused by Bubbles' return after breakfasting with the Eckersley Plumpfields.

"Why, Agnes, you look worn, too! Have you been to a party?"

"A party meeting. It's slightly different. Look here, will you be a darling and get me some tea and toast? Then I'll tell you my night's adventures."

She told them, extracting from them every ounce of drama; and when she had done, Bubbles said, "I say, how very sporting! I think you're simply splendid. What are you going to do now?"

"Report to Eggshell."

"Do you think—"

"Think what?"

"Well, we know who it is now, if Warrender's cleared." Bubbles frowned. "The other...he seemed nice, somehow."

"Don't you know Crippen seemed a love to the neighbours? That all the women liked Smith? That the girls went wild about Patrick Mahon? Bubbles, hand me the cigarettes. Gosh, I'm tired!"

"Look here, I don't think you ought to come trapesing back to Beanscot with me today."

"Fiddle-faddle, darling. I'm coming. I say, I wonder what Hilary will think of your new hair-do?" Hilary, she had learned, was the name of Bubbles' girl-friend.

"She'll think I look a bit fast," Bubbles said, rather apprehensively, "but I expect she'll get used to it."

When Agnes was rested, she telephoned Eggshell. "So I've cleared Warrender, haven't I? What are you going to do?"

He said gently, "Look here, Mrs. Kinghof, for all we know this F.B.M. business is a blind. If, as he says, last Saturday's meeting was early, he would still have had time to get to Hooham."

She was crestfallen. "I suppose so. But what about the other stuff?"

"The F.B.M.s? We know all about them. Miserable little crowd, no danger to Pussy, but they make a lot of noise. All the same, we'll watch Warrender on that score, because of his Government job. Doesn't seem the right man in the right place. Is Miss Ashton with you?"

"Right here. I'm going back to Warwickshire with her today."

"You are? For how long?"

"Oh, three or four days. It'll be a change."

"Yes. Be careful, Mrs. Kinghof. I shall notify the Warwickshire police, certainly, but keep a weather-eye on things. Good work last night, but don't do it again."

This Saturday was bright and mild, one of those January days that, aping spring, bring young women out upon the streets in unseasonable attire and make young men consider that success lies around the next corner. Agnes and Bubbles, at ease in opposite corners of a first-class carriage, looked with delight upon the unflowering country.

"It's nice to be going home," Bubbles said rather wistfully. "Not that I haven't had a lovely two days with you and Andrew, and I'm really terribly glad you made me cut my hair! But I can breathe in the country."

"Do you know," Agnes smiled, "I believe you've clean forgotten you're a wealthy woman."

"No. But it doesn't seem real yet, or even—quite pleasant. This horrible thing hanging over me—"

"Shut up. Nothing's hanging over you. Even if the police weren't going to loom about Beanscot till all this mess is cleared up, I don't believe you'd be in twopenn'orth of danger. Steer had a reason to—to kill your aunt. He has no reason to kill you. He wouldn't do it—"

"Out of revenge," Bubbles interrupted. "Do you think he wouldn't? I'm not so sure." And she shivered.

"Oh, piffle," said Agnes, the thought of the letter in the milk bottle lying uneasily upon her soul. "Look here, I'm just going along the corridor to wash. Always wash on trains. It's not a guilt-complex but simple cleanliness. Keep the door shut and your eye on the communication-cord."

"Why? You don't suppose *he's* following us?" Bubbles looked alarmed.

"Don't be ridiculous."

"Then why should I keep my eyes on the cord?"

"Because, dear," said Agnes with salutary rudeness, "before we cut your hair and bought you those *Couleur de Rose* stockings you would have been perfectly safe in an empty carriage. Now you're not." She grinned, threw the girl a new *Lilliput* and made off.

She washed herself thoroughly, combed her hair and made up her face, hitched her stockings and peered anxiously into the tiny mirror to see that her hat was at the right angle. Then she emerged at leisure, to find two furious women waiting outside. Apologizing mildly, she moved off, turning once to watch the ladies in collision, each snapping to the other that she'd been there first. In gay mood Agnes strolled back to the carriage where she had left Bubbles, enjoying on her way the fine panorama of albuminous cloud lying over the bare brown fields. Suddenly a voice said, "Good afternoon, Mrs. Kinghof. Everything O.K.?"

She jumped. Not a foot away from her, leaning against a carriage door, was Felix Lang, boyish and rosy, his light hair ruffled by the breeze that blew through the open window.

Her heart turned over. "What are you doing here?"

He smiled. "Don't scowl at me. I'm policing you, if you want to know."

"Why? What do you mean?"

Lang's smile faded. "Look here, I'm not going to play about. I know about the letter Miss Ashton got yesterday morning—or rather, didn't get."

"How do you know?"

"Your daily woman told me."

"Mrs. Hooker did? I don't believe it."

"Soul of discretion, you think? She sold me her discretion for half-a-crown. You see, when I looked out of my kitchen window, I saw your purple milk standing on the lift."

"What business is it of yours," Agnes demanded gallantly, "what colour our milk is?"

"It's not a nice colour for milk."

"It's a special pasteurized kind," she snapped wildly, "a new process."

"Quite unknown to medical science. Mrs. Kinghof, I'm travelling down with you whether you like it or not. It took me half an hour to get Ma Hooker talking, and fifteen minutes longer to know just where you were going, so—"

"I'll sack that woman when I get back."

"That's your business. Listen, I'm not fooling, and I've no time to fence. When I saw Miss Ashton on the stairs that day, I fell for her like a ton of bricks. I know she's in danger, and I'm going to see no harm comes to her. Please believe me, and let me come into your compartment for the rest of the journey."

Agnes's brain ran round and round like a mouse on the miniature treadmill. What, she thought, would Andrew say? Wouldn't it be safer to have Lang under observation than not to know what he was up to? "You're impulsive, aren't you?" she temporized.

"Yes, I suppose I am. But I'm not leaving Miss Ashton till I see her right back home. Look here, what harm could I do by just sitting with you? You can have the damned carriage door open if you don't trust me."

"All right," said Agnes, "you can come and we will have the door open. But if you breathe a word to Miss Ashton about that letter, I'll—I'll choke you."

"Don't worry, I'm not going to frighten her."

So they went into the compartment, where the very sight of him was enough to send Bubbles flying up in the direction of the cord.

"All right, dear, keep calm. You remember Mr. Lang, don't you? He's going to a medical conference at Warwick."

Bubbles flushed, and said lamely, "Oh. How funny."

"I don't think it's so funny," the student murmured, seating himself opposite her and taking out his pipe. "No, it's not funny; it's most pleasant. May I light this?"

She nodded.

"Thank you. Wonderful weather, isn't it? I always like getting out of town. You're glad to see the back of London, aren't you, Miss Ashton?"

"Very."

"And I," said Agnes between her teeth, "shall be happy to be back there."

They all sat in glum silence, while the train tore away great handfuls of the landscape. It was nearing twilight now, and the violet shadows were lengthening across the hills.

"We're in Warwickshire now, aren't we?" the student murmured. "Makes me think of Shakespeare."

"And what do you think of him?" Agnes demanded acidly.

"Oh… ags from old English lessons." His light eyes glimmered like steel in the growing dark. "Bits from the plays. They stick somehow.

> *"'Light thickens, and the crow*
> *Makes wing for the rooky wood.'"*

Agnes said, "I remember bits, too.

> *"'The raven himself is hoarse*
> *That croaks the fatal entrance of Duncan*
> *Under my battlements.'"*

"Who is Duncan?" Mr. Lang demanded slowly.

"I'm not sure," she replied, her gaze upon his face.

The lights went up. "That's better," said Bubbles. She seemed suddenly animated. "Mr. Lang, I didn't know you were literary!"

"I'm not," he answered cheerfully. "I know that tag, about 'light thickens,' because we had some crazy pedagogue who kept dinning into us that Shakespeare probably wrote 'bosky' wood, not 'rooky,' and the printer got it wrong. Barmy, of course. 'Rooky's' a good word. Yes, that's all I know. That and the Mercy Speech. Want to hear it? 'The quality—'"

"We know that, thank you," Agnes politely snubbed him. "Bubbles, we're nearly there. We'd better get our bags down. Is Hilary meeting us?"

"Yes; she'll have the cart there."

"Cart?" To Agnes, whose nerves were jumpy, this had a disagreeable connotation. She visualized a waiting tumbril containing priest and executioner.

"Dog-cart," said Bubbles, opening her wide eyes. "Can't have a car where we live. If we took one down our lane the springs would go in ten minutes."

They arrived at Warwick, and Mr. Lang bore their bags to the barrier, where they found a tall, upstanding girl with fouff teeth awaiting them. She wore tweed coat, sweater and jodhpurs and her greeting was hearty.

"Hulloa-loa-lo! Bubbles, darling, so glad you're back, rotten with wealth. Great glory, what have you done to your hair?"

"Oh, be quiet, Hilary. Agnes, this is my friend Miss Burton. Hilary, this is Mrs. Kinghof. She's going to stay with us for a few days. Did you get my wire?"

"I got it. All the beds aired, and the dogs bathed, and a shepherd's pie in the oven."

"Sounds grand. Oh, and this is Mr. Lang. He's going to a medical congress at Warwick."

"Congress?" Hilary wrinkled her fat snub nose. "First I've heard of it."

"These things are kept quiet," he whispered, "because of spying. Never know where you are, these days. Well, I'm going along now. Miss Ashton—"

"Yes?" she prompted him.

"If you should need me, I'll be at 'The Queen's William.'"

"Thank you."

"Good-bye. Good-bye, Mrs. Kinghof. 'Bye, Miss Burton." Picking up his suitcase, he walked swiftly off into the starry dusk.

Bubbles and Hilary piled with Agnes into the dog-cart, which was not, after all, so dissimilar to a tumbril, and they bowled off between the bare hedges on the four-mile drive to Beanscot. Bubbles whispered, "I say, do you think he's all right?"

"I'm sure he is," Agnes whispered reassuringly.

"I say, Boo-boo," Hilary shouted as she wielded the reins with large and expert wrists, "they're taking awfully good care of you. Had a policeman from Warwick up at the cottage this afternoon and he said I was to tell you that he's going to keep an eye on the place."

The two other women were much comforted. They might not have been so had they known about another passenger who had alighted unostentatiously from the Warwick train, and who, walking swiftly in the shadow, had gone first to a cycle shop, and then, wheeling the machine, had sought a bed in an obscure and shabby public house in a back street.

Chapter Thirteen

"I thought to be greeted by the deep-throated belling of hounds," said Agnes artistically, as Hilary and Bubbles led her up the path of Setters Croft, "or do I mean deep-belled throating of hounds?"

Hilary chuckled as she fumbled with her key. "Oh, we're short of dogs at the moment; only got two setter pups belonging to Mrs. Marston up at Shrews Manor—she's in Norfolk with her husband—and they're not old enough to bell yet. They can only squeak. Here we are. Come along in."

They went into a long, low-ceilinged room, its prettiness enhanced by the leaping light of a great open fire. Bubbles said, "Black-out down, Hilary?"

"Great John Scott, of course it is. You'd have seen the fire a mile away if it hadn't been." She turned up the lights.

"This is nice!" said Mrs. Kinghof appreciatively, and she meant it, although she would not have chosen such a home for herself. She liked high ceilings and modern sanitation.

"Glad you like it. Better see your room right away, hadn't you? Then you can have a wash and brush-up and I'll get supper on." Hilary divested herself of her tweed jacket, revealing a large, firm bust closely covered in canary wool. "I say, Bubbles, turn round! I want to look at that *chevelure*. Jumping snakes, there's plenty of lure about it. Were you responsible for this, Mrs. Kinghof?"

"I'd rather you called me Agnes. Yes, I was, really. I introduced her to 'Marquise,' who styles hair marvellously, and she couldn't resist styling Bubbles.'"

"Well, God alone knows how she's going to keep it in trim round here; but I like it." She slapped her friend heartily on the back. "Yes, Millais, I like it."

"Millais?" Agnes enquired.

"Bubbles. The picture, see?" Hilary rocked anew with mirth at this family joke.

"Oh, yes! Very slick."

"Well, come and see over the estate. This is an old place, but the last owner stuck pieces on it, making it look quite extraordinary, as you'll see by daylight. It was rectangular once, but now it's L-shaped, as this lounge has been extended by half its length again, and the two bedrooms above it, mine and the one you're going to use, were only added three or four years ago. Step along, and I'll show you the rest."

The lounge occupied the whole of the front part of the house. Hilary took Agnes through a door in the centre of the back wall and down a passage which, surprisingly, had rooms on one side only, the other side forming the outer wall of the house. "See what I mean? We're not nearly so wide as we look from the front. May as well see the downstairs rooms while you're here."

Next to the lounge was the kitchen, with a useful service hatch, next to that the bathroom, and next to that a narrow, cell-like chamber described by Hilary as the workshop. "I do a bit of carpentering," she explained. The room facing the garden was Bubbles' bedroom. "She hates sleeping upstairs; she's quite a sensible old baggage in all other ways, but she's got a holy horror of fire." Agnes peered through Bubbles' window, trying to see into the garden.

"See it better when the moon's up," said Hilary, "which it will be in about an hour. It's quite a pretty place. Nice belt of alders at the end, and a decent stream."

"Where are the kennels?"

"Oh, over that fence to the left there."

"Seems rather bleak for the pups."

Hilary belled deep-throated. "They're not out there. Sleeping on my bed, as a matter of fact. Millais says it's unhealthy, but I don't mind a few germs. Now, then, come and see your own room. We've got to go out in the yard to get to it."

Agnes wished faintly that she had not come. Following Hilary out into the starlight she climbed up a steep flight of wooden stairs towards something that reminded her unpleasantly of the Coldersbrook hayloft; but she found herself, to her surprise, in the first of two communicating bedrooms, pleasantly furnished and heated by electric bowl fires. "This is yours, the first room, and I'm next door. Hope you'll be comfortable, Mrs. Kinghof."

"Don't call me that, Hilary."

"All right. Queer sort of name, isn't it?"

"It isn't foreign, though Andrew—that's my husband—is always joking about his Austrian blood. The name used to be Kinghough, h-o-u-g-h, but Grandfather changed the spelling because he couldn't stand people calling him King-hore. He said it sounded like a contradiction in terms. I say,

Hilary…delicate question. What does one do here if—in the dead of night—?"

"Oh, that! I twig. Well, you can go down to the yard to the Nook—that's what we call it—or you can just make do." She kicked in explanatory fashion at the bed-valance.

"Oh. Yes, thank you. I think one would make do, don't you?"

"Please yourself," said Hilary. "Well, anything else I can do? Help you unpack?"

"No, thanks, I've brought practically nothing."

"Well, the bathroom's free when you want to wash, and supper will be in about twenty minutes. We'll have a spot of sherry first."

"Goody," said Agnes, suspiciously.

"I've bought some simply marvellous stuff, only two-and-six a bottle. Wait till you sample it! Well, I'll be seeing you."

Within ten minutes Agnes, refreshed and cheerful, rejoined her hosts in the lounge. Hilary was busy laying supper at a table in the far window, Bubbles was looking through a bunch of circulars all dealing with dog-foods.

"Can I help, Hilary?"

"No, thanks, Agnes, I've nearly finished. You can lend a hand with the washee-uppee, though, if you like. Sooner we get done the sooner we have peace. Bubbles!"

"What?"

"What the devil have you got on your legs?"

Bubbles wriggled those limbs awkwardly and attempted to sit on them. "Only stockings," she said defensively. "Why?"

"Did you buy them?"

"Of course."

"Great John Scott! You aren't going to fool around with the dogs in those, are you? I never saw such sissy things."

"I may want to do other things in life than fool around with dogs," was Bubbles' unexpected and spirited retort, for which Agnes mentally applauded her.

"Poor old girl," Hilary mourned, "money's turned your head. Ye gods! What did they cost?"

"A guinea."

"What rank waste! I say, Agnes, you've been degenerating the poor girl..." Hilary looked down at her own fine legs, encased in a drab hose of woollen check. She had discarded the jodhpurs in favour of a kilted skirt stuck through with a large safety-pin. "Wonder what I'd look like in those things?"

"I'll send you a pair for Christmas," Agnes said, "and we'll see. I never knew any legs look the worse for them."

"Better keep your money for a better object," Hilary said gruffly, but she seemed rather wistful. "Well, drinkee-time. One before tiffin." She poured sherry and came to sit with them in the chimney-corner.

Agnes offered cigarettes. "Do you smoke, Hilary?"

"Me? Lord, no! Got to keep fit. Can't afford coffin-nails. Bubbles doesn't, either...or does she, since she's been away?"

"I wouldn't mind," Bubbles said defiantly, "but I do choke so."

"Hope you continue to choke. Who was the man you were with today?"

"He lives in the same block of flats as I do," said Agnes, "he's a medical student."

"He looked nice. Open-air sort of chap."

"His looks belie him. He stuffs in overheated rooms smothered with books, and smokes himself yellow."

"Only because he doesn't know any better," said Bubbles, blushing.

The blush did not escape Hilary. "Ah, ha! A case?"

"Don't be ridiculous… And what about you? Seen anything more of Jack Jarman since I went away?"

"Saw him out riding with that egg-haired Hasleton piece."

"Is he your favourite young man?" Agnes enquired, disarming, by that smile, any attack upon her good taste. Agnes was never particular about taste.

"He's mine," said Hilary, with an entire lack of self-consciousness, "but I don't know if I'm his yet. I'll have to dislodge La Hasleton, and then we'll see. He's all right, but he's weak. Likes me when there aren't any tootsies from town about, but goes to the bad very easily. Not that I mind that. I'll stiffen him, when I marry him."

"If he likes tootsies," Agnes remarked, "he might like stockings of the type Bubbles is wearing."

"If you're hinting that I ought to descend to the Hasleton's level, I may as well tell you—"

"A nice young man is worth any loss of dignity," Agnes countered soberly. "Besides, it is not true love to put your own sartorial freaks above his. Andrew, for example, does not like a woman to wear court shoes in the winter. Consequently, I limp about like Lord Byron in bootees."

"I could show up in a pair when we go to his birthday do, next month," Hilary said thoughtfully, and Agnes did not spoil a good effect by pursuing the argument.

The supper was excellent, an admirable shepherd's pie served with parsnips and sprouts, and followed by a custard tart with bottled raspberries. The girls settled down to a game of three-handed whist until it should be time for bed.

Just before ten, when Bubbles and Agnes had retired and

Hilary was bolting the front and side doors, a policeman came round to say that he would be keeping an eye on the house. Pleased, she went to retail this to Bubbles. "So you're O.K., and you can sleep like a log. Feel O.K., old girl?"

"Yes, only I do wish it was all cleared up. Don't think I'm a beast for not saying much about it yet. I'll tell you everything from A to Z tomorrow."

"Tell me when you feel like it. Anyway, I can always get it out of Agnes. She's not a bad sort, is she? Ugly, but smart. Or is she ugly? Her eyes are good."

"She has wonderful clothes," Bubbles sighed, "and the most marvellous legs I've ever seen."

"Rather tootsy clothes, aren't they? No, perhaps not. Not like La Hasleton's."

"Wait," said Bubbles, "till you see the dress she made me buy. It's a dream… Good night, Hilary."

"Nightee-nightee. Sleepee-wellee. Bless you."

Good-hearted Hilary, whose mind was dwelling upon the dangerous sartorial thoughts put into her head by Mrs. Kinghof, went upstairs.

"I say, Agnes, a copper's just been round to say he's watching us."

"Hooray," Agnes called, from the adjoining bedroom. "I say, I'm not really used to these early hours. Mind if I read for a while?"

"Not a bit, so long as you shut the door between. You'll find some books on top of the wardrobe."

So Agnes made a difficult choice between *My Pal Towser, What Katy Did, A Warwick Wayfarer, Hard Times, The Kennel Book,* and *Warwick Wildfowl.* Selecting *Katy,* she read until eleven, when she turned out the light and fell at once into a soft, deep sleep.

———

Bubbles also slept deeply in her bedroom on the ground floor. Secure in police-protection, she had opened the casement windows to their widest extent, and was breathing in the sweet, cold air from the garden. The moon was at its full now, pouring over the grass, the bare brown earth of the vegetable garden, the alders fringing the stream. The clock on the passage wall chimed midnight, dropping its soft jangle through the quiet of the house. Bubbles was dreaming that it was Hilary's wedding day, and that her friend, simply and attractively clad in *couleur de rose* stockings, a long veil and nothing else, an attire that seemed strange to nobody, was coming down the aisle on the arm of young Jack Jarman of Crossacres. She, Bubbles, was a little troubled about her hair, which would not keep short; in fact, it grew a few inches with every step she took, and she was hard put to it to snip away, in the shadow of her bridesmaid's hat, at the superfluous growth. In another minute, she thought, someone will say, "Why on earth did you want to bring a pair of nail-scissors to a wedding?" And then her hand slipped and the scissors fell tinkling to the flags. Hilary, who, in the course of the procession, had somehow acquired a woollen vest, turned sharply and said, "Why on earth, Millais, did you want to bring…" And Bubbles woke sharply out of her dream, her heart pounding, her forehead and hands unaccountably moist.

The brilliance of the moon was so great that for a moment she did not know where she was. The night air froze the sweat upon her cheeks and made her gasp. She struggled up to a sitting position, rubbed her eyes and looked straight before her; and there it was, not a foot from the window, the grinning mask of the Pig.

He stood there, his stocky body, in some dark suit, firmly planted on the lawn, as if he had just grown out of the earth. The light was blue on the animal-head, glistening on the violet snout, the little, winking eyes. Bubbles saw all this, and she saw the glinting muzzle of the revolver, pointed neatly at her.

Icy-cold, sick, too terrified to move, she watched him as he advanced, thrusting his pig's head into the room. He said, quietly, but not whispering, "Well, what a nice cousin I have! Don't you budge, Joan Ashton, or I'll plug you where you sit. I'll plug you just where that charitable-institution nightie of yours is slipping off you… Did you get the note I left in Mrs. K.'s milk-bottle? I thought not. I said in it that I shouldn't think twice about killing you just for your *beaux-yeux*, without any regard to profit motives… Don't move! You'd like to remind me of the black cap, wouldn't you? But if they catch me for dear Pappa and dear Aunt Addie, why should I mind being caught for you? Get up! Do you hear me? Get up. If you make any noise, you'll catch it, dear Joanie…and if you speak! I don't want any talk out of you."

She said, dry-lipped, pitifully, "Maclagan, we were children together—"

"And now we're all jolly grown-ups together, aren't we? Get up and shut up. Come here to me."

Like a sleep-walker she crept from the sheets and went to the window, where he awaited her. Her thin nightdress clung to her body, and she shivered as the cold breeze touched her. He thrust the hideous head at her, butting the snout into her cheek. "Kiss your cousin, Joanie? Kiss Cousin Mac?" His voice, which had been soft, nondescript, changed. "Quick, do as I say. Come over the sill to me. You can get up, can't you? Quick's the word, sharp's the action."

He gave her his left hand, helping her with a savage aping of chivalry. He was a short man; as she stood beside him, her bare feet on flagstones moist with the night's dewfall, he was not quite so tall as she.

The cold ate through the soles of her feet. A sudden, fiercer wind whipped the nightgown about her, sticking it to the frozen sweat of her body. He said, "Get in front of me, and walk!"

As in a nightmare she obeyed him, and moved before him over the wet grass. The clouds were riding like witches across the moon, now and then obscuring her silver face.

Bubbles began to speak. "Maclagan, you're a coward, and I'm not frightened by childish tricks." Why not speak? For all she knew, she might still be dreaming.

He sang softly, sang a little jig.

> *"Sticks and stones*
> *May break my bones,*
> *But names will never hurt me!"*

"You're not only a coward, you're a lunatic. I'm sorry for you, Maclagan; civilized people are sorry for mad people."

She heard the soft brush of his feet behind her, knew he was moving up; and then the muzzle of the gun was dug into her ribs. "Hold your tongue, Joanie. Shut up, or I'll kill you, see? And this gun doesn't make much noise. Hurry up, and save your breath."

She was so cold now that she could scarcely stumble along. Stones cut her feet, her numbed toes could scarcely grip the earth. He forced her through the alders to the bank of the stream, where he made her turn and face him.

"Athletic girl, Joanie? You ought to be. Girls like you have to be good at games to cover up their lack of looks and to make the men at the tennis-club take notice of them. Mrs. K.'s improved you a bit, I will admit, but you're still a fat gawk. Do you know who I am, Joanie?"

She said, through chattering teeth, "Maclagan Steer."

"And who's he?"

She did not answer.

"You look funny when you shiver, Joanie; rather like that pink blancmange muck your mother made when I came to tea that day. Remember? 'We are but little children weak...' Do you swim? Well, we'll try you. Get into the water."

She moaned, half in protest, half in appeal.

"If you swim, you might live; if I plug you, you won't. Get into the water."

Blindly she turned and began to grope her way down the bank. The moon was bland again, showing every blade of grass, sparkling on the swift-purling water. As the stream ran over her ankles she cried out with the shock and agony of cold. "Get in," said the Pig. "Wade. How deep is it? They say you feel the chill less if you duck right in."

But she was now numbed past all feeling. Standing up to her knees in the ice-cold water she gasped, "Kill me."

"You'd like that? Always ready to oblige a lady, even a fat lady. Your friend's fat too, isn't she? What a pretty pair you make... Very well then!"

He stepped rapidly down to the water's brink and swung up the gun to strike; and as he struck, a great cloud swept across the face of the moon.

He heard the splash as she fell; and he drew a long, trembling breath, as of supreme and utter satiety. It was a matter of minutes to rip off the pig's mask, crumple it and bury it in the sand, under the gravel. Then he began to run, softly, at a leisurely pace, along the banks till he came to a foot-bridge, over the foot-bridge to the silent fields beyond.

———

Meanwhile, young Constable Yeldon, who at nine-thirty that evening had been attacked from behind, stunned, robbed of his helmet and tunic, tied, gagged and rolled into a ditch, was discovered by a late cyclist, a farm labourer coming home from a clandestine meeting with his employer's wife. He was not eager to appear in the case. He cut Yeldon's bonds, ungagged him, gave him water from a brook, then jumped on his cycle and rode away at top speed, leaving the dazed policeman to find his way back to the station.

Yeldon was picked up by a search-party, which had been looking for him ever since ten-thirty, when his helmet and tunic had been found decorating a signpost, contemptuously returned, as they did not then know, by the borrower.

When it was learned that he had been attacked not a stone's throw from the gate of Setters, two policemen came to knock up Miss Ashton. They were let in by Miss Burton, who arrived in agitated state followed by an equally agitated Mrs. Kinghof, and the party repaired to Bubbles' room: which was empty, the windows wide open, the curtains blown inwards by the force of the new-risen wind. It was then a quarter to one.

Hilary and Agnes, half-mad with distress, had barely begun their story when the local inspector pointed towards the window. They swung round.

In the bare and windy moonlight Felix Lang was advancing over the lawn, the body of a big, blue, wet girl in his arms.

He said, "I thought she'd be in danger, and I don't care a

hoot for the police. What good do they do? Did they stop the fun and games at Stewarts Court? So I prowled around the place."

Agnes said desperately, "Is she dead? For heaven's sake, Doctor, tell us."

The doctor, newly summoned, pursed his lips. "No, she's not; but it will be tough work pulling her through. She'll have to be tough to survive that exposure. She stunned herself falling on to the tree-root where Lang says he found her, and that was her luck, because if she'd missed it she'd have drowned. She's been struck a glancing blow on the shoulder too, but it wasn't that that laid her out. Miss Burton! Make this room as hot as you can and get hot-water bottles. And I want blankets."

"I saw a chap running," Lang persisted. "Couldn't make out anything about him, what he looked like or anything. I tore along by the stream, and then the moon came out suddenly and I saw Miss Ashton lying half-in and half-out of the water, her head caught between two forks of an alder root. It took me time to lug her out, because she's a weight, and I thought I'd never be able to carry her back. All right, Inspector, I know what you're thinking. I'll answer anything you like to ask. But I wouldn't harm Miss Ashton, not the nail of her little toe… I'm nuts about her. Mrs. Kinghof, do you believe me?"

"I want everyone but Miss Burton out of here," said the doctor.

In the lounge, before a fire hastily re-stoked, Lang repeated his question. "Do you believe me, Mrs. Kinghof?"

Agnes looked at him wearily, as if she could not understand him. "I'll give you a drink," she said at last; "you look as though you need that." She poured a liberal glass of Hilary's sherry. "It'll warm you, if it chokes you in the process."

The Inspector watched as he drank. Then he said, "Mr. Lang, you'd better come with us. Mrs. Kinghof, I am leaving a man here and shall be sending another. I shall want to see you first thing tomorrow morning."

When they had gone she sat down, lit a cigarette and stared into the fire, her heart heavy. In the ground-floor bedroom, heated now to the temperature of a Turkish bath, Doctor Sigourney and Hilary Burton fought for Bubbles' life.

Chapter Fourteen

THE FOLLOWING MORNING SAW A SLEEPLESS AGNES making coffee and cooking bacon for an exhausted girl and a doctor. It saw a large car sweeping down from London to the Midlands, sweeping majestically as if aware of its precious burden: which was Lord Whitestone. It saw Felix Lang trying to snatch a little sleep at "The Queen's William" after a long harassing at the police-station. It saw Bubbles Ashton breathing in a natural sleep, having fought death and come out on top.

"She'll be all right now," said Dr. Sigourney, rubbing his red eyes. "If she hadn't the constitution of six draught-horses she'd be finished. If Lang hadn't pulled her out when he did there'd have been no hope whatsoever. God knows what long-term results this thing will have, but for the present… Well, she's alive. It'll be a good time before she's on her feet again, though."

"Lang!" Hilary snapped, between ravenous mouthfuls of bacon. "Don't talk about him. I believe he put her in the water in the first place."

"If he did," said Agnes fretfully, "he damn' well saved her life by pulling her out again."

"Double bluff. He didn't think she'd survive."

Sigourney poured himself a third cup of coffee. "Do you think you can go on nursing her, Miss Burton? I was going to suggest that you had a trained nurse in the house, but you've done so well that I don't think it will be necessary."

"I'll nurse her all right. I've had a bit of experience, anyway; I was a probationer up in Leeds till I jacked in."

He said curiously, "And why did you jack it in?"

She answered sincerely and rather sadly, "Oh, I wasn't the type. I hadn't the right sort of sympathy. Used to get ratty with patients, think they could quite well get fit again if they'd only use their guts. Rotten of me, but there it is."

He smiled. "I think it's a pity you didn't stick to it. You'd have got over that. What do you mean to do, Mrs. Kinghof?"

"Me? Oh, I'll stay on here for a bit and help Hilary, if she'll let me. I may just as well. I could look after the house, and do the cooking and whatnot."

"It would be nice," Hilary said gratefully, "but I couldn't ask it of you."

"You could ask me," said Agnes grimly, "and with justice, to throw myself in the Avon. Why did I come down here? Because I wanted to see that nothing happened to Bubbles. What did I do? Fell for a fake constable, as poor Mrs. Sibley did, and let that girl sleep on the ground floor, with her window wide open, practically out of call."

"I'm more culpable there than you are. After all, you didn't know her damned window was open—Great John Scott, who's the fury coming up the path?"

They saw him through the leaded pane, Lord Pig,

distorted, but hideously recognizable. He wore his official suit of blue serge, and his collar was very stiff indeed.

"My cousin-by-marriage," Agnes said apprehensively. "Scotland Yard big noise. Oh, lord, this is the end."

She rose herself to let him in and, before he could pour his wrath upon her, introduced him to Hilary and the doctor. "Marvellous to see you; makes me feel so safe."

"Mrs. Kinghof!" This was the official voice, sharp as steel. "I want you, please, to return to London by the midday train. I'm not going to be responsible for you any longer, and you've no business here."

"Can I give you some coffee, Lord Whitestone?" Hilary asked, trying to divert the storm.

"Thank you, no. Agnes! What are you doing here, anyhow?"

She replied, "Look here, Herbert—" Pig looked faintly relieved that she had not used his nickname—"Look here, Herbert, I wish you'd come in the other room a minute, please."

"Pity," said Sigourney, who was too tired to observe the conventions of polite society, "because I could just enjoy a good row."

Pig, having glared icily at him, followed Agnes into Hilary's workshop. "Now then."

"Oh, I know. Curse me. Spit upon my Jewish gabardine. I've made another mucker. Or rather, I didn't avert one. I deserve all you're going to say."

"I am going to say very little. I am just going to order you home."

"Don't do that. Hilary's going to nurse Bubbles all by herself, and I offered to do the housekeeping. She was so glad of it! I've got to stay. I owe it to her."

"I don't care what you owe. It's time you stopped interfering in matters outside your province. You're doing no good and you're causing me personal embarrassment. Do you think I wanted to get up at dawn and drive down here? I needn't have done it if you hadn't been here."

She crossed and recrossed her legs, beautiful even when bare, and terminated by Hilary's red woolly bedroom slippers, but Pig did not respond.

"When the devil are you going to start behaving like an adult?" he demanded.

Agnes said, "All right, Pig. You've slapped me and I've said I'm sorry."

"I didn't hear you."

"Well, I'm saying it now. Don't be so particular! I inferred I was sorry, didn't I? You *do* niff-naff."

"Corcoran will see you get to the station in time to catch the train—"

"Is *he* here? Why, you ought to have brought him, too. He'd like to hear you smacking me."

Pig looked as if he could do this literally.

Agnes beamed suddenly. "Friends now?"

"Look here, Agnes, it's not the slightest use trying to wheedle—"

"Oh, Pig! I say, we did have fun at the Guide Concert, didn't we? I mean, it really was rather funny, and I believe you enjoyed it in a way. And then, you were so grand, not paying us back in our own coin. That showed you weren't vindictive. You aren't vindictive, are you, Herbert?... Yes, I think I shall call you Herbert. It suits you, and it's so much nicer than a ridiculous, childish nickname. Nicknames are all right for Andrew, but I'd rather not use yours when you've got such a lovely name of your own."

There was a thunderous silence, during which Lord Whitestone's resemblance to the animal grew more marked.

"I could," Agnes continued gently, for she had suddenly abandoned any hope of reconciliation, "call you *Porc*, in the French way, which would be quite chic and pretty; or then again, I could call you *Cochon*—Pierre Cochon, or Cauchon—the Inquisitor—isn't that appropriate? Yes, I think—"

And then something amazing happened. The features of her cousin-by-marriage became contorted by some remarkable emotion, something alien and overmastering. Before she realized that Pig was struggling to repress a grin he had drawn back his hand and slapped her quite hard upon the seat of Hilary's dressing-gown. She spun round. "You—"

"All right," said Pig, beaming, "all right. All over. But Corcoran will call for you at eleven-thirty."

He marched back to the lounge, where he astonished Hilary by asking in a most civilized fashion if he might now have some coffee. She gave it to him, exchanged a few generalities, and retired with Sigourney to look after the patient.

"Now," Pig said, "you can sit down, make yourself comfortable, have one of my cigarettes, and tell me last night's story."

Agnes did so.

He said, "And what do you think of Lang?"

"I don't know. What have you done with him?"

"The police here worked on him, couldn't get him to alter his tale and returned him to 'The Queen's William,' with instructions to stay there."

"Have you checked up yet on the Stewarts Court people? I suppose you haven't had time."

"Eggshell's had time. He's a good man, that, Agnes, and

we shall keep him taped. The train you took down here was
yesterday's last, so he checked up on the number of people
who were in Block 3 at the time it left London. Luckily, he'd
had Frankson hanging about all day."

"Well?"

"Lang went out at eight in the morning and didn't come
back. Well, we know where he went. Warrender left at nine,
as usual, and he, too, didn't come back. Mrs. Rowse left at
half-past ten, telling Blake, the porter, that she was spend-
ing the week-end with a friend. Sole occupant seems to have
been Madame Charnet, who at about ten let out the man
who came to replace her wireless batteries, and didn't show
a nose beyond the door for the rest of the day. That's all I can
tell you. By the way, I suppose you've heard from Eggshell of
the—ah, obscene cinema? Well, we have reason to believe
that there's something behind it. Can't say more now."

"What obscene cinema?"

He told her.

"I say, Pig," said Agnes wistfully, "I suppose you'll be
going on the raid. You wouldn't like to take me?"

He stiffened. "Certainly not. It appears to be no place
for decent women. I should no more take you than I should
take Mary."

"I didn't think you'd take Mary," Agnes murmured, and
abandoned the subject.

He rose. "Well, I must go. Be ready for Corcoran at
eleven-thirty sharp. Good-bye. And don't do it again."

She watched him as he walked briskly away. Hilary came
into the lounge.

"How is she?"

"Still asleep. Agnes, could you be a dear and run down
to the village? It's only half a mile off, and you can take my

bike. We've absolutely nothing in the house. Sausages, or anything. You'll find the ration books in the kitchen dresser drawer. I know it's Sunday, but if you go round to the side door of the grocer's and say you're from me, Mrs. Shallow will serve you."

"Of course I will, but I can't ride a bike. I'll walk. Hilary, could you possibly get some sleep now?"

"I will directly Mrs. Hepburn arrives; she comes in and does for us from eleven to twelve daily."

"Promise?"

"I'll be shut-eye by the time you get back. Snoree-snoree."

Agnes, reassured by this return to a dreadful but individual terminology, went upstairs to put her hat and coat on.

As she went down the road, in the direction Hilary had indicated, she felt refreshed by the cold, bright weather. I'll get my sleep in the train, she thought, with any luck. Damn it, I did want to stay and help Hilary; but as she says, she can have more help from Mrs. Hepburn, and if I don't get some rest soon I shall go mad.

Beanscot village was tiny and compact, comprising a row of cottages, a general store, a Norman church, a tin chapel and three public houses. The cottages were Tudor, delightful to the tourist, unpleasant for the inhabitant; but the most enthusiastic admirers of rural England do not, as a rule, have to live in it. If I were dictator, Agnes thought as she was cautiously admitted into the beetle-browed shop that smelled so nostalgically of sugar mice and real mice, of flour, liquorice, and cheese, I should acquire all those lovely old houses as national monuments, and put the late inhabitants into decent modern houses with good baths and good drainage. "Awfully nice of you to look after me. Have you any sausages?"

"Only for our registered customers," said the very old lady behind the counter. Her reply was a little ahead of the times.

"But I told you, I'm shopping for Miss Burton."

"Oh, yes! So you did. That's different. We've only beef, though."

"That will do. Half a moment—that looks nice galantine."

"Home-made."

"I'll have half a pound of that as well as the sausages. And I'd like some tomatoes, too. And a lettuce."

"No lettuces."

"Oh. Well, and three pounds of potatoes."

The old lady chattered amiably as she served Agnes. "Staying down here?"

"I'm going back today."

"Friend of Miss Ashton's?"

"That's right."

"Miss Ashton well? She's a right nice girl, she is."

"She's not very well, as a matter of fact. Got the 'flu very badly." This seemed to Agnes discreet.

"You know what my old mother used to say, whenever we girls had colds? Not that we called them the 'flu then. She used to say,

> "'An orange stewed in China tea
> Will draw the fever out of thee.'

"She used to boil the orange in the teapot, dry it out and hang it on a tape round our necks. And what the virtue was, I don't know; but the cold used to be gone by morning."

"Didn't it make a bulge?" Agnes enquired with interest.

"Lor'," said the old lady, "we was all bulge in the old days.

Now, you hide that bag as you go out, or you'll get me into trouble."

Mrs. Kinghof, her basket full, walked briskly back towards Setters. It was ten minutes to eleven, and she knew that the wrath of Pig would descend in unbelievable measure were she not to be ready when Corcoran called.

Her first visit to Warwickshire, she was disappointed in the country, which seemed to her without individuality; and she comforted herself by thinking that Shakespeare could have made an enchanted world out of Clapham Common. The leafless hedges were charming beneath a delicate lacing of frost, and there was ice in the puddles. It was a lonely part of the world and she passed no one save a young boy on a tricycle. She wondered what Bubbles' story would be, when the girl was well enough to tell it.

Her tiredness came in waves, left her, and returned with force redoubled. She thought, Oh, lord, what I would give for a good sleep!

Our prayers are not always answered in the way we would wish. At that moment someone, running on crêpe-soled feet from the coppice which had served as hiding-place, gave her the sleep for which she had so rashly prayed. Agnes went down heavily, and someone, putting back the rubber cosh, dragged her into the ditch, threw her packages on top of her, hooked the basket over her outflung arm and, before leaving, pinned to the breast of her tweed coat a little note, which read: "I'D KEEP MY BIRDY BEAK OUT OF IT, IF I WERE YOU. THE PIG-STICKER."

———

The bright morning saw something else, something we have not mentioned before; it saw Captain Kinghof riding happily in an Army lorry through the Warwick lanes, thinking how very pleasant it would be to give his wife a nice surprise. He had been transferred, quite unexpectedly, to an O.C.T.U. in a neighbouring county, where he was to act as instructor, and he proposed to take forty-eight hours' leave before undertaking the task of making R.T.U.-haunted cadets into confident officers. He was enjoying himself refreshing his memory on the subject of charges and how to make them, and he read the driver the following specimen:

"'Private Blank, when personally ordered by Captain Blank to take up his rifle and fall in, did not do so, divesting himself of his waist-belt and saying, "I'll soldier no more, do what you may!"'" Andrew said, "I wouldn't have the heart to charge a fellow who said that, would you, Lenscombe?"

"No, sir. Not that I've never heard no one say it."

"We must hope, Lenscombe. Life is before us. This is Beanscot, isn't it?"

"Yes, sir."

"All right, then, put me down. I'll find my own way now."

Andrew climbed out into the lane and looked for someone who might tell him his way to Setters. He found a small boy.

"I say, son! Know Setters Cottage?"

"Yeah, boss. Betcha." The Warwickshire tongue was heavily overlaid with Hollywood.

"Well, where is it?"

"Costya ten grand, bud."

"I was prepared for a request of the sort," said Andrew, "but not for its magnificence. You don't get ten grand. You get tenpence, by which you will be fourpence overpaid. Now then."

The boy scratched his head, and indicated the road

down which Agnes had gone not so long ago. "Well, that takes you straight there, only it's not so quick because it goes boogie-woogie."

"I think I see. What's the alternative?"

"Go across that field and you'll see a stile. Cross that, and you'll see a wood. Go through that and you'll find yourself in a lane."

"And what happens when I find myself in that?"

"You use your eyes, Slim. There's a green gate in the wall leading through a farmyard. Go through that, if you're not yellow about cows, and you'll find yourself within five minutes of Setters. Zowie!"

"How long will it take me if I go through the boogie-woogie way?"

"Ten minutes longer than if you go by the way I said."

"I'll trust you." He raked in his pockets. "Here you are."

The boy blinked at a shilling and a sixpence. "Jeepers Creepers! What's this for? I said tenpence."

"No. You said ten grand."

"Well, that's what I meant. What's the eightpence for, Dead Pan?"

"Entertainment tax," said Andrew, and strode away towards Setters.

He arrived at eleven-thirty sharp and met Corcoran on the doorstep. "Good heavens, fancy seeing you here! What's up? Anybody dead? Pig here, too?"

Corcoran frowned and said with some disapproval, "Lord Whitestone came down with me this morning. No, sir, no one's dead, but Miss Ashton was pretty near it. I've called to take your wife back to London."

"You have? Well, she's not going. She's staying here till I go back from leave. Is she all right? What's she been up to?"

"Nothing, sir."

"Then what's up with Miss Ashton?"

Briefly Corcoran told him, and Andrew said a short, bad word.

"We'll go in now, sir, if you don't mind. We were going to catch the noon train."

"I tell you you're not going to catch any train! If you want Mrs. Kinghof out of the way, and I can't blame you for that, I'll take her to Warwick, or Stratford if you like."

"Lord Whitestone said—"

"Listen, Corcoran, I don't care what he said. If he snorts at you, refer him to me." Andrew knocked at the door, and Hilary opened it.

"I'm Agnes's husband," he said, stepping into the lounge and looking around for his wife. "I suppose you must be Hilary. I say, I'm terribly upset about Bubbles! How is she?"

"How do you do?" said Hilary distractedly. "Oh, she's doing all right and they say she's marvellous to pull through, but—Captain Kinghof, it's your wife I'm worried about. She went to Beanscot to do some backdoor shopping—you can do it on Sundays, if you know the ropes—and she should have been back quite a quarter of an hour ago."

He swung round. "What?" Quickly he strode to the door, opened it and yelled to Corcoran, who was just starting up the car.

"Hi! Come back. My wife's got lost."

The detective came running. "Lost, sir? How? When? Isn't she here?"

"Of course she's not here," Hilary snapped. She was unspeakably tired, and the prospect of sleep seemed further off than ever. "Captain Kinghof, how did you come? By car?"

"No, over the hill and across the farmyard. Would she have come back that way?"

"No, she didn't know it. She was coming by the road."

"Come on, Corcoran, we've got to make a search." He glanced briefly at Hilary and his face softened. "You're dog-tired. Can you lie down?"

"Not until—ah, here she is." The daily woman was going round the side of the house.

"Your woman? Let her look after things. Please. You must have some sleep."

"I think..." said Hilary. She walked to the sofa, lay down on it and immediately fell into heavy slumber.

"Blast!" Andrew said. "Now I'll have to explain things to the woman. Corcoran, you explain, will you?"

"If you like, sir. I won't be a tick."

Andrew did not wait for Corcoran's tick. He ran to the car, commandeered it and drove off, paying no heed to the roar of rage that followed him. Up and down that half-mile of winding road he went, sick with fright, blind with anxiety; but he saw nothing. At last he ran the car back to Setters, took hold of the furious detective by one arm and said, "We've got to search the ditches. You one side, me the other. Can't see anything driving."

It was Andrew who found her, flat out on her back, ticketed, sausages and tomatoes about her feet, potatoes nestling in her ribs. She was half-hidden in weeds, and her clothing was sodden with mud.

"Agnes! Hey, darling! You're all right. I say you're all right! You've got to be. Here, wake up. You can wake up if you want to." Characteristically, he swore at her as he lugged her out on to the road. "Come on, come on, damn you, you're all right. You're not hurt. Here, Corcoran, get the car, will you?"

When the detective drove back in the Lanchester they laid her on the back seat and Andrew knelt on the floor at her side. "Agnes. Listen to me. It's Andrew. Come on, darling, snap out of it. You're missing all the excitement. Corcoran, take this damned note and give it to Pig.—Agnes! Do you hear me?"

Her long lashes fluttered delicately, and lifted. Big blue eyes, extremely surprised and quite guileless, looked into his. "Andy? What the devil are you doing... Oh, Great John Scott, my head hurts!"

Relief made him angry. "Where the hell did you learn that disgusting oath?"

"Hilary. Andrew, what's happened to me?"

"Someone conked you out. You were lying in the ditch, smothered in sausages."

She moaned. "Oh, not sausages!... Pig again. Oh, re Pig; don't tell Lord Pig about the sausages. He'd laugh. I don't want anyone to laugh."

"Darling, you're all right, aren't you?"

"I suppose so... Ow, my head! Andrew, you know my tweed hat, the one I had on when I got hit? It was too large, so I'd stuffed cottonwool in the lining. Looked awful, but I think it helped..."

He thanked heaven, intensely and without irony, for cottonwool.

The car drew up outside Setters and he bent to pick her up.

"All right, I can walk. Anyway, you always drop me." Her arm round his neck, she made her way into the house. Then she saw Hilary, recumbent, her mouth open, her big limbs sprawled at all angles. "My God, he's got her, too!"

"He hasn't," Corcoran reassured her, "she's just gone slap off to sleep. Mr. Kinghof, I'm going to leave you now, and I'd be obliged if you'd get Mrs. Kinghof out of this house just as soon as she feels strong enough."

"I want a drink," Agnes murmured as the door closed behind him. "I want a drink, and there's nothing but some awful sherry."

"Is there a room where Hilary is *not* sleeping?"

"Bedroom upstairs."

"I'll get you there. You're going to be wrapped up, kept warm and given nice, hot tea."

"Don't want tea."

"That's what you're going to have."

How he got her up the wooden steps he never knew, but he did it; and when she had drunk her tea and had been put to bed, she said, "You're quite good at things, Andrew. What have you done with my clothes, by the way?"

"Slung them on the floor."

"As good a place as any. Oh, my head!… How long are you on leave?"

"For as long as you need me," said Andrew.

She beamed faintly. "What pretty things you say!"

He quoted, "'I'll soldier no more, do what you may'… Go to sleep."

"Aren't you hungry, darling?"

"Of course I am."

"No food in the house."

"Not an egg?"

"I believe there's one egg, but that's for Hilary. You didn't pick up the sausages?"

"Don't be a fool."

"Don't eat the egg, will you?" She was drowsy.

"I'll send the daily woman to the village. She can do some backdoor shopping for a change."

"Always resourceful," murmured Agnes, and was within half a minute the third person at Setters sleeping through the noonday.

Chapter Fifteen

CORCORAN SAID TO THE LANDLORD OF "THE QUEEN'S William," "Where's Mr. Lang?"

"In his room, sir."

"Where's he been all the morning?"

It was a delightful bar-room, not too sunny, not too gloomy. A great fire glowed on the Tudor hearth, and the wood floor was traversed by the beams of muted light filtering through the leaded panes. The landlord, conventionally ruddy, but unconventionally small and lean, looked worried. He did not like police in his hotel.

"In his room, so far as I know."

There were a few early Sunday customers in the bar. The landlord lowered his voice, and Corcoran tactfully did likewise.

"Not been out of it?"

"Well, he came down about ten-thirty and went to the lavatories in the yard. I was in the kitchen at the time, so I saw him. He said, 'It's full of old ladies on my floor.' Which was ridiculous, sir, because we've only two ladies here."

"Did you see him go into the yard?"

"Yes."

"See him come back?"

The bar was getting full.

"Hey, Mr. Riderhouse! Don't you want my money?"

"Two old-and-milds, please! Oi!"

"Ginger beer shandy, please." This was a scrawny boy in shorts, spectacles halfway down his precipitous nose.

"'Scuse me, Inspector. Got to attend to business. Short-handed this morning."

Corcoran waited patiently until Mr. Riderhouse was again at his disposal. "See him come back?"

"No, sir. Being Sunday no one was around and I'd stepped upstairs to have a word with the wife... Ah, here you are, Harry!" This was to the potman, who had made belated entry. "Take over, will you? Now, Mr. Corcoran, if you'll step in here—"

He led the detective into a little dark parlour hung with pictures of Grand Elks, Buffaloes and Druids long dead. "Yes, sir. Go ahead."

"I was asking you if anyone had seen Mr. Lang come back from the yard."

"No, sir. As I was saying, I'd stepped upstairs to see my wife, who's in bed with 'flu, and Harry was in the smoke-room cleaning up, and the chambermaid was doing the top floor."

"Sure she didn't see him?"

"Don't think so, but I'll ask her."

Riderhouse went out, and in a minute appeared with the girl, who was the perfect pattern of any lass Shakespeare might have slapped, *en passant*, across the back breadth of her green serge skirt. There are two Warwick types, the dark square-heads, the red long-heads, and she was of the latter type, red as Queen Bess, tall-browed as William himself, her little chin receding to a dimple, her cheeks rosy, her eyes long and exploratory.

"Mary, this is Detective-Inspector Corcoran, who wants to ask you a few questions."

She smiled, nipping her lower lip with her little white teeth.

"Have you been on the top floor all morning, miss?"

"That's so, sir. I had to do the passage and the bathroom, because they'd got left somehow and Mrs. Riderhouse said—oh, she is queer, poor dear! But she manages to run the house wonderful—she said—"

"All right, miss. Weren't you at any time on the second floor?"

"No, sir."

"Would you have heard anyone go into a room there?"

She giggled. At forty she would be a Mistress Quickly. "Oh lor, sir, yes! Those two ladies were banging away all the morning, in and out like dogs at a fair. They never go out till after lunch, which is why I can't get their rooms done. People are so thoughtless."

"You don't know if Mr. Lang entered or left his room between, say, ten-thirty and eleven forty-five?"

"Oh, him! He went out about half-past ten. Never knew if he came back, though. I suppose he did. He's there now."

"How do you know when he went out?"

"Because I was shaking my duster over the top banisters and I saw him come out of his room. He said—" She blushed and was silent.

"What did he say?"

"Oh, he fancies himself with the girls, he does. Always

saying silly things, I should think. He said, 'You look pretty this morning, fair wench. Want me to buss you?' I don't know what he meant by that, unless he wanted me to go on the Green Line with him. I said, 'You mind your own business and I'll mind mine.'"

Mr. Riderhouse nodded moral approbation.

"All right," said Corcoran, "you can go now, miss, and thanks."

"Thank *you*," said Mary, raying her black eyes at him, and she pranced gaily back to her work.

"Look here, Mr. Riderhouse, is there an exit from the yard?"

"There's a gate, sir, gives on to Lordship Street."

"Better show me."

They walked out into the cobbled yard, stacked with crates of empty bottles and strewn with mudded straw. In one corner was a row of four brick-built lavatories, in another a bicycle shed, and in the far wall a wicket gate. Corcoran inspected it silently. "All right. Thanks very much, Mr. Riderhouse, and I'm sorry to have taken up your time. I'll go and see Lang now. What's his room?"

"Number 11. Know your way up?"

But as Corcoran walked back through the lounge the landlord pointed to a young man drinking Guinness in the corner by the fire. "That's him, sir. That's the chap you want."

"Give me a brown ale," the detective said, and when he was served, carried his tankard over to the great chimney-piece.

"'Morning, Mr. Lang."

The student looked up. "Oh! Morning. Who are you?"

Corcoran gave him a card.

"H'm. Another of you. What have I done this time? And how's Miss Ashton?"

"Going along nicely, sir. Where were you between ten-thirty and eleven-thirty?"

"Oh, hell! Here we go. Why? I say, nothing else has happened, has it?"

"It would be easier if you answered my questions, Mr. Lang."

"All right. I was here, of course."

"In the bar?"

"Of course not. Doesn't open till twelve, and even residents aren't encouraged to sit around in it before then. I was in my room."

"All the time?"

"Yes. No; I went out once to the lavatories in the yard."

"Why?"

"Full on second floor, potman changing towels on first floor, quicker for me to go out the side door than all the way round to the one on the ground floor. Satisfied?"

"Did you come straight back, sir?"

"Of course I did. Do you imagine I stood in the yard giving myself P.T.?"

"What were you doing in your room?"

"Reading. What was I reading? *Reynolds' News.* A Penguin thriller. That all? Now tell me what's happened."

"Mrs. Kinghof was attacked between eleven and eleven-thirty this morning on the road between Beanscot and Miss Ashton's house."

Mr. Lang roared. "Well, *I* didn't do it! I wasn't there! Is Mrs. Kinghof all right?"

"Luckily, yes. Her husband's with her now."

"What hit her?"

Corcoran drank deeply of the beer, wiped his mouth and gently enquired. "How did you know she was hit?"

Lang danced impatiently up and down in his seat. "You said she was attacked! Don't people usually get hit when they're attacked?"

"Sometimes they're stabbed," Corcoran said.

"Wasn't my question natural? Suppose I'd said 'who stabbed her'?"

"It might have looked better, in the circumstances."

"By which I gather she wasn't stabbed. What did hit her?"

"Rubber cosh, or piece of hosing, or something of that sort. As luck would have it she was wearing a tweed hat that was too big, so she'd stuffed some cottonwool in the lining. The wool saved her."

Lang wiped his forehead and pulled his chair further from the fire. "Stewing in here. Well, look here, Inspector, how long have I got to stay in Warwick? I must be back in London by tomorrow morning."

Corcoran rose. "I think you can catch the four o'clock. We can't hold you. I'll confirm that with the Chief Constable and let you know."

The young man gave a deep sigh and, with a hand that was not too steady, raised his glass for a long, final gulp of Guinness. "Good. How nice of you. Well, Inspector, dear, if you've finished with me I'm going to have an early lunch."

"Right. I won't keep you." Corcoran watched Lang as he put his tankard on the shelf above his head, straightened his tie and walked off jauntily towards the dining-room.

———

Agnes said to Andrew that evening, "I'm going back to town Tuesday morning, as soon as your leave ends. I've just remembered I promised Clem Poplett quite three weeks ago that I'd be a casualty in their big A.R.P. exercises."

He said, in slow admiration, "Haven't you had enough of being a casualty? Here, take another aspirin."

"Darling, I can't fail him. I promised to have a broken jaw. He said I could lie in a crane, if I liked—it's down on the wharf—and that the Rescue Party would lug me down. Don't be difficult, Andrew! I don't suppose I shall ever have a chance to lie in a crane again."

"But why on earth—"

"My aunt, General Sidebotham, was campaigning once on the slopes of Mount Ida when Jupiter appeared to her, disguised as a crane. The bird, I mean, not the machinery. He was always appearing as something odd—bulls, or swans, or showers of gold. Anyhow, he picked up my aunt in his beak (which proved he was a god, by the way, because no ordinary bird would have had a hope with her) and carried her off to Olympus, where, I believe, she laid an egg."

"And for which deity are we indebted to your aunt, Pet?"

"Oh, for none of them; it didn't hatch. But anyhow, we were so proud of Auntie that cranes became an absolute mania in our family."

Andrew powdered the aspirin and gave it to her. "Now you just sleep it off, and don't worry about nasty cranes, and I'll go and enquire after Bubbles. Hilary's a fine braw piece, isn't she? I might deceive you with Hilary."

"No use. She's in love with a local young man. Why not deceive me with Bubbles?"

"Not now. I might have thought about it before you glorified her like a Ziegfeld girl. I like natural women."

"I'm sure you do," Agnes said dreamily, reaching for her

lipstick. Reassured by this certain sign of recovery, he left her and went downstairs.

"Supper!" said Hilary, who by this time had recovered sprightliness. "Only salmon fishcakes, but thank your stars you can get 'em. Agnes feel like eating?"

"Oh, surely. I'll take a tray up. Bubbles O.K.?"

"Marvellous. Doctor Sigourney's just left, and he says he's absolutely flabbergasted. It would have killed ninety-nine women in a hundred. Come on, Andrew, and I'll fix up the tray. We've got one policeman in the kitchen, one at the front and one at the back, and I must admit it's a darn' fine feeling."

As they sat down to their meal Andrew said, "Agnes has got some mad idea of dashing back to town Tuesday morning to take part in an A.R.P. practice. She wants to be a casualty."

"Great John Scott, what a hoot! Of course you won't let her?"

"Of course I can't stop her. No. She's made up her mind. So can you bear with us one more day and tomorrow night?"

"Pleasure. Wish it were longer. I say, have they arrested Lang?"

"No. I saw Corcoran for a moment just before tea; he came round with a message from my cousin that I was to take Agnes home as soon as she could put one foot before another; and he said they'd no evidence on which to hold him."

"Could he have attacked Agnes this morning?"

"It seems possible."

"Then what do they want evidence for? Red tape, that's what's wrong with this country," Hilary snorted as she helped herself to tinned apricots.

After supper Lord Whitestone arrived, smooth, conciliatory. He accepted sherry from Miss Burton and looked at her with approval. He really did admire natural women. He sipped his drink, turned a sour grimace into a smile and tucked the glass tidily away behind a pottery group representing an old balloon-seller beaming upon three Dickensian children.

"Now, Miss Burton, I hope you'll use your influence with Mr. Kinghof to persuade him to send his wife back to town."

"Why," said Andrew merrily, "should you even think I need persuading after that very courteous and prettily worded note you sent me by Corcoran?"

Pig had the grace to look ashamed. "Oh, well, you know how it is when there's a rush on. Frankly, Andrew, I thought the moment after I'd sealed it that it would be enough to make you buy a cottage and settle Agnes down here for life."

Andrew crossed his legs, put his fingers tip to tip, in the manner of Sherlock Holmes represented by Sidney Paget, and observed that he would be generous. "She's going home on Tuesday morning, because she's got a date as casualty in an A.R.P. practice. I tell her she ought to join up in some form of national service soon. What do you think of the A.F.S., Pig? For Agnes, I mean."

Pig spluttered. "Now listen; if your wife got within a mile of a fire she'd manage to spread it. Put her in a Rest Centre, or a canteen, or anywhere reasonably quiet, but don't add to your country's defence problems."

"I'm joining the Women's Land Army," said Hilary. "Why not get her to join up at the same time I do? Fresh air's what she wants, and a good crowd of pals."

"I could ask her," Andrew agreed politely; "certainly I could ask her," and Pig choked on his cigarette.

The next visitor, surprisingly, was Felix Lang, who walked in, nodded to Pig as if he had been a commissionaire, and said to Hilary, "How is she?—All right, don't glare at me. If you were right, I'd be in clink with gyves upon my wrists. Hullo, Kinghof. Perhaps you'll tell me how she is?"

"O.K.," said Andrew, "and—"

"And mend your manners, Lang," Pig snapped.

"Look here, sir, my probable murders are the business of the police: my manners are not. Miss Burton, does she know that I—I got her out? She might as well know something decent about me."

"Yes, she knows," Hilary told him, grim-lipped, bestriding the narrow carpet like a Colossus in jodhpurs.

He smiled suddenly and his face shone. "Then perhaps she'd see me for a few minutes! And there's no point in scowling like that, Miss Burton, since you're likely to be '*in loco* sister-in-law' one of these days."

She gasped. "You mean—"

"I'm going to marry your best friend."

She shot at him, "And get the money that way!"

Lang advanced towards her. "Be quiet, you large hoyden! Hold your tongue!"

Pig arose majestic. "Lang, control yourself, please, and leave here at once."

"I'm sorry, sir. Mr. Kinghof, you're not such a—a thumping ass as everyone else, are you? Make them ask Miss Ashton if she'll see me."

There was silence in the room, broken only by the crackling of the logs in the hearth. Then Andrew said: "You know, we could but ask her. I don't believe it would hurt."

Hilary looked at Pig.

"All right, Miss Burton, go ahead."

She stumped off, grumbling, down the passage and said, returning, "She'll see you for a minute. I'm coming, too."

"Must you? I'd rather have Kinghof."

"That will do, Lang," said Pig.

When Hilary had taken the student to Bubbles' room, Andrew murmured: "It's wiser to let him, isn't it?"

"Can't do any harm. Be interesting to see how she feels about it."

After some ten minutes they heard the door open, and Hilary's gruff voice calling: "O.K., Millais, guest's got to go now. Come on, Mr. Lang, quickee-quickee." Then Bubbles' voice following, an eager voice rather plaintive: "It was nice of you to come… owe a lot to you, more than I can repay."

Then Lang came into the lounge, nodded briefly to Andrew and Pig, and marched out of the house.

Hilary appeared then, flung herself into a chair and glowered at the fire. "She's fallen for him. Isn't it crazy? Looking at him as if he were Robert Taylor, not that she can endure Robert Taylor, but looking at him as she would look if she could endure him."

"Miss Burton," Pig said, "please tell us what happened in there."

"Oh, not so much. He went in and gaped at her, and she smiled, and then he said, 'What's your name beside Bubbles?' and she said, 'Joan.' So then he sat on the bed, by her, and said, 'I hope you're better, Joan.' Then she thanked him—heaven starve the crows, I could have killed him where he sat!—for saving her, and he said, 'I wish you'd call me Felix, although it's a silly name.' She said, 'Can't you shorten it?' and he answered, 'Well, you can't call me Fee or Licks. I used to be called Fix at school sometimes.' Then he asked her again if she was all right, and she said she was, and he told her he had meant to go back to town that night, but couldn't leave till he knew how she was. 'I'll be back soon,' he said, 'and please eat, drink and take your bath with policemen till I'm here to take care of you.' Then I broke the party up, and about time too."

Pig said, "Thank you; that was very well remembered. Well, I give you my word that Corcoran will see Lang on to the first London train tomorrow, and that I shall keep two men on guard at Setters, day and night, until this business is cleared up. Well, I must go now. Got to drive back tonight. Agnes must go back definitely on Tuesday, Andrew."

"I'll see she does. Good night, Herbert."

"Good night. Thank you for your hospitality, Miss Burton, and don't worry."

Andrew, who had escorted his cousin to the car, said—"I say, don't you want to see Agnes?"

"She's in bed, isn't she?"

"Not asleep, though."

"Oh, I don't think I'll go up," said Pig, blushing faintly. For a policeman, he was a modest man.

———

Next morning, the local inspector watched Felix Lang depart for London on the noon train. There had been a train much earlier, carrying business people back to town, but this departure had not been watched by the police. There had seemed no need. Nevertheless, one of the passengers might have been of some interest.

Monday passed uneventfully; Agnes was quite well enough to spend the afternoon with Andrew in a Warwick picture-house, and the evening with him and Hilary in

Bubbles' bedroom, into which they had brought the wireless and some good Irish whisky. Bubbles, induced to believe that the latter was good for her, became very gay, tempting Hilary also to a glass. Hilary became not gay but wistful, and she listened with something approaching eagerness to Agnes's advocacy of a good Rachel foundation lotion and a Hunting Pink lipstick for country usage.

"What's so remarkable about Bubbles," Andrew said, as he lay in bed that night with his wife, "is how little the horrific aspect of her adventure has upset her. It would have given me a complex. She's a superwoman in her way, and I hope she joins the Army."

"Shall I join it?" asked Agnes. "I think I'd rather be a Wren."

"You think carefully before you take any rash step," he warned her, "there's no flaming hurry for you to decide." And at that time, the period of "sitzkrieg", there was not.

On Tuesday, at the bleak hour of eight o'clock on a morning of khaki fog, he saw her off at the station before going on to the O.C.T.U.

"Promise me, darling, not to do anything silly, and don't fall out of the crane. Can't you be as good a casualty on a packing-case?"

"No, darling. But I will be careful. Oh, Andrew, I'm so fond of you! And it always makes me happy to think you're not one of those men whose ears stick out."

"You," he replied generously, for it might be a long time before he saw her again, "are beautiful. Don't listen to people who say you're not. I say you are, and I know."

"And you," she said, seeking to repay him with equal generosity, "are clever."

He was not so pleased.

She waved until his long form was lost in the wreathing fogs.

She arrived back at Stewarts Court at a quarter to one and on the stairs met Mrs. Rowse, who was just going out.

"Oh, Mrs. Kinghof, I'm so glad to see you! I only got back yesterday from a week-end with a friend in the country, and the police have been asking me questions—where I went, who I was with! *Has* anything dreadful happened?"

"Who were you with?" Agnes enquired with interest.

"An old friend who lives in Leamington. Do tell me, what—"

Agnes gave her a brief account of the week-end's excitement.

Mrs. Rowse stared at her, eyes bulging. "Oh, how shocking! Miss Ashton, and then you too, poor, brave Mrs. Kinghof. Truth is stranger than fiction, say what you will. When I wrote my last chapter, where Fernia Prideaux saved the Prime Minister's life and became a Dame of the British Empire on her seventeenth birthday I thought, Is that too far-fetched? Will my public accept it? But now I know that it would be impossible for my poor imagination to compete with the marvellous invention of life. So I shall proceed with confidence to Chapter the Last, where Dame Fernia unmasks Miss Herring, the geography mistress, as a Nazi spy by the name of Hermann Uberflung—"

"Lovely," said Agnes dimly and went slowly upstairs, not pausing even to admire the incredibly hideous new turban belonging to Madame Charnet, who was polishing her door-knob, or to wonder what Mr. Warrender had been doing in the upper reaches of the flats, from whence he was now in retreat.

Chapter Sixteen

AGNES, WHO DEPRECATED THE WEARING OF SLACKS BY women of all figures, thought it as well to abandon her principles temporarily when it came to lying in a crane; so at two o'clock she set out, in cherry corduroys, brown sweater and camelhair coat, to Tegman's wharf, where she found Clem Poplett trying to give some seventeen or eighteen small boys an idea of their duties.

"Gor', it's nice of you to turn up, Mrs. Kinghof. These kids are all very well, but they do lark about so, and you never know whether they'll stay where you put 'em. Wouldn't like to give me a hand with these labels, would you?"

"Of course I will. Hand them over." She was instantly mobbed by the perky, bright-eyed children who lived around the powerhouse. They swung on her shoulders, played touch round her legs, breathed down her neck and were vociferous in demanding the most gruesome injuries.

"Eh, miss! I don't want no broken leg. That's for girls. I want a compound fraction!"

"'Ere, I 'ad a severed art'ry last time."

"'Ooray! I've broke me ribs."

Patiently she attached the labels, bearing details of injury, to buttons and buttonholes, and she whispered soberly to Clem, "This is what gets me, the beastliness behind it all. To think those kids might one day...bear out those tickets."

"Still, they're 'appy," he replied. "Let 'em 'ave fun while it lasts, even if it's pretty mucky fun."

Her attention was diverted by the sight of a large gloomy man arrayed in a white coat and wearing a steel helmet over which was draped some pale-blue butter-muslin. "Mr. Poplett! Who's the gentleman in the pretty hat?"

"Incident Officer. He's chief one on the spot."

"I see. Can I get in the crane now?"

He regarded her anxiously. "Look, that's no place for a lady, that ain't. You'll 'ave an awful job getting up there, and it's all dirty. Spoil your nice trousers."

"I've put them on to be spoiled. It's all right, I've made up my mind. Crane for me."

"Well, what part are you going on? Up the top, where they work it?"

"Well, no. I'm going to hitch myself into the bucket-thing. It'll be quite comfortable."

"That you're not, ma'am, not if I know it. It's all full of muck, and gawd knows 'ow the Rescue Party would ever get you out."

"But isn't that just why we're practising? Besides, how do you know that some day someone mightn't be blown into the bucket?"

Clem's Post Warden, a tall young man of classic features and shining red hair, who looked like the Discobolus, came through the gateway into the wharf. "Anything wrong?"

"Mr. Carton, sir, Mrs. Kinghof wants to go in the bucket."

"What bucket?"

"The one on the crane. I tell 'er it's not a nice place for 'er to go, all mucky like it is, and besides, you couldn't get blown up there."

Mr. Carton knew the Kinghofs well. "I'm afraid Clem's right. Look here, Mrs. Kinghof, there's a perfectly beautiful rubbish-tip that would make a marvellous hide-out for you. And it's a good place to be rescued from."

"I don't doubt it. That's why I prefer the crane."

The Post Warden led her aside. "No crane."

"No? But suppose someone did get blown—"

"That counts among War Risks. No, the main reason I won't let you go in the bucket is that the foreman down here says we're not to touch the crane because they'll be working it. It spoils the illusion of reality, but there you are."

"Jim Carton," said Agnes sternly, "you are more impressive in that get-up than you are in the 'Green Doe' on Sunday mornings telling Andrew and me frightfully obscure stories that sound dirty and turn out frightfully clean: but you'll have to do better than that rubbish-tip. You've disappointed me bitterly about the crane. Now you can just damn' well find me a decent substitute."

"The exercise is due to begin in five minutes. Mrs. Kinghof, you are a saboteur. Or Teuse."

"And you'll need practice in dealing with them, too. Go on. Suggest."

Most of the children were already disposed artistically on iron dumps, woodpiles, ladders, and roofs. Mr. Carton looked around, narrowing his eyes against the sun that had burst through the fogs of the earlier day. "Here you are." He led her to a shed, up the side of which was a ladder. Around the shed were chalk-marks, but these Agnes did not notice.

"You go up there and you'll have a good view of the game. Will it do?"

"Just about. Oh, all right, Mr. Carton; but I'll give your best stories the horse-laugh for the next six months." She climbed up yet another ladder, thinking that her life had been set recently in Freudian ways, and the Post Warden went grinning to report to Mr. Poplett that Mrs. Kinghof would have a thin time, as she was lying in the middle of the supposed crater and would therefore be presumed, by any intelligent reporting warden, to be not only dead but most probably invisible. "So no one, I fear, will bother to collect the lady."

Clem said, "Hard lines! And she was dead set on that crane. Don't you think we ought to get her off there and put her some place where at least she'd get a nice ride in the ambulance? Doesn't seem quite fair."

"Mrs. Kinghof," said Carton happily, "will thereby learn the useful lesson not to be obstructive." He strolled off leaving Mr. Poplett, who was also acting as casualty, to choose his own pitch.

Agnes decided that, having a broken jaw, she would neither speak nor open her eyes while the exercise was under way. Below her, the waiting children shouted, laughed, and boasted their injuries, and she had to quell the uprush of depression that took her when she considered a world that had made such ghoulish fun a commonplace.

The shed roof was dirtier than she had expected and she sighed for her camelhair coat; then, reflecting that she would have been worse off on the rubbish-tip, she achieved a degree of comfort. After what seemed an interminable wait, the exercise began.

Through the gates two wardens came running, wardens

in gas-masks and protective clothing. "Lumme," one of the boys shrieked, "we're supposed to be gassed!" and all put on their own masks with admirable promptitude save three who were warned sternly by their comrades that as they had, respectively, right arm broken, ribs broken, and fingers crushed, they would be unable to perform such an operation and must therefore lie where they were.

Agnes was interested and impressed by the efficiency of the men, one of whom made rapid notes while the other put gas-masks on the three children exposed to danger, then ran to make a closer survey of the wharf. She heard them checking the report: "Air Raid Damage, Tegman's Wharf. Bombs, H.E., Gas, phosgene. No fire. No mains"—which last she thought unlikely—"twenty casualties." She was rather surprised that no one came to put a mask on her, nor to inspect her injuries at close range, but she reflected that Rome was not built in a day.

Then one warden ran off to send in his report, and the other prowled around making the giggling children as comfortable as possible.

The Rescue Party was first on the scene. An R.S.D. lorry drove through the gates, and wardens could be heard parking other vehicles in the street outside. Time, she thought, to act my part: so she closed her eyes and waited.

It would have surprised Jim Carton had he known how rapidly help came to her. Agnes felt herself gently handled, she blinked up once into the snout of a gas-mask, and then put her trust in the two men who seemed to be tying her to a board. The next thing she knew was that she was lowered gently over the side of the shed, untrussed, and transferred to a stretcher. Then she felt herself swaying in smooth, sickening fashion over the ground. In a few moments she came softly to rest, and was surprised to hear squeaks of laughter, delighted comment.

"I say, Les, look at the lady's pants!"

"Coo! Eh, missus! Where did you get them trousers?"

"What's wrong with 'er? She dun' 'alf look a treat."

"Wotcher, me old cock robin!"

Opening her eyes, she found herself laid on the ground outside the gates, surrounded by a crowd of pleased juvenile spectators. She was one of a long file of stretchered casualties, and she hoped the ambulance would not be long. I am extremely glad, she thought, that Andrew cannot see me now.

"Hey! Oh, you, miss. You, Farver Christmas. Give you fourpence for them red pants."

"Go away, you rude little boy," said Agnes.

"Wotjer talking for? You've bust your jaw."

"I'll bust yours if you don't stop kicking my shins," she countered simply.

A warden who was passing drove her tormentors away. Clem Poplett, the next casualty to be borne out, recognized the cherry slacks and thought, I'm glad they got her out after all, though it spoils old Carton's lark.

Agnes had, in fact, been removed in error; but the driver of an ambulance car, an ordinary four-seater saloon, chose her quite deliberately from the waiting list against the wall.

"Here, Spiggot! Put that one in here, will you? Lady in the red pants."

She felt herself lifted and shoved lovingly into the back seat of a car, which drove away at once. Relieved, she sat up and called to the masked driver, "Thank God that's over. I needn't go on playing now, need I? Mind if I smoke?"

The muffled voice replied. "Sorry, miss, exercise won't be over for you till I get you to hospital."

"All right. Where are we going?"

"What's your injury?"

"Jaw."

"Very well, then, you mustn't talk."

"Oh, flumdiddle," said Agnes rather crossly, feeling she had endured enough; but she held her peace and relaxed, closing her eyes in fulfilment of her role. It seemed a surprisingly long drive. At last the car stopped and the driver got out, raked for her and picked her up bodily. "Don't you," she said, lying over his shoulder, "have people to do that for you? It seems very inefficient. And I must be a frightful weight, because you're not a big chap."

"You can't talk, miss. Remember that."

So she jolted and swayed in silence, feeling the cold air on her face, wondering when she would smell the hospital odour of rubber, radiators, and iodoform.

Suddenly she was slumped so roughly on to rough ground that she cried out in protest, and opened her eyes. She gazed about her. She was in the rank, sour-smelling yard of an empty house, sprawled on the gravel between a stack of rotten timbering and a scrap-heap of rusty corrugated-iron roofing. The driver squatted before her, and even as she asked her angry question, whipped off his mask.

"You!"

"Me," said Mr. Warrender, "and if you're wise you'll shut up while I'm talking. If you don't, I may have to quieten you." He showed her a length of rubber tubing.

"Why the hell are you playing at wardens?"

"Because I am a warden, or a driver, to be precise, and I'm taking legitimate part in the exercise. Got half a day off to do it. When I've finished with you I'm going to pick up another body from the wharf and take it to hospital. Real hospital."

"You very nasty piece of work!" said Agnes slowly. She felt, to her surprise, not scared but very, very angry. Her temper had not been sweetened by early references to her trousers. "Where are we?"

"In the dump-yard of an empty house in Cross Street, if you want to know. We've done exercises here, and I know it's quiet. Now listen—"

"You don't suppose I'm going to keep quiet about this?"

"Who's going to believe you? It'll sound a silly story. Now you listen to me, and if you're good I'll let you go home. I saw you at the barn last Friday night."

She replied coolly, "Did you? And a fine fool you looked in that idiotic cape. And a fine fool you're making of yourself now, with your kidnapping idiocies."

"That's brave talk, Mrs. Kinghof; you hear a lot of it from democratic statesmen these days."

"Suppose I scream now?"

"You won't be heard. If you were, they'd only think it's the children who play here sometimes. And long before you'd finished screaming I'd give you this." He held up the tubing. "Listen to me. Did you tell the police about last Friday?"

"Yes."

He flushed. "Are you lying?"

"You do seem a stupid man. Why should I lie?"

"They haven't been on to me."

"For what?" She was crafty.

"Illegal political activities, maybe…"

"I suppose they think you're too stupid to matter."

"You are lying. They would have arrested me. Tell me the truth!"

She thought rapidly. "All right, I haven't told them."

"Why not?"

"I was afraid to."

"Why should you be afraid?"

"I don't know…but I was. Don't you believe me? If I had told the police, wouldn't they have raked you in?"

He glared at her. "You're not lying now?"

"No," said Agnes and, because she was an honest woman, crossed her fingers.

He sat back on his heels and seemed to consider.

She remarked, "The A.R.P. people are going to ask questions if you're away so long."

Suddenly he rose to his feet. He looked sick and bewildered, and there was an ugly yellow tinge in his cheeks. "Mrs. Kinghof, I'm going to throw myself on your mercy."

"It's no good your doing anything of the kind till you give me that bit of tubing."

He handed it over. Agnes, who felt suddenly that had he failed to do so her self-control would have broken down, drew a long breath of relief.

"I've been a fool. I don't know what good I thought I'd do hauling you off like this, except that I was worried. Mrs. Kinghof, don't tell the police about—Friday. I'm not really in touch with these people. I was once, but since war broke out they've made me sick. I'm a patriot, Mrs. Kinghof. I only go there because they've threatened me with exposure if I don't stick to them, and I can't face being dismissed the Service. Besides, if I do tag along with them I might learn things that would help my country—"

"Which country?"

"England," he said, and his face was unpleasant to look upon.

"So you'd turn King's Evidence?"

It was crazy this conversation, this bleak yard, in the heart of a busy district, yet lonely as a desert, the rotting iron and timber, the dull red sun, the man's pale face, the length of tubing in her hand.

"For England I would."

It seemed to her essential to terminate the interview at all costs. The excitements and shocks of the last few days were telling on her, and she felt she could endure no more. She said disgustedly: "Take me to the hospital and dump me there, and for heaven's sake let's hope they don't ask you where you've been all this time."

"You aren't going to tell?"

"No, you ridiculous little swine."

"You swear?"

"Oh, let me out of here. I swear. What a contemptible thing you are!"

He bowed slightly, once more the quiet and Civil Servant of the Circumlocution Office, as we have chosen to call that essential ministry, and pushed her before him, out of the yard, across the pavement and into the car. He drove in silence to the hospital and waited while two men came to carry her inside. He turned, and his eyes flickered. "Contemptible?" he said.

The door opened. Agnes was hauled out, her ticket was inspected and she was borne into the warmth of the building. When she got inside, to her surprise and horror, she fainted.

Kindlily they revived her, made her rest for a while, gave her tea and a cake, and found an idle driver who was pleased to take her home.

Alone in her flat, she tried to sort out the curious events of the day. She had promised Warrender not to reveal the secret she had revealed already, nor to expose the madness of the kidnapping. Oddly enough, she was troubled by conscience and, because she had lied to him in one respect, was eager to play fair in the other. How would the silly story help Eggshell? It did nothing to connect Warrender with the murder of Mrs. Sibley. And perhaps the fool had been telling the truth and was innocent of all save his connection with a rather childishly "subversive" political body. And yet, why this fear of the police? The Free British Mussolites, so far as she knew, were on no list of banned organizations. She felt thoroughly tired and muddled, and she longed for Andrew's advice. She was just preparing to go to the "Green Doe" for a lonely drink when there was a knock on the door. She opened it to Mr. Warrender.

"Oh, I say, Mrs. Kinghof, they didn't deliver my *Evening Standard* to you by mistake?"

She was flabbergasted. Mild, correct in his black suit and striped trousers, she could hardly believe he was the violent, excited man of the afternoon.

"You—you dare!"

"I beg your pardon? I don't understand."

"How dare you come here, after this afternoon—"

"Why, Mrs. Kinghof? I only took you to hospital. Nothing odd about that."

"You—you—"

"You haven't got my *Standard*? I'm so sorry I troubled you." He turned and went smartly off downstairs, and as he reached the stair-head of the flight below looked swiftly up at her; in that second he was not contemptible, but frightening.

Agnes, her heart beating, backed into Number 8 and, absurdly, double-bolted the door. What should she do? Twice she put out her hand to the telephone, meaning to call Eggshell; twice withdrew it. Panicked, she thought, I'm besieged here. I shan't dare go out. If it is him, he'll finish me somehow. The voice of common sense, that sounded surprisingly like the voice of Andrew, said: "Don't be a fool, my girl. A word to Eggshell and you can have a police convoy to the 'Doe' and back again, and a policeman sitting in the hall all night." But somehow she dared not move. She felt exhausted, incapable of thought and action.

For comfort she lingered in the window that she might watch the people in the streets, ordinary people with no obscene menace hanging over them; and soon she saw Warrender leave the flats and go briskly off down the road.

Craving for a drink overcame her fears. She slipped out of the flat, ran to the "Green Doe" as if the Hound of the Baskervilles were after her, and had three nips of Dunville's whisky. She felt braver when she returned to Number 8, and this was as well; as just outside the door her foot slid on something greasy, and she would have fallen had she not gripped the handle. It was a small, disgusting piece of pig's flesh.

This, thought Agnes, is the end. She rushed inside, bolted herself in, put up the chain and made for the telephone.

She waited, while jiggling noises assaulted her ears. She dialled 0.

"Operator! This is Carlyle 01706. Will you get me Carlyle 68410?"

A long silence, and more jiggling. "Trying to connect you. Hold on."

Jiggle. Jiggle. Jiggle. "Sorry. Line's out of order."

"But it can't be! It's—"

"Line's out of order."

Agnes, in despair, hung up the receiver. "But it's

disgusting!" she said aloud, afraid almost of the sound of her own voice. "A police-station has no right to have its line out of order!" It was not until days later that she realized that, in her agitation, she had asked for Carlyle 68410 instead of Carlyle 64810.

It was a nightmare evening. She had no heart for the wireless, no concentration for the book she was trying to read. She went to bed early, took a bromide and tried to sleep, but it was not until half-past twelve that sleep came to her.

She was aroused from a thick dream by a persistent tapping on the window.

Awake at once, she sat up in bed, her heart pounding like a drum, and stared at the black-out curtains. Three floors up. Was he clinging to the rainpipe, there in the dark and windy night, his pig's snout tapping the pane?

Too numbed by fear to move, she listened to the insistent knocking. She mumbled to herself. "What would Andrew do? He'd get up, get something heavy, open the window and sock it hard... Don't be a coward. Do you want to be a coward, Agnes? Something heavy."

Seizing the moment of resolution, she leaped out of bed and fled into the kitchen, where she pulled the rolling-pin out of the drawer. With this pantomime weapon she returned to the bedroom, and then, summoning the last dregs of her courage, whipped the curtains apart.

He was there, one knee on the sill, the other leg curled about the pipe, his face furious in the meagre light of a torch.

Agnes pushed up the sash.

"Damn you, girl!" said Andrew, jumping down into the room, "can't you hear a bell?"

Chapter Seventeen

"Why all the locks, bolts and bars?" he added. "Couldn't get in with my key, so I rang like a maniac, and then I thought, Well, I'd done some climbing before, so why not again? I tried the door of Number 6, below us, hoping Blake might have left it open, which he had, and I hoiked myself up the pipe from there—"

He spent the next fifteen minutes bringing his wife round from a fit of lusty hysterics.

When she had recovered she asked weakly, "Oh, darling, what are you doing home again? I do hope they haven't cashiered you or anything," and being deluded by her recent shocks into believing that this might, indeed, be the case, she burst into tears.

"Don't be an ass, Agnes!" He gave her a handkerchief. "Here, blow." She blew. "No, I haven't been cashiered—which would be a long process anyway and couldn't be managed in the few hours since I last saw you—and I haven't deserted. What's happened is that I was supposed to take charge of a new draft of cadets, but they won't be arriving till

Friday—some muddle of some sort. There was damn all for me to do, and no one seemed to mind me taking a holiday till I was wanted. I've got to go back Thursday night. Now tell me what's been happening to you, and for Great John Scott's sake, stop sniffling!"

She gave him an account of her day's adventures, lucidly and attractively presented. When she had done, she began to feel better, and not a little proud of herself, so she asked her husband tentatively if he did not think she had behaved well. He gave her a long, dark look charged with all manner of mingled emotions and said damningly: "So far as I can see, you behaved just like Fernia Prideaux."

Feebly she countered, "But surely it takes a Fernia to cope with a Fernia situation?"

"She never does cope. That sort of girl is helped out of messes, not by her own efforts, but by the God in the Machine. I can't conceive anything sillier than your conduct throughout. A. When you were in that yard, why didn't you yell like stink? No matter what Warrender says, it was a 99 to 1 chance that you'd have been heard. B. When you were at the hospital, why didn't you make a complaint there, or go straight to the police-station on your way back? C. If the line was out of order, which I doubt, why didn't you dash out into the street and hare round to Eggshell at once?" He softened, seeing her woebegone face. "My poor, poor darling, your legs are wonderful but your brains are pitiful. Now go back to bed and wait for me while I cook up a fried-egg sandwich. You can go to sleep if you like, and I"—he added in a burst of generosity—"I won't even wake you!"

She did, and he didn't.

———

The next morning he took her round to see Eggshell, who, on rising to greet them, said dryly to Andrew, "Army doesn't seem to be so busy these days, sir. What brings you?"

Andrew sat down, eyed the Inspector stonily and said, "I am a ratepayer. One of the reasons I pay rates is that my wife shall not be struck on the head by a rubber cosh, abducted in broad daylight in the middle of A.R.P. exercises, and made to slip on pieces of cold pork outside her own front door. I take a poor view of the police. As a citizen, with home and hearth to protect, I demand that you round up all the lunatics in Block 3, with the possible exception of Mrs. Rowse and that frequenter of obscene cinemas, at the earliest possible moment."

"All, sir? You don't leave many."

"Well, stick those two in jail! If I were writing a letter about this to the papers, I should sign myself 'Disgusted.'" Andrew briefly related the tale of his wife's adventures, concluding with a hope that the entire London constabulary would die of a surfeit of pork before the year was out, and waited for this to sink in.

"Quite right," said Agnes, settling her furs and giving emphatic tilt to a hat made of one three-inch circle of felt, one bow of candy-striped ribbon, an eye-veil and half a yard of elastic.

Eggshell sighed deeply, lowering his eyes in acceptance of rebuke. The air was heavy in the little room with its barred window, its walls of lavatory green, and its hammy carpet. Then he sat up, glared, and struck the table.

"Captain Kinghof! I should be glad if you'd let us do things in our own way."

"So that you can festoon the neighbourhood with bodies and let maniac pigs run loose in every front garden."

"Now listen, sir, and hold your horses."

"I want you to hold your pigs."

The tension tightened in the room. At last Eggshell made a grimace, and relaxed in his chair. "All right, sir. Give me a few minutes of your time and I'll explain, though I've no call to, what our game is. First, Warrender. We may be fools, sir, but we aren't idle. We've found out a great deal about the Free British Mussolites and Lord Whitestone has arranged for a watch to be kept on Warrender, especially when he's at work."

"I wish you'd been watching him yesterday," said Agnes stiffly.

"Yes, ma'am. I regret that. We knew he was going to the exercises, and thought he'd be all right there. However. To continue: We have definite information that Stevens, the leader of the Coldersbrook Group, is an enemy agent, and instructions have come from Scotland Yard for his arrest. We intercepted correspondence from him—it was posted from Coldersbrook on Sunday night—written in a code that could have been read by a one-eyed ninny. It fixed a F.B.M. meeting for tonight, seven o'clock, at a private house in the Coldersbrook district. We're going to look into that, now, so we can't alarm Warrender yet awhile."

"Did you find out where he spent the week-end?"

"No. No lead on that. He was back here on Monday night, and we learn that he did turn up at the office at his regular time—ten to ten that morning. As for the others, we know what happened to Lang, and Madame Charnet didn't go out. Didn't move out all the week-end, or at any rate, not up to Sunday midday, when I took my man off the flats. We don't yet know where Mrs. Rowse was."

"I do," said Agnes, "she was staying with friends at Leamington."

"Leamington?" Eggshell's brows shot up. "Not far from Warwick."

"Look here, the old lady was out when Mrs. Sibley had the Punch-and-Judy shock, and in the bungalow when she was murdered."

"We've only her word for the latter," Andrew interpolated, looking excited.

Eggshell said, "We'll check up on the Leamington friends. Now then, to continue once more: We can't hold Felix Lang because we've nothing against him but a set of funny circumstances. Also, take a look at this." He routed through a file, and after a moment handed to them a cutting from the *Daily Recorder*, of yesterday's date. "What do you make of that?"...

Andrew read it, and passed it to Agnes, who mumbled aloud, "'It is announced that the marriage between the Honourable Roderick Furnivall, younger son of Lord Sheepcote, and Miss Kathleen Smith will not take place.' I don't make anything of it."

Andrew shrugged. "Nor I. Do you, Eggshell?"

"Well, sir, it's early to say. Seems interesting, though."

"It refers to Lang's reluctant young lady?"

"Yes, sir."

"Well?"

"Nice to have on record," Eggshell said vaguely, and returned it to his papers. He rose. "Well, Mr. Kinghof, Mrs. Kinghof, I hope you'll trust us a little longer. Things are moving, and we hope to make an arrest soon."

"If only you'll make it," said Andrew, tamed by the Inspector's kindness, "before I go back on Friday, I'll forgive you all. Will you forgive him all, Agnes?"

"All," she replied fervently, "every little bit. In the meantime, can we have a policeman in the hall?"

"You certainly can, Mrs. Kinghof. Good morning."

"Bless you. Good morning."

———

That afternoon Eggshell and Frankson drove down to Coldersbrook, where they met, as arranged, the local Inspector, who was called MacAbbott.

"We knew there was a branch of the mob round here," said the latter, "but we haven't been able to get anything on them. They cover their tracks pretty well and keep in touch with their members, as a rule, by personal contact only. I should think something pretty urgent was up, to make them risk correspondence. Anyhow, if they're no better at sabotage than they are at codes they won't be any great danger to the country. Stevens, so far as we can tell, is the only one in actual communication with the Nazis."

"Wonder why they aren't holding their meeting at the usual place?"

MacAbbott flushed. "Well, I hate to confess it, but it's probably through a blunder by one of my men, a youngster who hasn't found his feet yet. We set him to watch the barn, and according to his story he let them catch sight of him, when they left rather earlier than he expected from one of their meetings. Good thing for us it happened, though, because at least we know who another of them is, besides Stevens and Warrender. The meeting's being held in the house of a Mrs. Cottenham, well known round here. A real fly bit, I tell you, though she was only widowed a year ago when her husband, commercial traveller, was killed in a road accident. Everyone knows her, because she's to the forefront of all the local charities. Very patriotic, she is. You know her house, because she's got a Union Jack on the flagpole in the front garden. She was going to stand for Parliament as an Independent Conservative, whatever that may mean, but when war broke out she cut away from politics and put a statement in the local rag that she would withdraw her candidature in the name of national unity. I was surprised, because we had a by-election shortly afterwards, and I thought she'd rather choke than miss showing off on public platforms."

Eggshell nodded, in token that he had digested this information. "Well, what's the procedure? You know the lie of the land better than I do."

MacAbbott said, "Mrs. Cottenham's got a small place, single-fronted, semi-detached, with parlour downstairs and kitchen at the back, two small bedrooms and bath upstairs. A garage has been built on to the house, which means that the side parlour window gives in to it. My idea is that you, your constable, and Grigson here secrete yourselves in the garage and listen-in to the meeting. I know you can hear all right, because Grigson's brother, who's a motor-mechanic, was in there one day tinkering with Mrs. C.'s two-seater, and he says he heard every word she was saying to a visitor she'd got in the front room with her."

"Yes, and probably she'll know that too, so most likely she'll hold the meeting in the bedroom."

"I am banking," said MacAbbott simply, "on my belief that asses big enough to send a code like that would be asses in other ways. We'll give them time to get started, and then you can sneak into the garage under cover of the hedge. It's never locked now, since she put the car up for the winter. It'll be risky, but it can be done."

"It can be tried," said Eggshell, "but I don't fancy it."

"I'll be across the way with two of my men, and we'll raid when we get your signal."

They set out. Mrs. Cottenham's house was the last of a row of mean, elaborate villas disagreeably blotched with fake half-timbering and unexpected gables. To the right of the door was the garage, and beyond that, separated from the house and front garden by a high ragged hedge, was a strip of vacant land on which stood a notice-board describing it as an attractive site for building. Facing the row of houses was Coldersbrook Common, a square half-mile of rough grass adorned by furze bushes and unnecessary iron railings over which latter, presumably, it was hoped that strangers might tumble in the dark and break both legs. It was a clouded night; even Eggshell, whose eyes were sharp as a cat's, could do no more than make out the shape of Number 16, Greenlands Grove, which was the highly suspect home of Mrs. Cottenham.

The policemen found an excellent cache behind a mass of furze, and MacAbbott, looking at his watch, announced that it was seven-ten. He grinned his satisfaction. "Knew I was right, Eggshell; meeting's in the front room, just as I said. I can just see the glow round the edge of the black-outs. Better be going, hadn't you? We'll wait here. When you want us, flash your torch 'C' in Morse—umpty iddy, umpty iddy."

"Right. Frankson, be ready to come with me. You too, Grigson."

The three men crossed the road softly, glanced about to see that all was clear, and advanced velvet-footed in the shadow of the hedge up the path and into the garage.

"We're in luck, sir," Grigson breathed, as he moved cautiously in the dark, "they haven't quite closed their curtains. You can see through the middle chink."

Eggshell whispered, "You and Frankson get right to the back. I'll watch here."

They obeyed him, and for a moment his heart was in his mouth when Frankson, banging his knee against a derelict iron bedstead stacked up against the wall, incautiously swore. Eggshell listened, but all was quiet. And there was no sound from the room beyond.

Crouching, he put his eye to the gap between the curtains; and almost fell over backwards with surprise.

He had thought the room would be empty, that the members had not arrived, or that the meeting was indeed being held in some other part of the house. He saw a room full of people, all silent, all, save one, standing. Wearing their capes, they were ranged about the table, a blond man, obviously the leader, at the head, a black-haired woman on his right, a disdainful-looking boy and an elderly, broken-nosed man on his left, a pimply, red-haired youth facing him from the far end. No sign of Warrender.

But the thing that most arrested Eggshell's attention was this: that upon the table itself was a struggling object in a sack, trussed securely as a spring chicken.

As he watched, the scene sprang to life and sound. Stevens, the leader, drew from beneath his cape a length of yellow material and tossed it over the sack. He said, "Disgrace and death to the traitor in our midst."

"Disgrace and death," boomed Mrs. Cottenham.

"Disgrace and death. 'Ail Doosey," said broken-nosed Jones.

"Disgrace and death," echoed the young men, dainty voices chiming.

"He is dead to honour."

"Dead to honour," they agreed in concert.

"He shall be dead to life."

"Dead to life."

"Whether he die soon or late."

"Soon or late."

Doesn't look like murder on the spot, anyway, thought Eggshell, in some relief.

"We will have vengeance. Our hand is against him."

"We will have vengeance. Our hand is against him. Hail, Duce! Hail, Free British Mussolites! Hail, Stevens!"

This litany concluded, the leader motioned his followers to sit down. He himself remained standing. "Fellow Troopers, I have called you together this night to witness the condemnation and punishment of a traitor. Not, I regret to say, the final punishment; that must wait, until Wotan himself wreaks his punishment upon this creature, or until the Free British Mussolites are in power in England's green and pleasant land"—he corrected himself—"I mean, are in power, and have the power to make it a green and pleasant land. The minor punishment will follow immediately I have recalled to you the circumstances of the crime. This man, once our trusted fellow Grouper, the repository of our secrets—those secrets more potent than any locked in the criminal breasts of Freemasonry or world Jewry, for ours is the white magic that must defeat their black magic as the sun defeats the storm cloud—"

There was some murmured appreciation of this rhetoric.

"—this man was heard, in a public place, jeering at our aims—"

"Wot a bleeder!" interjected Broken-nose.

"Quiet, Trooper Jones. Jeering at our aims and, more beastly, hinting at our membership and our meeting-place."

One of the disdainful young men leaned forward and

smote the sack hard where he presumed the head to be. The others—apparently this was a ritual—followed suit, Mrs. Cottenham delivering her blow with an ebony ruler, at which the sack writhed more convulsively than ever.

"You all know our laws," said the leader. "You know our aims; to tear from the fair face of England that filthy veil called 'Democracy,' that loathly fabric which mars her beauty and keeps the bright sunlight from her eyes, and, shot through with the courage imparted to us by that great Leader from whom we take our name—"

" 'Ail, Doosey. Doosey, Doosey, Doosey," chanted Trooper Jones, who had learned how to chant from the Rome wireless.

"—shot through with the courage, I say, to fight against the tyranny of the Democrats, the Socialists, the Trade Unionists, the Co-operators, the Communists, the Jews, the Freemasons, the plutocrats, the bureaucrats, the atheists, the Protestants and the Scotsmen—ay, the degenerate Scots, who wear women's skirts in the streets of their Babylonic cities. Shot through, I say, to fight…to fight…" He had lost the thread of his discourse. "Oh, yes, to fight the warmongers and all others to a—to a finish. I give you our toast, Brother Troopers: may Wotan sustain our friends in High Places and give preferment to our friends in Low! Trooper Cottenham, bring out the Cascara Sagrada!"

While the lady found the big black bottle and a large-sized tumbler, the F.B.M.s amused themselves by striking at the sack. Then they resumed their seats while the leader filled the glass and gave it to Jones to hold.

He said, "We are ready to mete the first stage of punishment. When the traitor has received this all-too-meagre warning he shall go free, remembering that our eyes are on him by day and night, and that his doom, be it swift or slow, is inevitable as tomorrow's sunrise. Sit him up and show us his filthy face!"

At that moment Eggshell, who had not been so enthralled since, as a small boy, he had read *Dracula* by torchlight in bed on an extremely foggy and malevolently silent night in late autumn, awoke from stupor, shouted to Frankson and Grigson, and flashed "C" through the open door of the garage. In a second he had broken the window and, followed by the two young constables, was jumping down into Mrs. Cottenham's parlour, while MacAbbott and his two men hammered at the door.

The room was in turmoil. While Grigson ran to admit his Chief, Eggshell and Frankson fought four men and one crazy woman, who was laying the ruler about her with painful effect. The sack gave one great writhe and fell with a thud from the table, bringing down the cascara bottle and tumbler with it into one great, messy smash. "All right, Warrender," Eggshell shouted, hitting Trooper Jones with the left hand while Mrs. Cottenham bit at his right, "I'm coming for you."

Then MacAbbott, Grigson and the two constables came to join battle; and in less time than it takes to tell the Free British Mussolites, or such of their representatives as Mrs. Cottenham's room could contain, were under arrest.

Meanwhile, Eggshell had out his knife and was hacking away at the ropes bound about the sack. Then he gave a grunt of fury and disappointment. Regarding him was the white, blubbered face of a seventeen-year-old whom Grigson at once, and with commendable promptitude, identified as the boy who ran errands for the grocer's on the corner.

———

Back at the station, Stevens, the leader, under arrest for espionage, the Mussolites lodged in the cells upon a charge of assault and battery, MacAbbott interrogated the weeping lad, whose name was Nifferson. "I only joined for a lark," he wailed, "and then when I saw that they were up to funny stuff I just didn't go any more. But they kept at me, and threatened me, until I was scared barmy. So one night I 'ad a drink to make me feel better, and I'm not used to drink, so I suppose it went to my 'ead, because I was in the 'Red Lion' telling a chap that I knew a bit about them, when I saw Mrs. Cottenham standing right by me talking to some fellow. Didn't think she'd 'eard me, but I was real scared all the same, and when they told me there was a special meeting tonight and I'd got to come, I didn't dare stop away. So I got there, and they fell on me and roped me up, and you saw what 'appened then. I say, sir, I'm patriotic, honest Injun I am. I've joined the L.D.V. I thought it would be a lark to join them b——F.B.M.s, and maybe if they was traitors I could give them away and 'elp England, but you see what a mess it got me into. Ask anyone if I'm not patriotic. Don't be 'ard on me, sir. I'll lose my job as it is."

"All right," said MacAbbott gently, "all right, son, I think you're more fool than rogue. Can't help your job, though. It'll have to come out. If I hear good reports of you—and only if, mind—I'll do what I can for you."

When the boy had gone, Eggshell turned wearily to Frankson. "There you are. No Warrender. Wonder why he didn't show up? We're no wiser than before, my lad, and God knows when there'll be an end to this case. We'll watch him for a couple of days longer, and then we'll just have to drag him in on some charge in connection with the Mussolites. No option. Oh, hell, when shall we really get a lead?"

———

Had he known it, that lead had already been given. It had been given that very afternoon, in curious fashion and by a rare chance.

It was mild in Warwickshire that day, and Bubbles was sitting, in dressing-gown, blanket, and slippers, by the lounge window, watching the sunlight on the pleasant fields. Hilary was out of doors, messing around with the summer-house. At lunch she had chanced to say: "Hell, we do need a new cupboard in the kitchen, to keep wood in. It gets so damp out in the shed."

"Why don't you make one? You're good with your hands."

"What of?"

"What happened to that old wardrobe we put out there? Couldn't you chop it up?"

Hilary regarded her roughened hands. "Could, I suppose; though I'm getting fed up with carpentering. I say, Millais, don't wear those silly stockings round the house. You'll only tear them, and you look a hoot, farthing head and penny tail. Wonder if Agnes really meant to send me some?" She pondered for a moment, admired her friend's sleek head. "Yes, your hair isn't bad. Wonder how I'd look with mine done like that?... Oh, yes, we were talking about cupboards. Suppose I could hack up the wardrobe. Where is it? In the summer-house?"

So she had gone out there to rout around; and now she returned, smothered in grime and very grumpy.

"No jiggering good. It's all rotten and simply full of woodlice. What filthy things they are!"

"Maclagan hated woodlice," Bubbles said dreamily, "they simply drove him mad. That's about the only thing I remember about him. When he came to tea at our house we were playing in the garden and we sat on a fallen tree. One of the woodlice got on his hand, and he went white as chalk and came out all of a sweat. I've never seen anything like it. He nearly fainted… Why, what's the matter? Never seen me before?"

But Hilary went on staring, and, still staring, she rose slowly to her feet and groped for her hat, which she had flung on to the couch.

"Where are you going? What on earth—"

"I'm going out. To the post-office."

"Hilary! Don't be mad. You've got to tell me what's up."

"To the post-office," her friend repeated dreamily, her rather fine eyes blank as two slabs of toffee, "to send a telegram…"

Chapter Eighteen

WAR-TIME HAS ITS MANY UNAVOIDABLE DELAYS. IT would not have been surprising had the post-office officials elected to give priority to telegrams announcing births and deaths rather than to telegrams of the kind Hilary sent to the Kinghofs. Indeed, it might well have stimulated efficient officers to test it for code; but whatever the cause for delay, it was not received by the addressees until eleven o'clock the following morning, Wednesday, 31st January, seventeen days after Mr. Reginald Coppenstall had been discovered by Clem Poplett in the Stewarts Court shelter.

Agnes and Andrew who, having had no news from Eggshell and having that morning seen Mr. Warrender walk out of the flats unscathed on his way to work, were putting on outdoor clothes preparatory to risking a snub at the police-station when the wire came. Agnes read it first, and her brows puckered. "Darling, everyone's mad. Would you have said Hilary was unbalanced? I suppose people who say 'Great John Scott' and 'it's a hoot' are unbalanced in a way, but not in a—a surrealist way, if you see what I mean."

"I shall see what you mean when you give me that wire," said Andrew. He took the paper and read aloud "MACLAGAN TERRIFIED WOODLICE BUBBLES SAID DROVE HIM MAD WHEN CHILD WILL THIS HELP HILARY BURTON."

Many things may be said of Mr. Kinghof—that he is not very fond of work, that he spends too much money on personal comfort, that he smokes too much, that he drinks too much Irish whisky (though this is not true, for he drinks not too much but quite enough), that he is scatterbrained, reckless, and impertinent, that he does not respect authority, that he does not admire the Ballet nor read books that are good for him—but not even his worse enemies have accused him of being slow in the uptake. Andrew is not very good at long, liquid whistles; but he performed a creditable one on this occasion, stubbed out his cigarette, seized his astonished wife in his arms and bore her in a boisterous polka round the room, smacking her into the wireless cabinet on the second round.

She pulled herself away from him, howled with pain and began to rub her injured hip. "What on earth do you think you're doing? You've hurt me. You've bruised me. I bet I'm bleeding internally."

"I've no time," said Andrew, whose face was patchily flushed with excitement, "to hear a tale of petty ailments. Great J.S., girl, can't you see the point? Don't you understand? We've got him at last!"

"Got whom?"

"That peculiarly disgusting murderer of ours. We have him on the hip, Agnes, my good wife—on the ruddy hip. Both hips."

"Now look." She sat down, her injuries forgotten, and patted the settee. "You come and sit by me, and tell me all about it. Perhaps I'm dense. It wouldn't be surprising if I were, considering the appalling time I've had being chased and coshed while you were cosily tucked up in the Army; but I think I shall be able to understand you if you explain, very very slowly, in words of one syllable."

Patiently he took the seat she had indicated, and solemnly kissed the back of her neck just where the curling hair sprang upwards from a childish peak. "How pretty you are from the rear... I love you, Agnes. 'What e'er betide, I shall be at your side, Your spouse and your guide.'"

"Don't be *greasy*, Andrew," said his wife severely, "and don't spit down my neck. Now then, I'm waiting."

"Do you know what we're going to do within the next half-hour?"

"No?" She was expectant.

"We're going out, and we're going to buy half a dozen pairs of *Couleur de Rose* stockings for Hilary and post them off to her."

Steadily she rose and began to walk up and down the room. "No, Andrew, please don't trouble to tell me your little secret. I'm not curious. I have no time for conundrums, so we will talk of something else. Have you seen Aunt Lucy lately? Poor dear, I do think you should write to her more often. How would you like to have herpes? A trying complaint, especially when one is widowed. A trouble shared is a trouble halved, and since your Uncle Hector died, poor Lucy has no one with whom to share her herpes. And don't you think you should persuade her to leave Cheltenham for a more bracing climate? I always said that a woman of her age should—"

"All right, all right," he shouted, "I'll tell you. And immediately after I tell you we're going to write some little notes."

So he explained the plan in his mind, and when he had done she sat silent, admiring, unnerved.

"Well, what do you think?"

"Oh—I don't know. It seems a ghastly thing to do!"

Andrew replied, and his voice was steady, cold, without flippancy. "Do you think anything could be bad enough for that brute? Have you forgotten that he's a parricide, who shot his father in the back, that he deliberately scared an old and unhealthy woman to death—the foulest form of murder possible—and that he tried to kill Bubbles by one of the cruellest methods a killer could devise? Good lord, you know all that and you want to be humanitarian!"

She accepted the rebuke. "But will they come?"

"Of course they will. The innocent because there's no reason why they shouldn't, the guilty because they, because he, wouldn't dare stay away. Besides, bravado's up his street. He'll come. They'll all come."

"Don't you think we should tell Eggshell?"

"No, because the police would never dare use the methods we mean to use."

So they sat down to write four notices. "I think we'll send a fifth," said Andrew, "to Blake. He's the porter, after all, and any decisions would have to come through him. Besides, he's hefty."

The notices read as follows: *There will be a meeting tonight, 16th instant, at 8 p.m., Flat 8, Block 3, Stewarts Court, to discuss further precautions against fire that might be taken by tenants for the protection of this building. It is a fortnight since our last meeting, and we feel it important to attend without delay to this matter of security. Your presence is urgently requested.*

They addressed the envelopes and delivered them to

respective addresses. Then, as they walked across to the "Green Doe" after buying and despatching Hilary's hosiery, Andrew said, "Where would it be best for us to spend the afternoon? Richmond Park?"

"Wimbledon Common would be nearer."

"Battersea Park nearer still. I suppose that would do."

"Better not risk it," said Agnes, "we can't afford to fail."

They were both strung up, consumed by their secret. Jim Carton, walking across the bar to stand them a drink, found them extremely jovial.

"Such a marvellous exercise!" Agnes told him. "You're wonderful at A.R.P., Mr. Carton, really you are. Honestly, Andrew, you'd never believe just how wonderful he is."

"So are you," said Mr. Carton, "quite wonderful. How you managed to get rescued when I'd left you for dead in a crater I can't imagine. I'd have blown somebody up for that, if I could have caught them. Your health, Kinghofs."

"Your health," they replied.

"By the by, I've a good story for you. An Oxford don, holidaying in Greece, came suddenly upon the ruins of the Parthenon—"

"You can't come suddenly upon the ruins of the Parthenon," said Agnes coldly, "it's impossible. They aren't round a corner."

"Came suddenly upon the ruins of the Parthenon, and found his wife, in the nude, wreathing a heifer with flowers."

"How ridiculous," said Agnes, "even to suppose there would have been a heifer around."

"If you'll excuse me—So he said, 'My dear, this is most extraordinary behaviour. If the animal were Jupiter I could understand it, but this—' She replied, 'It's not Jupiter, my dear, but Io.' So he looked at the heifer closely and finally observed—"

"We must be going," Agnes interrupted. "Thank you so much, Mr. Carton, that was an extremely funny joke."

"But I haven't got to the point!"

"Oh, don't spoil it! It's frightfully funny as it is. Ha, ha, ha! Isn't it delicious, Andrew? You must tell your Aunt Lucy. Really, I've *never* heard a better. Good-bye, Mr. Carton, and it was such a nice drink."

"You are a very revengeful woman, Mrs. Kinghof," he told her, grinning pleasantly, "and to pay you out, I won't finish that joke for you. You can wonder about it till your dying day."

"I apologize," said Andrew, "for my wife. I don't understand her behaviour, but I must assume she has reason for it. Next time I see you I'll atone for her freakishness by telling you what the hat said to the brassière."

"I've heard that," Mr. Carton called after them, as they left, "and it is extremely crude and vulgar."

In the street they met a pretty young lady in a boiler suit and lemon turban, wearing green eyelashes stuck to her lids by strips of transparent paper. "Hullo, Larida," said Agnes.

"Hullo, Agnes, my sweet. How are you?"

"All right. You?"

"Oh, tearing busy, and darling little Hartlebrass is run off his feet. Besides, we're always having police bothering us about a little man called Henry Race who's supposed to be mixed up in a murder, or something, but of course we never saw him again after the day he stole the uniform. Sweetie, I can't stop. Going to have a wee drappie at the 'Doe,' and then I'm simply haring off to a fire practice. God bless." She hared off, pursued by the whistlings of soldiers driving by in a lorry.

"Pretty girl," said Andrew, looking after her.

"You think so?" his wife replied, somewhat coldly; but it was coldness on principle. Another of Mr. Kinghof's virtues is that of fidelity. No other woman is so pleasing in shape as his wife.

They lunched in a cursory fashion at their customary restaurant, and went immediately afterwards to Wimbledon Common. It was a very cold day with a grey frost on the grass and a mournful wind whistling through the bare boughs; but they were too busily employed to notice the weather. The afternoon was an exhausting one, and several times they nearly despaired. Not until a quarter to five were they successful in their quest.

Ten to eight. The Kinghofs had set out their lounge for a committee meeting, with settee and chairs in a ring and before the big armchair a table on which was a fountain-pen, a blotting-pad, and a thick block of lined paper. It was comfortable indoors with the fire leaping in the grate, though outside in the streets the wind had risen and was screaming in the chimneys. Agnes, though she had put on her nicest black dress and her new shoes to give herself confidence, was sick with nerves. She was so nervous that Andrew had to take away the decanter and lock it up. He himself had put on his uniform. "I find it heartening," he explained, "in any sort of crisis."

She fidgeted about the room, straightening cushions and pictures, rearranging a vase full of great, golden-bronze chrysanthemums. "I wish they'd hurry up! Why are people always late?"

"They're not late. It isn't quite eight yet."

"I can't bear waiting, can you?"

"Don't fidget," he said irritably, "you're getting on my nerves, now."

"Oh, damn your nerves. I wish we'd told Eggshell. I wish we'd never started this. I simply can't bear shocks. Oh!" She jumped as the door-bell rang.

"I'll answer it."

He admitted Mrs. Rowse, resplendent in semi-evening dress with little pieces of chiffon trailing from all manner of extraordinary places. She held out an arm heavy with bangles, the trophies of many a Mediterranean cruise, and told him how very kind it was of him to convene the meeting. "And you, too, Mrs. Kinghof. Public-spirited. That's what I said when I had your note. Believe me, I've been thinking and thinking about the matter, but somehow I couldn't bring myself to have another meeting in my flat, remembering what happened last time…"

"Come and sit by the fire, Mrs. Rowse, or will you be too hot there? How's your book? Is it finished?"

She smiled. "Finished, and with my publisher. And I've just started a new one. Aren't I a busy bee?"

"I should say you have been B. busy," Andrew told her jocularly, "if I weren't afraid of being scolded for the Shavian jest."

Agnes gave him a look of contempt.

"You're a wit, Captain Kinghof," Mrs. Rowse pronounced, "and a naughty wit at that. Oh, my dear Mrs. Kinghof, the new book is going simply splendidly! The title is *The Bravest Girl at St. Basil's*, and the heroine is Vineyarda Grey, the orphan who was found in an Italian vineyard, adopted by an English M.F.H. and brought up as his very own. She grows up thinking he's her father, and then, when a malevolent schoolgirl called Minna Wolfe finds out the truth, the bottom drops out of Vineyarda's world, and she— but I mustn't give away my secrets, must I? Or you won't want to read it."

"You shouldn't whet my appetite like that," Andrew teased.

The bell rang again, and Agnes admitted Madame Charnet, who was rather grubby in a tarnished lamé coat and a turban of green chenille.

"I would rather not be too near the fire, if you don't mind," Madame said. "The leetle chair will do vairy nicely. I'm so glad you've called this meeting, Mrs. Kinghof, as I am afraid of fire, and so vairy nervous of being trapped. Don' you think we ought to 'ave a pirrup-pump? And I spoke to Blake about the bran—sand, but 'ee was so un'elpful."

Blake and Lang arrived together, the former neat in his blue uniform with gold braid, the latter cross and untidy.

"Sorry if I'm late, mum," Blake said, "but I got 'ung up with the black-out of Block 2. Always falling down. No, thanks, I'd just as soon stand."

"You can't stand," Agnes said firmly, "you'll be tired to death, and anyway, the meeting may last some time. Take this chair, will you? Mr. Lang, where are you sitting?"

"Oh, any old where. I say, what's this all about, anyhow? We aren't going to have any raids. It's all Government guff."

Andrew pushed him on to a firestool. "Guff or no guff, we must get something done. And I shouldn't bank on 'no raids' if I were you, Lang."

"I was in Paris in the last war," said Madame Charnet, "when the Boches tried to shell it with Beeg Bertha. You are a young man, Mr. Lang, or you would not speak so lightly."

"Big Bertha was a flop. Good lord, I remember the Zepps here, though I was only a kid. They used to stick me under the sideboard during raids, and sing nursery rhymes to me in shaky voices. Heard from Miss Ashton, Mrs. Kinghof?"

"No. She was better when I left her."

"She is a plucky young bit, isn't she? I think she's marvellous. Should have died like a fly, myself."

Mrs. Rowse said quickly, "What's that?"

Andrew said quickly, before Lang could answer, "She fell into the river. Our friend lugged her out again."

"No one told me that! Poor girl! How did it happen?"

"Missed her footing in the dark," Agnes lied.

Andrew said, "Well, shall we make a beginning? Mr. Warrender's not here, I know, but he's often kept late at work. Shall we elect a chairman?"

"I propose Mr. Kinghof," said Madame.

"Seconded with enthusiasm!" Mrs. Rowse exclaimed archly. "We must be led by the military men. All in favour say 'Ay'!"

Andrew was duly elected, so he took the big chair and drew the table towards him. "Mrs. Rowse, you kept the minutes of the last meeting. Can you read them to us?"

Delighted, she drew the little note-book from her bag. "Minutes of meeting held at Flat 10, Block 3, Stewarts Court, Wednesday January 17th, 8 persons present, Mrs. Sibley in the chair." She paused, and touched her eyes with her handkerchief, while they remained silent for a moment out of respect to the dead woman. Then Mrs. Rowse continued her reading, and when she had done Andrew thanked her.

"What was done about these proposals?"

They looked vaguely at one another.

"Madame Charnay asked me to stick sand in the attic," said Blake, "which I'd have done gladly, only there weren't no sand, and the landlords wouldn't give it us."

"I move we all sign a request to the landlords," said Agnes, "they'll have to act on that."

"Seconded," said Lang, moodily lighting a cigarette.

This motion was agreed.

"But they are soch tairrible people!" Madame exclaimed. "They made the most dreadful bother before they would even let me 'ave my leetle cats 'ere, even though I said they were soch clean pussies and never went out."

"My dear madame," said Mrs. Rowse profoundly, touching her knee, "don't talk to me of landlords! When my cistern was leaking so badly, could I get them to move? Threats, tears, entreaties, nothing would shake them. Little Hitlers, my dear. I said to the agent, 'How can we truly boast that we are fighting for Democracy, when democracy is denied us upon our own hearths?' I said—"

"It's the tenants, too, sometimes," Blake said moodily. "Flat in Block 1 got their lavatory bunged up, so I poked and poked around, and what do you think I found? An 'ole cod's 'ead!"

"Order, order!" Andrew banged the table. "We must proceed with business. Blake, have you any suggestions?"

"Well, sir—Your bell, sir. Shall I go?"

"That will be Mr. Warrender," said Agnes. "No, I will."

But it was Pig who stood on the mat, Pig bland and sociable, Pig cousinly.

She gave a gasp of dismay. "Oh!"

"Hope I haven't come at the wrong time. Have you a party? I had to go to cocktails with a friend in Carlyle Street, old Hugh Rivenham, and I thought I'd look in on you."

"No, Pig, not a party; only a tenants' meeting to discuss fire precautions. I'm afraid you'd be bored."

He looked at her sharply. "What tenants?"

"Oh...all of them. All Block 3."

He said slowly, "I don't think I'd be bored," and hung up

his hat. "Agnes, not all of them know me. Don't say anything about my position."

"No, I won't," she said, baffled and furious, and as she took him in, noted the stricken despair on Andrew's face.

Mrs. Rowse, Madame Charnet, and Blake bowed to him politely. Felix Lang started, and growled a brusque acknowledgment.

"Don't let me interfere with the proceedings," said Pig easily, sitting down by Agnes on the settee and hitching his trousers neatly.

He watched, with narrowed eyes, as the company dismally debated means of saving Stewarts Court from flames.

"It's the spirit that counts most of all," said Mrs. Rowse, "and faith. If we believe we shan't be hurt, we shan't be. If we remember we're English, nothing can touch us. Of course we must make our plans; but the spiritual counts most of all."

"I'd as soon have a stirrup-pump," Lang said rudely. "Blake, can't we get one here?"

"Landlords won't give it, sir. Might get the A.R.P. to let us have one in the flats, but they're a bit slow."

Again the bell, and Agnes let Mr. Warrender into the flat. He stared straightly at her, his eyes blank, said, "Evening, Mrs. Kinghof, patriotic of you," and walked past her into the lounge. Here he acknowledged the company, and, when introduced, gave Pig a cursory "How d'ya do?"

"Well," he said, looking at Andrew, who was regarding him with a gaze of cold murder, "done much yet? Sorry to be late. Work of N.P., national importance. Anyway, they say it's important. Move up, Lang, and I'll draw this chair forward." He sat down.

Andrew recapitulated the business to date. Mr. Warrender

was helpful that evening. He made several suggestions, said he might be able to obtain a load of sand at a reasonable discount. He told a joke about Hitler, another about Mussolini. By nine o'clock they had come to the end of business, and Agnes went to get tea. When she returned with the tray, Pig was standing before the fireplace telling a long story about a Scotsman and an Irishman, Mrs. Rowse and Madame Charnet were discussing the advantages and disadvantages of central heating, Mr. Warrender was guffawing at Pig, and Lang was scuffling irritably through the pages of an old *New Yorker*. Andrew was sitting quite still and looking desperate.

When tea had been drunk, he flashed to Agnes a look that said: "No help for it. Pig or no Pig, we've got to go on."

Clearing his throat, he began with fair deftness a conversation dealing with the reconditioning of local workmen's cottages, which were then rented as small modern houses at fabulous sums.

"I know," Madame said indignantly, "they are 'ovels, mere 'ovels, and yet people pay the mos' tarrible lot of money! It is a scandal."

"And what's more," Andrew continued, "though I don't like to bring up such an unwholesome topic, most of them are verminous. People rent the houses, move in, admire the nice new decorations, and a fortnight later they find things on the wall."

"How very disgusting," Mrs. Rowse boomed.

"But look here," said Agnes, "there's that danger in all old buildings. Whether I should tell you all this I don't know, but my husband and I had an awful shock last night. We found a most extraordinary animal in the kitchen, on the pipes just below the sink, and we can't think what it is."

"Silver fish?" Lang suggested.

"Oh, no! They're quite pretty. Andrew, you caught the thing, didn't you?"

"Two of them," he replied. He drew from a jar on the mantelpiece a small jeweller's box.

"Oh, darling, don't show them round! You'll make everyone quite sick!"

Pig's eyes were curious. He sat quietly down and watched his cousin.

"My dears," Mrs. Rowse whispered, "I do hope they're not… Well, I mean, most people who have been brought up decently don't recognize…vermin…when they see them."

"Good heavens, wouldn't you know a bug?" Lang exclaimed.

She flushed. "Only from what I've heard."

"You're fortunate, Mrs. Rowse," said Warrender. "When I was living up north, lodging in a very old house, I had the unlucky experience of making their personal acquaintance. I moved at once, but I was afraid they'd got in my luggage."

"You could tell the landlords about that, Mrs. Kinghof," said Blake earnestly.

Agnes was delicate. "But honestly, I don't think these are…well, bugs, if we must say it."

> *"'Big as your fist and as broad as boats,*
> *Wearing mahogany overcoats,'"*

Warrender quoted gaily.
Lang added, knowing the song,

> *"'In one line they reached*
> *From here to the Marble Arch,*
> *With a packet of Keatings*

Over the sheetings,
They were on the march.'"

"Please," said Mrs. Rowse. Pig looked shocked, then smiled tightly.

"Well," said Andrew, "just to put an end to this unlovely controversy, I'll show you our find. Blake, you have a look first."

The porter stepped forward, looked in the box. "Coo! You know what I'd say they were? I'd say they were ordinary—"

Agnes stopped him. "No! Let the others guess. Herbert, you're not to look till the last. You're always so clever, you'd guess at once."

And she gave him a glance of appeal. Though Pig did not understand it, something in her eyes made him respond. Quietly he stepped back, and went on watching.

Andrew said suddenly, "Come on, the rest of you, all together. Let's see who guesses first." They crowded to him, Mrs. Rowse, Madame Charnet, Lang, and Warrender, and with a swift movement he thrust the open box beneath their noses. There was a gasp.

Warrender said, "Take the filthy things away! They're woodlice, you ass. Disgusting," and he backed away.

Lang looked and laughed.

Madame Charnet said, "What nasty leetle things! I think you call them… I forget what, in French…"

Mrs. Rowse gave a little screech and said, "How horrible! Yes, I'm sure they are. You really should complain."

But it was Agnes who was looking at a certain pair of hands tightly clenched, the knuckles pearl-white; and allowing her gaze to travel upwards she saw something that froze her blood: from beneath the fringe of dry hair that bordered the chenille turban a little trickle of sweat was creeping, wandering in an uncertain runnel round the rim of the eye, towards the grey, damp cheek of Madame Charnet.

———

And as she saw, Andrew saw. He stepped forward, thrust the woodlice under the two terrified eyes, and with his left hand wrenched away the turban and the wig.

Bared now, without its disguise, the face sweating beneath the ochreous make-up was undoubtedly a man's, and a young man's. Steer, ridiculous in the long dress, seemed incapable of movement. The centre of a horrified, only half-comprehending circle, he stood still, and the sweat crawled out of his skin like worms out of the earth, to pour down his face. He whispered, "Take them away! For Pete's sake, Kinghof, take them away!…"

Agnes looked at Pig, whose eyes were bright with shock and understanding. She looked from Mrs. Rowse to Lang, from Lang to Warrender, from Warrender to the stricken Blake, who understood less than anybody else: and then she said boldly, "Andrew, don't let him go."

Andrew pushed the man down into a chair, held him with one hand, and placed the box carefully between the skirted knees.

Agnes said, "Listen, everybody. You don't need me to tell you what's happened. This is Maclagan Steer, the murderer of his father and of Mrs. Sibley, the attempted murderer of Miss Ashton and myself. I can't tell you everything now. We've caught him, and he's going to talk. This isn't a legal proceeding, and it may seem to you a cruel one; but this wretched object isn't a man—he's a monster of beastliness.

I'm going to implore you to do something you'll hate—to go away quietly, say no word to the police until we tell you, and leave this to us. Will you?"

They were silent. Then Lang said, "I will! I don't care how you're going to do it, but I wish you luck. You've got me out of a mess, Mrs. Kinghof, and I'll do what you want of me. I'm going. Will you come, Warrender?"

Mr. Warrender was grey-faced. He said, his lips scarcely moving, "Yes," and without a word followed Lang from the room.

Mrs. Rowse shrieked, "Oh, heavens, nothing would make me stay in this dreadful place!" She was trembling, the fat of her cheeks shaking violently. Suddenly and unexpectedly, she stepped up to Steer and struck him a soft, flabby blow on the cheek. "That's for you, you—foul murderer!" And with queer, startling dignity she walked quickly from the room.

Agnes looked at Blake, and lastly at Pig.

Blake said, "I don't know as I ought—" He was bewildered by the shock of the situation, not knowing how he should answer her.

But it was Pig who settled the question. "Blake," he said sharply, "you can go, and I'll take full responsibility. Wait downstairs till I speak to you. Go now."

The porter, startled by the tone of authority, turned on his heel. "Right, sir." They heard the door slam behind him.

Andrew, Agnes, and Pig were left alone with the half-fainting parricide.

Pig drew Andrew aside and said slowly and very distinctly, "This is enough to smash my career; but I'm going to let you have your head. Heaven help me, but I know you've the only chance of breaking this man, and I'm damned if I can feel a ha'porth of pity. If I stayed I'd have to stop you. So I'm not going to stay. I'll be downstairs with Blake. I want a written confession, if you take all night to get it, and Andy, if you ever reveal my part in this…or my voluntary lack of part in it…"

Agnes said faintly, "Pig, you are a sportsman… I'll remember that…"

He walked deliberately from the room. They heard the door close behind him.

Andrew wiped the sweat from his own brow. He pointed to the table. "Steer, you see that writing-pad? That nice blotter? That pen? That's for you. It was meant for you. You'll sit down and write a full story, a life-story, with details of your beastly killings, and if you don't… See these woodlice? Nice little things, aren't they? Pretty grey colour. Corrugated undersides. Well, they go on your face…or one goes on your cheek and the other down your neck."

Maclagan Steer looked at him, his eyes almost childish. "If I do…will you take them away?"

"We promise," said Agnes, for a second oddly touched.

Andrew, in token of good faith, withdrew the box from his knees.

Steer rose. He seemed almost jaunty. "Well, if I've got to do it I'll make a good job, damn your filthy eyes. All right. Give me the pen."

"And if you try any tricks, down your neck they go," said Andrew. He watched the trembling hand go towards the pen. "Agnes, you'd better get the whisky. And bring cigarettes. We're going to sit here a long time." They watched Steer as he began to write. Andrew took the jeweller's box upon his knee and now and then tapped on the lid with his finger-nail. There was no sound save the scratching of the pen.

The night wore on.

Chapter Nineteen

"My name is Reginald Maclagan Steer.

"I was born at Tunis, April 4th, 1908, the son of Mary and Reginald Coppenstall. My mother ran away from Coppenstall in 1911, and quite rightly too, because, from all she told me, he was a beast of a man. My only early recollection of him is a damn' good lamming with a strap for some childish misdemeanour. I always hated his memory, and I hate it now. He was a violent man. My mother used to tell me the whole Coppenstall family were devils. I grew up to hear a lot about Adelaide Sibley, my father's sister, who had clung like a leech to a half-lunatic aunt till she persuaded her to leave her fortune away from my father. I loathed her too. They were a wretched crew. If my father had inherited, I should have been a rich man upon his death.

"My mother lived with Stephen Steer till 1913, when she persuaded my father to let her divorce him. He didn't mind. He was a loose-living devil himself and wasn't sorry to be rid of her. He never paid any alimony, as she knew he wouldn't.

She didn't expect it. Steer was a decent man. I wasn't an easy kid to get on with, I know, but he did his best. He meant me to be an actor. When I was six or seven he used to teach me to recite long speeches from Shakespeare and yell at me when I lost the sense of them, but I didn't mind that. When I was seventeen I joined a repertory company, playing small parts. I wasn't first-rate, but I was expert at make-up and a reliable character actor. I played Engstrand in *Ghosts* when I was eighteen. I never wrote to my father or heard from him. When I was 21, I changed my name by deed-poll to Steer, and dropped my Christian name.

"The next year, I got a chance to go out on a Canadian tour. It was all the same to me. As I said, Steer was a decent chap, but my mother was wrapped up in him, and anyway, I wasn't overfond of her. All this stuff about blood being thicker than water makes me sick. I never could feel anything towards her, though she was all right. I felt more strongly towards my father, though that was hate. Hate is stronger than love. I've found that out. He'd led her a dog's life and he'd have led me one, given half the chance. He couldn't keep money, either, made it and lost it; and I suppose his blood may be responsible for my gambling.

"I did all right in Canada, but then I got keen on a fat fool of a woman and let job after job slide while I ran around after her. She was ten years older than me, and when I saw someone I liked better she wouldn't let me leave her. Made scenes, screeched and yelled till the sight of her made me sick, and said she'd write to the other girl's father telling him all about me. I got mad with her one night and thrashed her with a strap, as poor dead dad, of blessed memory, had thrashed me. She howled so much that I had to shut her up somehow, so I knocked her down and left her to cool off.

The next thing I knew, she'd charged me with assault and battery, and they gave me six months.

"Of course I didn't write home about that. I never wrote home again. When I came out I couldn't get a job for love or money, so I started using my savings trying to win a pile. I did well for a bit, then went smash. Then I took up with another woman, and she kept me going for a time. She was a beauty, but a slut; kept her house in a filthy state, was always losing things and leaving money around. It was too much temptation for me, and one night I took a couple of quid hoping to win a fortune with it. Next thing, I was in trouble again. I got away from the police when they were taking me to the station, ran for it, and hopped a train. I spent the next three years as a waiter, a gigolo—that always makes me laugh, me crawling round all the vain old women who like a man to cuddle them even if they have to pay five dollars an evening for the treat—and a fairground barker; I barked for six months, then lost the job through another tart, a girl who used to do the hula-hula. When I was twenty-seven I thought I'd like to get back to Europe, so I stowed away on a liner going to France.

"Not many people get away with that, but I did. I was half-dead when I got ashore, starved, sick and thin as a rake. That was March 1938. I lived until June by tramping round Normandy, getting food and a bed where I could. I'd learned French from the French Canadians, and after I'd been in France for a month could pass off as a Frenchman pretty well anywhere. One night I broke into a house and got away with two thousand francs in cash. That was near Louviers, a wretched little town not far from Rouen. On that I took myself to Paris, as I wanted to see the capital and felt I could muck along for a bit.

"One night, in June, I crossed the river to Puteaux, a suburb where I'd got a cheap bed before. It was eleven at night, and the house I'd once gone to was empty. I wandered around the place, and finally stopped and asked a man where I should go. He told me that Madame Charnet, who had been a café proprietress up to a year or so ago, still took people in sometimes for bed and breakfast, and that I could ask there.

"To cut this part of a long story short, I knocked her up and she took me in. I told her I was English, as I never liked to work the French stuff too hard, and she seemed to like it. She was a funny old duck, very made-up and dyed, and I think she'd taken a lover or two since her husband kicked the bucket. Well, I stayed with her till my money gave out, then told her I was broke and said I'd have to push on. She wouldn't hear of it. I was her dear little boy, her '*soisoif*,' she used to call me, and I was to make her house my own. I thought there was nothing else for it but to make love to her, so we settled down in a nice cosy little *ménage* all among the *meubles rustiques*.

"I took care not to seem more than a paying guest where the neighbours were concerned—'paying' is funny, when you come to think of it, because if I didn't pay cash I certainly paid for my hospitality by having to endure her smarmings. We had fine fun together sometimes, though, and I told her a bit about my life, leaving out the unpleasant items. She was tickled to death about me being an actor. One night I made her laugh by putting on her clothes, and she said, 'You could look just like me if you chose! You're my height. A small-sized man makes a middle-sized woman, *n'est ce pas*?' That gave me an idea. I bought make-up and all I needed—she didn't know what she was paying for, that time—and she used to shriek with laughter when I made myself a double of her. I forgot to say she'd come into quite a bit of money. She was generous with it, but it gave me ideas. I've always had ideas.

"I started keeping house with her, as I said, in June. By August I was pretty fed up with having to dance round her, and I got it into my head that I could put her away. It wasn't difficult, though I had to make plans carefully. The house was the last in a dead end, with high fences on either side, and no one to overlook the backyard. I told Jeanne the garden shed was damp and that it needed new flooring. She swallowed that rot whole—she'd have swallowed anything—and asked me what I thought ought to be done. I said I'd dig it up, and then try and re-brick it. I tell you, that woman was dumb. She used to watch me while I dug and beg me not to tire myself.

"The next part was easy. On August 20th I stuck a knife into her while she was asleep—it was so sudden I don't think she felt much (anyway, I hope she didn't, because she'd been kind in her way, had poor old Jeanne)—and buried her out there in the shed. That was a nasty business, but I must have done the job well because the damn-fool police never had a suspicion. I suppose they'll dig for her now, but that doesn't matter. Nothing matters. The next five days were the most ticklish, and the first day was the worst, because I had to go out for the first time made up as Jeanne and draw her money from the bank. I did it, though, which shows you that I was a good actor within limits. I'd practised the signature a lot, too, and they swallowed that without a murmur. For the next three days I kept pretty closely within doors and didn't do any shopping, though I showed myself at the door to the postman and the milkman, and I went out latish in the evening to post letters. On the fourth day I shut up house and went to tell the half-blind, half-deaf druggist on the corner of my—I mean, Madame's—intention to go to England to live. I said I'd got relations there. Luckily she'd few intimate friends; if it had been otherwise, I might not have got away with things so easily. Still, it takes skill to do what I did. On the fifth day I sailed for Dover, using her passport. That was the 25th. For safety's sake, so that I'd be noticed and remembered, I made a fuss at the Customs, acted so suspiciously that they searched my bags thoroughly and found some scent.

"I came to London, and two days later took the flat at Number 5, Block 3, Stewarts Court. I came here because I'd seen old Addie's name in the 'phone book, and had vague ideas of getting something out of her later on. I felt like a pig in clover (funny, that—'a pig')—and by gosh, furnishing the place just as a silly middle-class Frenchwoman would furnish it was fun. I got a bit tired of hanging about in skirts, so I used to alter my appearance a bit sometimes, and go about the place quite freely. Going in and out of Number 5 in trousers wasn't easy, but I could usually pick a time when the coast was clear, or when it was dark.

"Then, by pure chance, I found out that my father was in England. I saw him one day in Piccadilly. At first I wasn't sure it was him, because I hadn't seen him since I was three and children's memories are worthless; but I'd seen pictures of him, and I'd have known that scar of his anywhere.

"It set me thinking. When you've done one murder, another doesn't seem to matter. My money, I knew, wouldn't last for ever and I had no plans for the future. One of the things I had dinned into me by Mother, when I was a kid, was that Addie intended to leave my father her money when she died, which meant that I'd get it some day—or most likely I'd get it. I thought, If he was dead, and she was dead, I'd get it now; and that started me off. First of all, I managed to trace him. When he was in England he'd always stayed at some wretched hotel on the London outskirts, so I thought he might go there again, knowing how mean he was. My first enquiry struck lucky. There he was.

"I began to wonder who I should do in first, him or Addie; but it didn't seem to matter. I'd seen her about in the flats, and she made me sick. My mother used to call her 'that pig,' and I always thought she looked it. That gave me another idea, and I started to make my plans.

"I think I was pretty thorough. The first thing I did, when I'd got the ground plan worked out, was to set about details. First, I gave myself the identity of Henry Race, and started putting in a few hours' voluntary work at the Town Hall. Then I bought a wireless battery-set. That was useful, because I could often go out or in as the chap who changed the accumulators, and it came in useful later as an alibi; I'll come to that.

"On December 26th, I wrote to my father suggesting a meeting. I told him frankly that I'd seen him in town, and explained that Mother had so often told me where he used to stay that I'd taken a chance on finding him there. I said that as she was dead and there was only him and me left, I'd be glad of reconciling myself to him, so I asked him to come and see me on New Year's Eve.

"He wrote a cautious letter back, as if he was suspicious of me; thought I wanted to borrow cash, I suppose; but he agreed to come. Meanwhile, as Henry Race, I'd pinched a boiler suit from the Town Hall—that was easy, as they're slack as the devil up there—and bought a pair of Wellingtons. He arrived at eight, and a surlier old devil you wouldn't wish to meet. No Auld Lang Syne about him. No one would have thought I was a long-lost son. 'What the hell do you want, Reggie?' he said. 'Because I've got no money, if that's what you're after. If that pig of an aunt of yours hadn't robbed me of what was mine it might have been a different story.' Well, I soothed him down—he was a wreck, I can tell you, looking old as the hills and completely gone to seed—saying I only wanted his goodwill and friendship. I found that he'd checked out of his hotel, meaning to spend the night with me and then find London digs the next day. When he was more or less mollified I said I'd mix a drink. I turned up the wireless at full blast and went out of the room. As I expected, he crossed to the set to turn it off, or down—doesn't matter which. I came back and shot him. I used a silencer.

"It was easy, that part. The next part wasn't. I stripped off his clothes and put him into the boiler suit, stuffed him into Wellingtons and bundled up his own things. Later on, by the way, I went right to the other end of the borough and stuffed them into some sandbags in a shelter there. They haven't been found yet. It's the Platts Crescent shelter, if the police want to dig them out.

"I waited till two in the morning. Then I got him into my small bedroom, which overlooks the well, put a rope round him, tied the other end to the bedpost and lowered him neatly. A bit of A.R.P. training is a good thing. I followed at once and lugged him into 3 Block's shelter through the well exit. It was then I went a bit crazy, though it didn't make any odds later on; I suddenly thought that he was a bit too near home. God knows how I took the risk, but I did it. I got him up the steps into the street, supporting him as if he were drunk, and pushed him down into the No. 2 shelter instead. No one met us. If they had, the game would have been up.

"The sandbags here were better for my purpose. It took me an hour and a half, sweating all the time, but I got him inside then and replaced them neatly. I had a bad moment when a warden flashed a torch down there, but I stayed doggo and he didn't see me nor what I was hiding in the corner.

"Then I went back to bed, and I slept soundly. That's what makes me proud; I slept soundly. I don't think many people could have done that.

"Of course, I'd meant the body to be found, after a decent time-lag. My idea was to get Addie properly rattled before I started on her; I didn't mean the fat pig of a woman to die easily. In the meantime, I was carrying on with my plans. I got two pigs' masks from Baggot, the costumier, and later, as you know, I got the policeman's helmet and tunic. The fool didn't think to tell you that. I'd made myself up elderly when I bought it, so I suppose he didn't connect me with his other visitor. I could change my height with elevators, when necessary, which is why reports of me varied so much.

"The next thing I knew, Coppenstall's body had been discovered. Knowing it would set up a train of thought in Addie's mind, I played the first trick on her, the one with the service lift, that night. It went astray rather, because I hadn't realized that the corpse wouldn't have been identified. The best of us make mistakes.

"I left her alone for a bit and then, on the day of the inquest—I knew she'd have no illusions by that time—I borrowed the Punch-and-Judy. That was a risk, if you like; but I brought it off. I'm proud of that, too. I bought the pig's head from a butcher in West Street.

"Ever since I was a kid I'd heard of Addie's weak heart. They'd been expecting her to die for years. But that heart was stronger than I'd bargained for, because she popped up again like a jack-in-a-box. The next thing was a facer; Addie left Stewarts Court suddenly, and I couldn't find out where she'd gone. It was by pure luck that, just as I was going out in my ordinary clothes, I intercepted the telegram she sent to those blasted Kinghofs. All right, then, I could push on again. I went to Baggot and bought the policeman's get-up. Then I came back and fixed my alibi for the evening; it was a tricky one, but even without it I didn't see the police could get anything on me.

"In the afternoon I went to the High Street cinema, the Classic, and took great care to be seen going in. This was a double bluff, as I'll explain. Inside, I changed my appearance by the simple device of removing my very conspicuous turban and putting on a mackintosh and a blue felt hat, and I left unobserved. Then I went to Currie's smutty film show—it's a cover-up for dope-passing, by the way—and slipped out after ten minutes. Next, I returned to my flat, changed into men's clothes and turned on the wireless at full blast.

"I'd rigged up a Heath Robinson arrangement of tins and bits of string, so that when enough water had dripped from one tin into the other the weight would pull the lead out of the plug and turn the wireless off. I had worked it out to happen round about eleven in the evening, which it did; and Blake was practically ready to swear blue-blind, on account of it, that I'd been at home that night. *Boy's Own Paper* stuff, I know, but very handy. Of course, you'll realize that it was my intention to be spotted at Currie's cinema. I knew it would divert the interest of the fat-headed police, who could never believe in anyone being concerned in more than two diverse crimes at a time.

"I went down to Hooham on the Green Line, arriving at eight o'clock. I had the mask, helmet, and tunic in a brown-paper parcel under my arm. You know what happened then. When I'd finished Aunt Addie off I threw the mask down near her, as a jeer at the police, and chucked the rest of my disguise into the reservoir. Then, it's true, I had a bad time, because I had to sleep in a barn all night, and catch the first bus back to town in the morning.

"What else? Yes, nothing more until the shock of old Addie's will. If Mrs. Kinghof thought her trick would save that fat idiot of a Bubbles, she was wrong. I'd killed two people—three, if you count dear Jeanne-Louise—for gain; it was no odds to me if I killed a fourth for the sheer fun of it.

"One more trick only; the Warwick trick.

"The police guard stuck around Block 3 helped rather than hindered me. They were watching to see who went out. Did Madame Charnet go out? Oh, no. At about ten o'clock on the morning of Saturday 27th I opened my door, said in my pretty French accent loudly enough for the imbecile Frankson to hear, 'Zank you, they weel do vairy well on Tuesday,' then stepped out dressed as a workman with an accumulator under my arm, and went off to Warwickshire. Madame Charnet didn't leave. She didn't step out of her flat the whole week-end, bless her heart. It was easy enough for me to get in again on Monday as the dear police had relaxed their watch. Stupidly easy. I should have liked a higher hurdle.

"Well, I suppose that's all. Any more details I can supply at leisure to the police.

"It is customary, at the end of a confession of murder,

to express regret. I can't. With the best will in the world, I can't feel it. (By the by, if you enquire at 14 Cordelia Street, Warwick, you'll find the lodgings to which I went when I left the train—it's a pub, but I've forgotten the name—and the cycle shop on the corner will tell you they loaned a bicycle that wasn't returned. I left the bike in a wood on the Beanscot road.) No, I can't feel it. I am a parricide; if I'd been a Roman they'd have put me in a sack with a cock, a dog, a monkey, and a viper—if I'm correct with my fauna—and thrown me into the sea. And it doesn't bother me. My father was a brute, my Aunt Addie a greedy pig who died as she deserved. As for Bubbles Ashton, she was a stupid little girl who screamed at me because I wouldn't have her smelly dog yapping at my ankles. Ask her if she remembers that, as well as the insects—I suppose you got that from the beastly female? Anyhow, she'd have been better off dead. As for my attempt on Agnes Kinghof, nosey-parkers are always better out of the way and a woman with a face like that is no ornament to the earth. Not that she isn't the best of the lot. At least she's fairly intelligent.

"Nothing more to say. Do your damnedest. I had a good run for my—I was going to say 'my money,' but that didn't come off. But I shan't need money where I'm going.

"(*Signed*) R. Maclagan Steer."

When Andrew, red-eyed, had finished reading this document and had glanced up at his wife, who, equally weary and not quite sober, had been peering at it over his shoulder, he said: "Gee, I've never read anything so sickening!" His eye strayed to the jeweller's box.

Steer flinched. He said, "I had your promise."

Andrew stood up; his face was quite grey and his hands were twitching. "You're lucky, you know, that one is brought up to a rather B.O.P. sense of honour… If I hadn't been, and if some of the teaching hadn't stuck, I'd treat you to the woodlice just the same."

In that moment the small man had darted forward, and had knocked the box into the dying fire. Then he sprang for the window; but it was Agnes who, plunging forward in a burst of alcoholic courage, grabbed him by the ankle. Andrew struck him, and he went down. He said to his wife, too exhausted even to praise her, "All right now. Go ahead."

So she went to the door of the flat, opened it and called down to the man waiting patiently on the lowest stair.

"All right, Pig. Bring your policemen up. You can collect the body."

Chapter Twenty

Miss Kathleen Smith, returning shaken and tearful from a painful interview with the police, flung herself on Mr. Lang's mercy.

"But Felix, darling, I couldn't help it! Can't you see what an awful position it was for me? I'd never told you of my engagement to Roderick because I didn't want to hurt you; but darling, he was so *proper*! If it had come out that you spent the night on my bath it would have ruined everything. Anyway," she added forlornly, "everything was ruined anyhow. He found out about you—read one of your letters that I'd left lying around—and we had the most terrible quarrel. I'd no option but to give him his freedom... You do understand, don't you? I'm so fond of you, Felix. I wouldn't have hurt you for the world, you know that. That day at the police-station, I suffered so dreadfully *inside*... Please forgive me, and let's start afresh. I feel so dreadfully upset, and honestly, this has been as bad for me as for you—"

Coldly he regarded the ladylike girl, looked at her Harris tweeds, her sensible shoes, her smooth hair, and he said:

"My dear Kay, do you seriously imagine I'm going to forgive a nice-minded, respectable tootsy who has done her damnedest to get me hanged?"

"But Felix—oh, Fix, my dear—"

"Don't you 'dear' me! The worst thing I can wish you is reconciliation with your stuffed-shirt Roderick, you—you nasty little hypocrite!"

Miss Smith dried her eyes and assumed belated dignity. "I can do no more than apologize."

"No. If you committed hara-kiri, it still wouldn't be enough. Go home to your arty friends, and offer your bath to someone more chivalrous than I'm prepared to be."

She said, "You loved me once."

"Dear, dear," said Mr. Lang, "what funny things we boys do do!" Stepping to the door, he flung it ajar. "Outside."

"What?"

"Outside. I can't stand any more of you."

"You're aware you're behaving like a cad?"

"Don't be more of a fool than you can help, and please go home. I've got a lovely girl waiting for me in Warwickshire. She's not arty, and she'd scream with fright if I suggested sleeping on her bath. She's not even very clever, and she has rather a large nose. But I love her, Kay, and I'm quite sure she wouldn't try to hang me to save her miserable pride. Outside."

And Miss Smith, white with rage, departed.

It is not surprising that within a year she married Roderick. She is now the Honourable Mrs. Furnivall, and is prominent as a patron of the Ladies' Guild of Pluck and Honour.

———

Felix Lang, seated at Bubbles' feet in the lounge at Setters Croft, said, "You are going to marry me, aren't you?"

She looked startled.

"Oh, if it's your money that's bothering you, I'm quite comfortably off myself, and anyway, you needn't give me any."

Outside in the cold garden Hilary walked with her new fiancé, Jack Jarman of Crossacres. Her hair was cropped, and dressed in loose curls all over her head. Her mouth looked well under a layer of Hunting Pink. She wore a scarlet dress, a leopard's-skin coat and, rather absurdly, *Couleur de Rose* stockings of cobweb fineness.

Bubbles murmured, "Well, it would be rather jolly to be with you. Are you going to be a doctor?"

"I'm afraid I've mucked about such a lot that I'll flunk my exams…but I'll start all over again if you'd like to see me carting babies around in a Gladstone."

She flushed. "Honestly, Felix, you do say dreadful things."

"Do I? I'll be saying worse when we're married, so you'll have to get used to it. How nice your hair is, Joan! It's a grand colour. May I kiss you?"

"Oh, not just yet," said Bubbles, in a fright.

"You are a duck," he admired. "I've never met such a stuffy girl in my life. Won't it be fun degenerating you! Why won't you kiss me? Wouldn't you kiss a bloke till you were engaged to him? Well, let's be engaged, shall we? I've got a ring."

He drew from his pocket a box, and from it took a large, carved amethyst set in small, fine diamonds. "I thought it was better to get you that than some pimping emerald you could hardly see."

He held it in his palm. Bubbles gazed at it as longingly as

a child gazing at the fairy doll in a shop window. Finally, he slipped it on to her unresisting hand.

Mr. Lang gave his promised wife a brief but excited kiss. Then he left her, opened the windows and shouted into the garden, "Hey, Hilary! Jack! What about a double wedding?"

"Quick work, old-boy-old-boy," said plump, handsome Jack Jarman, hurrying in with Hilary to offer his congratulations. The latter came to Bubbles and embraced her warmly.

"Great John Scott," she exclaimed, "how ripping! Darling, what a hoot!"

———

Mr. Warrender was arrested on a charge of espionage the day following the fire-precautions committee meeting, and taken off to prison.

"Lord knows he's played his cards badly," said Eggshell to Pig, "and that there are bigger fish than him in that particular sea. Still, people like him, sir, are safer in than out. I only wish we'd got his mistress, that Mrs. Cottenham. We've got her for assault and battery all right, but if you ask me she's the most dangerous of that gang politically."

Pig agreed. "We're keeping an eye on the other Free British Mussolites, and the sooner we get them behind barbed wire the better. We reckon there's about forty-two of them, in all. Not very successful people. As for Stevens, we'll be glad to have him out of the way. He's an infernal nuisance, singing, shouting, and hailing the Duce from one day's end to another. It's mostly bluff, too, because he's no fool. Hitler's his boss, not Mussolini, but he's trying to throw us off the main track. By the by, how did you get on with Kathleen Smith?"

"I have never," said Eggshell, "suffered from such an itching palm. Once or twice I felt I'd even sacrifice my career to get in one good slap on the place where it stings—if you'll excuse me, sir."

"Don't apologize. Should have felt the same myself."

"Anyhow, I gave her a good bawling-out, and she was grizzling when I let her go... Well, sir, in a way I'm sorry we've come to the end of this. It has been a great honour working with you."

"It's been a unique experience for me," said Pig. He sat down, crossed his plump legs and assumed an expression of inscrutability. "Out of order for me to say it, Eggshell, but—er—I think there may be a leg-up coming for you."

His subordinate went pink, looked down his nose and murmured confused gratitude. He added, more distinctly, "We owe a lot to your cousin and his wife, sir."

"Now look here, Eggshell! I don't deny they've had their uses, and they certainly got Steer by methods we could never have used. Nevertheless, if they ever show signs of getting mixed up in murder again I'm going to have them both arrested on any charge that will hold water. Committing a nuisance, or..." Pig's voice trailed away into indeterminate mumbles. He flashed a glance, through sandy lashes, at the Inspector, hoping he had noticed nothing; but Eggshell's amiable face was blank.

"Well, I must be going." He held out his hand. "I hope you'll be working with my men in the near future." And clamping down his *chapeau melon* on his round fair head he went out, leaving the Inspector to entrancing dreams of the good time coming.

———

On Thursday evening, as Agnes was preparing to go with her husband to the station, Mrs. Rowse looked in upon them.

"Ah," she said, pausing on the threshold and standing with hand upraised while the fluttering scarves subsided about her, "I am *de trop*! You don't want me now."

"No, no. Come in. We haven't got to leave for half an hour yet. Andrew, give Mrs. Rowse a drink."

The old lady stepped in, walked slowly into the lounge and came to rest upon the settee as smoothly as a barrage-balloon. "I have come," she said, "to bid you farewell. I'm going early tomorrow to my friend in Leamington, with whom I shall stay until I have found another flat in London. This building holds too many sad memories for me. I suppose you'll both be doing the same?"

"Oh, no," said Agnes, "we like it here. I can see your point of view, though."

"I don't think"—Mrs. Rowse took a long pull at the Irish—"I don't think I can claim to be psychic; and yet I have seemed to hear poor Addie's voice in my ears, telling me to seek pastures new. Yes. It has been quite insistent sometimes, and I should not have the temerity to ignore a message from such a source. Besides," she added, "I am having *such* trouble with the cistern, which has left such a nasty damp stain down the wall. It disturbs me. I can't work in an atmosphere of petty annoyance."

"And how is your work going?" Andrew enquired politely. He was wondering whether he should wear his forage-cap or his cheese-cutter. He decided that the latter was more suitable to his age, decided to wear the former.

"My work? Oh, fair to middling. I have been much distracted. Only this morning I noticed that I had given

Vineyarda auburn curls on page three and raven braids on page fourteen. Well, just a tiny little spot, Mrs. Kinghof."

"Say when."

"When," said Mrs. Rowse, after a long time. She finished her drink and rose. "Well, I won't be keeping you two dears. Allow me to express my gratitude for all you've done. I know poor Addie would wish me to thank you."

The Kinghofs swallowed the sour thought that Mrs. Sibley had little for which to thank them. "Wish we could have done more," said Agnes.

She escorted the departing guest to the door. Mrs. Rowse seemed a little unsteady on her feet. "Well," she beamed, "I hope we may all meet again soon in happier shircum-circumshtances. What a dreadful war this it!" She proceeded upstairs.

"She's rather a darling," Agnes remarked. "She deserves a quiet life, and I hope she's going to get it. Yes, I do love Mrs. Rowse."

"Better get a cab," said Andrew, and he rang up the nearest rank.

They set off, both in melancholy mood.

"It's been fun, hasn't it?" Agnes murmured, adding, "I suppose that's not the most tasteful of remarks."

He put his arm round her. "Anything we do together is fun, however horrible it may be. Anyhow, we've made three people happy: Bubbles, Lang, and Hilary. I suppose Bubbles and Lang will get married?"

"I suppose so, but it seems *most* unsuitable."

When they reached the station they found they had three-quarters of an hour in hand, so they went into the buffet for a drink.

"I'm hungry," said Andrew. "Wonder what they've got?"

He peered into the glass bells at the sandwiches, sausage-rolls, and pies. "To pie would be an awfully big adventure," he mused, indicating a sienna-brown object adorned with parsley.

Agnes addressed the waitress. "Miss, what's in those?"

"Them? Pork."

"Oh, no," Andrew said, shuddering, and he announced that his appetite was gone.

Time passes quickly enough when there is a long separation ahead.

They found themselves on the bleak platform, before the yawning door of a first-class carriage. "Go on," said Agnes irritably, "get in. We don't want to protract things."

"What a callous beast you are! Don't you want to wave to me?"

"Don't like waving. Besides, there's no earthly point. It's so pitch dark I'd never see you. Kiss me."

He kissed her. "That's an awful hat."

"Think so? It's a Deanna Durbin model."

"It's too old for you. Burn it. I don't want to see it again. Good-bye, darling. No more murders."

"No more. Good-bye, Andy. Don't do anything I wouldn't do."

"That gives me a wide margin of possibilities."

"Am I beautiful?"

"Terribly," said Andrew, moved almost to tears. The whistle blew. He jumped into the train. Agnes turned, snuffled into her handkerchief, then squared her shoulders and marched briskly from the platform.

———

She was not best pleased, returning to her lonely flat, to find awaiting her a note from Pig.

My dear Agnes,

I suppose I should thank you both for the assistance you have given in the case of Maclagan Steer. That I can only do this half-heartedly is due to my distaste for the meddling of amateurs in affairs that are perfectly safe in the hands of the police.

Like hell they are, Agnes thought. Who caught the brute, anyway?

I cannot but think, my dear girl, that you might have been serving your country better in one of the Civil Defence or Auxiliary Services than in causing a great deal of trouble to everyone by exposing yourself to the attacks of homicidal maniacs. As for Andrew, he has too much leave, and all I can say is that the Army needs a great deal of tightening up.

However, I am, within limits, grateful, and am most relieved personally that you have escaped this affair without bodily harm.

My regard to you both, in which Mary joins me,

Very sincerely yours,
Whitestone.

There was a P.S.

Mary wishes you to convey her regards to Miss Ashton,

whom she thought a most charming young woman of splendid type.

But best of all there was a second P.S., and it was this that restrained Agnes from pitching the letter into the fire.

Come and have lunch with me one day soon, and I'll show you over the Black Museum. You deserve some sort of reward, I suppose.

And this was signed, *Pig*.

——

At the end of the week Eggshell had the, for him, dismal experience of attending the private cinema in Welwyn Studios. A modest man, not especially gifted with humour, he found the indecency of the films less trying than their intolerable dullness, and he was not amused. He had an adult's mind; had always been adult. Not at fourteen years of age would Eggshell have got a kick from strip-tease.

But the afternoon was not unprofitable. It ended in the taking of names all round—one little gentleman in pin-striped trousers fell to his knees in an effort to persuade the police not to take him—and in the arrest of Mr. Currie, who, on being searched, was found to be carrying on his person enough cocaine to keep three or four addicts happy for a fortnight. It was a sad business. One or two young people were scared into decency for several years to come, one prominent business man was ruined, and Mr. Currie received a good, long sentence.

Harris and Frankson, who attended the raid, were able

to 'dine out' on the story for an indefinite period. So far as the films were concerned, both policemen worked out a circumlocutory description designed to fascinate, but not to terrify, the most modest of their girl friends; to produce, in fact, the inward but not the outward blush.

———

This should have been the end: but it is not. Not quite.

The year had worn into the spring, and the "sitzkrieg" was showing signs of drawing to a close. Agnes, who, though she had not yet made up her mind to join the Service women, had become a full-time warden at the Featherstone Mews Post, now saw little of Andrew, and was extremely lonely.

One afternoon, when she had returned exhausted from a 6 a.m.–2 p.m. session of which three hours had been spent on the practice ground putting out fires and making ten-foot drops, the door-bell rang. Agnes swore, and heaved herself off the settee, where she had lain down to rest with tea, sandwiches, cigarettes, and half a dozen copies of *Life*. She looked down at the old cotton overall with which she had replaced her dungarees, and wondered if it was anyone "who mattered." Deciding that nobody mattered, she went to open the door, anticipating by a second another ring.

On the mat there stood a very little, plump old lady with a face like a pekinese, eyes round, protruding and clouded, snub nose, and mild low brow. She was dressed remarkably in violet marocain. On her dyed red hair was a little toque fronted with mauve and magenta flowers, round her neck three strings of amethysts, a double loop of seed-pearls, and an enamelled cross. Her stumpy hands were brilliant with diamonds, and in them she held pencil and a sheaf of papers. Her manner was both fierce and cordial.

"Is your mistress at home?" she enquired unexpectedly.

Agnes swallowed, collected herself. "This is my flat."

"Oh! How silly of me! I really must apologize. May I take up just a wee tippet of your time?"

"I don't want to buy anything," said Agnes, rude in her turn.

"Of course you don't! And I've nothing to sell. My mission is purely humanitarian, and will appeal to any *enlightened* person that manages to survive this dreadful day and age.—Oh, thank you!"

Lack of an invitation did not deter her from crossing the threshold, where her smile and her diamonds seemed to light up the somewhat gloomy hall.

"You must be wondering who I am, my dear. Let me introduce myself. I am Mrs. Bawford-Bishop, Secretary of the B.R.S."

"The what?" Agnes demanded severely, her back to the lounge door. She had no intention of letting this mauve woman move a step further.

"The Burn the Rope Society. We are pledged to remove from this grand old democracy of ours the blot of capital punishment. Such foul, unworthy barbarism! We have a membership of nearly four thousand and we are growing day by day. Take a leaflet. Er...where was I? Such unworthy barbarism. The murderer should be treated as a mental case, not punished with mediaeval ferocity. Would you murder? No."

"How do you know I wouldn't?" Agnes, thinking of her tea getting cold, her cigarette burning to ash, her beautiful *Lifes* lying unread, was belligerent. "How do you know I haven't?"

"My dear! I am a student of human nature." Mrs. Bawford-Bishop drew a long breath and showed all her teeth. "Would you murder? No. Would I murder? No. Ergo, or 'therefore,' if you prefer it, a murderer is a lunatic. We no longer beat or chain our lunatics. Why should we hang them? But I expect you're wondering to what I lead."

"I was wondering, yes."

"I have a petition here, to which I hope you will append your signature. It will appear among the many hundreds already collected. Petition for what? You may well ask it."

Though Agnes had asked nothing.

"It is a petition for the reprieve of that sad, unfortunate, and most pathetic mental case, Reginald Maclagan Steer. Doubtless you have read the papers and followed the details of this bizarre crime. Who could doubt that it was a crime of a lunatic's making? Indeed, who? And so—" She held out paper and pencil invitingly. "—I hope you will sign your name, here, where I'm pointing."

But Agnes made no move, nor did she take her hands from the pockets of the disgraceful overall. Something in her expression may have tied Mrs. Bawford-Bishop's tongue, for she said nothing, while Agnes squared her shoulders and prepared to let fly.

"Look here, Mrs. Bishop, on principle I agree with practically everything you've said. I'm a form-signer by nature. I can't resist dotted lines. Anything there is to fill up, I fill. Yes. But, Mrs. Bishop, this is just one form to which I am not going to append my signature…"

To her astonishment and fury, the mauve Pekinese found herself firmly gripped by the plain, rather grubby young woman of the beautiful legs and torso, and propelled, slowly but implacably, out of the flat and towards the stair-head.

Before she had recovered sufficient wind to make a protest the door of Number 8 slammed behind her, and Mrs. Bawford-Bishop had no recourse but to retreat ignominiously downstairs, muttering as she went:

"The rudeness of these savages! But they will learn. Ah, yes. One of these days justice will prevail."

THE END

Praise for the
British Library Crime Classics

"Carr is at the top of his game in this taut whodunit... The British Library Crime Classics series has unearthed another worthy golden age puzzle."

—*Publishers Weekly*, STARRED Review,
for *The Lost Gallows*

"A wonderful rediscovery."
—*Booklist*, STARRED Review, for *The Sussex Downs Murder*

"First-rate mystery and an engrossing view into a vanished world."
—*Booklist*, STARRED Review, for *Death of an Airman*

"A cunningly concocted locked-room mystery, a staple of Golden Age detective fiction."
—*Booklist*, STARRED Review, for *Murder of a Lady*

"The book is both utterly of its time and utterly ahead of it."
—*New York Times Book Review* for *The Notting Hill Mystery*

"As with the best of such compilations, readers of classic mysteries will relish discovering unfamiliar authors, along with old favorites such as Arthur Conan Doyle and G.K. Chesterton."
—*Publishers Weekly*, STARRED Review, for *Continental Crimes*

"In this imaginative anthology, Edwards—president of Britain's Detection Club—has gathered together overlooked criminous gems."
—*Washington Post* for *Crimson Snow*

"The degree of suspense Crofts achieves by showing the growing obsession and planning is worthy of Hitchcock. Another first-rate reissue from the British Library Crime Classics series."

—*Booklist*, STARRED Review, for *The 12.30 from Croydon*

"Not only is this a first-rate puzzler, but Crofts's outrage over the financial firm's betrayal of the public trust should resonate with today's readers."

—*Booklist*, STARRED Review, for *Mystery in the Channel*

"This reissue exemplifies the mission of the British Library Crime Classics series in making an outstanding and original mystery accessible to a modern audience."

—*Publishers Weekly*, STARRED Review, for *Excellent Intentions*

"A book to delight every puzzle-suspense enthusiast"

—*New York Times* for *The Colour of Murder*

"Edwards's outstanding third winter-themed anthology showcases 11 uniformly clever and entertaining stories, mostly from lesser known authors, providing further evidence of the editor's expertise…This entry in the British Library Crime Classics series will be a welcome holiday gift for fans of the golden age of detection."

—*Publishers Weekly*, STARRED Review, for *The Christmas Card Crime and Other Stories*

Poisoned Pen
PRESS

poisonedpenpress.com